# Carl Weber's Kingpins:

## The Dirty South

# Carl Weber's Kingpins:

## The Dirty South

*Treasure Hernandez*

*www.urbanbooks.net*

Urban Books, LLC
97 N18th Street
Wyandanch, NY 11798

Carl Weber's Kingpins: The Dirty South

ISBN 13: 978-1-62286-948-0
ISBN 10: 1-62286-948-6

First Trade Paperback Printing December 2015
Printed in the United States of America

10 9 8 7 6 5 4 3 2 1

Distributed by Kensington Publishing Corp.
Submit orders to:
Customer Service
400 Hahn Road
Westminster, MD 21157-4627
Phone: 1-800-733-3000
Fax: 1-800-659-2436

# Carl Weber's Kingpins:

## The Dirty South

*by*

*Treasure Hernandez*

# Prologue

"Five . . . four . . . three . . . two . . . one! Happy New Year!" The crowd cheered as confetti fell from the ceiling of the Columbia, South Carolina, nightclub. Champagne flutes, bottles, and cups with assorted light and dark liquors filled the air.

"I'd like to wish a special Happy Thirtieth Birthday to the queen bee of not only the South but also the BK! Kafisa the Don! I see you, baby girl! If you don't know, you better know now, 'cause she one badass bitch!" Mister Cee, the DJ, shouted through the microphone as he switched songs. "This one's for you, ma!" he added.

Just then the sounds of Biggie Smalls's classic track "Juicy" boomed through the massive speakers that lined the nightclub's walls, and shook the building. It was her thirtieth birthday, and Kafisa felt she deserved to go all out and splurge for her special day, which was why she had chosen Club XS.

Club XS had exactly what the name implied, excess. Excessive was all that it was hyped up to be, from the walls to the luxury VIP sections, to the gigantic bathrooms and the twenty-thousand-square-foot building. The three main bars and the two service bars were designed to meet the supply and demand in the high-energy hot spot. The sound and lighting system was state of the art and was truly mind blowing. The owners had poured over one million dollars into the establishment to give partygoers the ultimate nightlife experience right in the heart of Columbia.

Kafisa loved that Club XS was four clubs in one: a nightclub, a live music venue, an ultra lounge, and an outdoor oasis with cabana seating. On any other occasion, she and her crew would be chilling in one of the cabanas, but tonight was a special occasion. You turned thirty only once, and Kafisa wanted to make sure it was memorable, especially with all that was going on back home. And that she did.

In her VIP section Kafisa held her glass up higher than she already had it raised, and nodded. Her birthday was one of the best times of the year for her. Being born on New Year's Day meant that she really gotten to celebrate on the ultimate party night. Because her dad observed the Islamic faith, she had never got to indulge in the luxury of receiving gifts on Christmas, like other children, but on her birthday, she had always been showered with more gifts than she knew what to do with.

All the while that she had been on her own, she'd made sure that she went all out on her birthday, the way her father had when she was under his watch. Tonight Kafisa felt she had everything she had ever wanted or could possibly need in three lifetimes: good health, a loyal team, an unlimited drug supply connect and, most of all, more money than she knew what to do with. She was glad she had made the decision to leave the Big Apple. After she'd left Brooklyn, things had fallen into place for her.

In just one year she had managed not only to lock South Carolina down in the coke department, but also to cut into a piece of the action in Atlanta, North Carolina, and Virginia. She felt like she was on top of the world. The two hundred grand she had dropped to rent out the club and pop bottles of Cîroc and rosé all night long was nothing to her, especially on her special day. She knew the DJ, Mister Cee, personally from back home and had flown him in to rock her party, which was why she was not surprised to hear her favorite song, by one of her hometown's hip-hop legends.

Her female entourage followed suit. They held their glasses in the air to toast with their boss. Most of them were from the borough of Brooklyn, also known as BK, and had joined Kafisa's team of money getters in the South. Kafisa turned and smiled approvingly in her team's direction, and the whole while the camera-man shot away. His flashing lights added to the ballin' ambience surrounding Kafisa and her female entourage. They were indeed the center of attention in the upscale club. Kafisa held her hand up to her eyes to block the flash from the camera as she raised her glass to her lips. Between all the rosé she had consumed and the flashing lights, she was getting light-headed. She dismissed the cameraman with a wave of her hand. He nodded and directed his attention to the crowd.

Kafisa took a sip of her rosé. Just before she tilted her head back, something caught her eye. In a New York minute, she went from party mode to combat mode. Her smile was quickly replaced with a scowl at the sight of the two bodies standing up in the VIP section next to theirs. The glare from the chrome weapon one of the men was brandishing was what caught Kafisa's attention. One look at them and she knew they weren't local. Kafisa instinctively reached for her weapon tucked in her LV belt, despite the fact that the two unidentified gunmen already had their weapons raised and pointed in her direction. By the time her crew realized the imminent danger surrounding them, Kafisa had already sprung into action, and the sound of gunfire filled the air.

# Chapter One

*1995 . . .*

"Fee, I want you to put all of these ones together for Daddy," thirty-four-year-old Kafis Jackson instructed his daughter, Kafisa Jackson. "Take your time and count to a hundred. Then put one of these rubber bands around each stack and put 'em in there." He pointed to the black drawstring bag lying on the floor of the living room in their Brooklyn brownstone, next to a mountain of singles.

Kafisa listened as her father gave instructions. At ten years old, she thought the assignment was the most important task her dad had ever asked of her. She was always ecstatic when he asked for her help. Since she was old enough to crawl, she had been curious about her father's job. Every chance she got, she managed to make her way into their living room or kitchen while her father worked.

She reflected on the times when her father picked her up off the floor and sat her on his lap while he was working. One time when he was counting money, he grabbed a brick of bills and said, "This is all for you, baby girl." Another time, when they were sitting at the kitchen table with product in front of him, he warned her, "Don't ever let me see you use this. It would break Daddy's heart, you hear me?" And like an obedient little girl, she nodded her head yes. Still, she would try to reach out and grab the substances and objects on the table, like any little child would do. She remembered how her father would pop her hands and then put her down, sending her off to her mother. Now, years later, Kafisa knew better than to disturb anything without permission, let alone touch it, when her father was "at work."

"This pile right here." Kafis pointed to the stack of five-dollar bills opposite the singles. "I want you to do the same thing, but count by five. "Can you do that?" he asked his daughter.

"Uh-huh!" Kafisa shook her head repeatedly. She was determined to prove to her dad that she was now old enough for him to count on her.

She had never seen her mother help her father with his work, not one time, and she was happy that her father had chosen her over her mother for such an important task. Kafisa believed her father took his job very seriously. She couldn't understand why her mother did not understand. She recalled staying up and listening through the wall that separated her bedroom from her parents' to the arguments they would have over the late-night hours he kept. She remembered hearing her father telling her mom, "I'm out here puttin' all this work in for you and Fee, and all your ungrateful ass can do is complain? I work hard for the shit we got, and instead of appreciating it, you worryin' about what time I'm comin' in the fuckin' house."

Some of the words Kafisa was too young to understand the meaning of, but in her young mind, her father was right. He did work hard at what he did. She couldn't figure out why her mother couldn't see that. Kafisa resented her mother for the way she stressed out her dad. The feelings drew her closer to her father. In her eyes, Kafis Jackson was the best daddy in the world.

"A'ight. I'm going to be in the kitchen, baby girl. If you make a mistake or forget your count, start all over again, okay?"

"Okay, Daddy." Kafisa nodded. She tried to match her father's stony facial expression.

Kafis smiled at his daughter, seeing what she was trying to do. There was no denying, even if he wanted to, that Kafisa was his child. When he looked at her, all he saw was a female version of himself. She had inherited his deep-set brown eyes and his wide-flared nostrils, along with a mouth that was the same shape. She even had his dimples when she smiled. Like him, Kafisa was dark skinned and had dark brown hair. Over the years of traveling the continent, both Kafis's skin tone and his hair had darkened, but still anyone could see that Kafisa was all him. She was a certified Jackson, one he had made.

Kafisa began to smile to herself when she saw her father shoot her his famous wink, followed by a smile all his own. It was times like this when they shared a father-daughter moment.

"Come here," he said to Kafisa.

Kafisa moved closer to him. Kafis bent over and gave her a kiss on the forehead.

"I love you, Fee."

"I love you too, Daddy."

After flashing another smile at her, Kafis turned around and headed for the kitchen. For a brief moment, he wondered whether it was a bad idea to have his ten-year-old daughter counting his blood money, but just as quickly as the thought had appeared, it excused itself.

He knew that he was pressed for time and couldn't count money and do the other thing he needed to do all at once. He had been up most of the night, counting all the hundreds, fifties, twenties, and tens. The count had reached 380 Gs. He still had to cook up the last ten bricks of cocaine he had sales for, so he could meet his quota and pay his connect. By two in the afternoon, he had to come up with six hundred thousand dollars to give to his Colombian coke connect.

To cut corners, Kafis took the one hundred thousand in cash he had inside his safe and added it to the 380 stacks he had counted, but this still left him with 120 Gs to come up with. In singles and fives alone, he had over two hundred grand, but his connect, Pepe, would allow him to give him only fifty thousand in small bills. Kafis had already intended to get the other seventy from the three bricks he would sell, which would be at around 1:00 p.m. He knew his options were limited. The only way he could pull everything off in time, and effectively, was if he let Kafisa count the money while he finished cooking up kilos of cocaine. She was the only person in the world he could truly trust.

Camilla, who was his longtime girlfriend and the mother of his only child, on the other hand, could not be trusted when it came to his money. Camilla's behavior had led Kafis to this conclusion. He knew he was some-what to blame for this, because he had practically raised Camilla and had made her the way she was by spoiling her and refusing to let her work a regular nine-to-five.

Kafis was three years Camilla's senior. The two had known each other forever but got together when Kafis was on the rise. When he'd come up and made it out of the projects, he'd taken Camilla with him. In the beginning, everything had been all good. He'd spoiled her rotten, lavishing her with gifts, trips to anywhere she desired to go, and vacations beyond her wildest dreams. He'd put her up in an American dream house, bought her an expensive car, given her an unlimited credit card and access to a healthy supply of cash, all on the basis that she had been with him from day one, when he'd first got in the game.

She'd known him before the streets named him "Big Fis." She had been there when he was just little bum-ass Kafis from the projects. Once upon a time, she had known him for him, and not for what he had or what he could do for her. When the paper started rolling in, Camilla had begun to change. Instead of sending her back to the ghetto, like he'd wanted to, Kafis had let her stay, especially after she told him that she was six weeks pregnant with his child. It was because of that, and that alone, that they stayed together for the last seven years of their eighteen-year relationship.

Kafisa took her time, just as her father had suggested. With each hundred-dollar stack of singles she rubber banded, she felt confident she had not messed up the count. *There must be millions of singles in this pile*, she thought to herself, deciding that the twenty-five rubber-banded stacks she had already counted didn't even make a dent in the pile. She had yet to start on the pile that contained only five-dollar bills. She wondered if her dad was a rich man, like all the kids at her private school talked about their dads being. She figured that he had to be. She drew her conclusion based on the elite school she attended and the clothes he could afford to buy her all year round, along with any and everything a young girl her age would want.

Kafisa was just about to rubber band her twenty-sixth hundred-dollar stack when she heard her mother's voice. The unexpected sound startled her.

"Kafisa Martisha Jackson!" her mother shouted, calling her by her full name. She could tell by her mother's tone that Camilla was angry at her. She had no clue as to why, though.

"Ye—" Before she could get the words out of her mouth to answer her mother, she was met with an open-hand slap to the face. The blow sent her flying across the room.

"What the hell do you think you're doing, little girl?" Camilla Daniels yelled. She was now standing over top of Kafisa.

"Nothing!" Kafisa cried. She honestly had no idea what her mother was talking about or what the cause of the slap was.

Tears had already begun to stream down Kafisa's face. She grabbed her right cheek. The pain from her mother's slap was intense. It felt like her right cheek was on fire. She feared what her mother would do next. She had never seen her mother so upset at her before. She didn't know what she had done to deserve a slap to the face like that. Neither her mother nor her father had ever beaten her or even slapped her in her life. Whatever the cause, she knew it had to be something serious for Camilla to react the way she did.

Camilla snatched Kafisa by her arm and yanked her up off the floor.

"Mama, I didn't do anything!" Kafisa sobbed innocently, fear and shock in her tone.

"Shut up, Kafisa! Don't you ever let me catch you . . ." Camilla's words were drowned out by Kafis's.

"Yo, what the fuck you think you doing?" he barked. He had entered the living room after hearing Kafisa's cries from the kitchen.

Camilla swung around in Kafis's direction, still holding Kafisa tightly by the arm. "What does it look like? I'm chastising my daughter!" she spat.

"Take ya muthafuckin' hands off of her!" Kafis spat back as he moved in closer to Camilla.

His request went unheeded.

He repeated himself, only this time he made sure Camilla knew how serious he was. "I said let my mutha-fuckin' daughter go!" Kafis grabbed Camilla by the throat.

Instantly, Camilla released Kafisa's arm. She gasped for air. With one hand, Kafis seemed to be choking the life out of her. He had cut off her air passage. Were it not for his daughter's cries, he would have surely killed Camilla in front of his only child.

"Daddy, no!" Kafisa cried out.

As much as she was angry with her mother for what she had done to her, Kafisa did not want to see her father hurt her. She loved them both, but she loved her dad more. She knew that when it came down to her or her mother, he loved her more also, which was why she believed he would listen to her cry.

With his hand still wrapped around Camilla's throat, Kafis looked over at his daughter. He could see the hurt and the fear in her eyes as he applied more pressure to Camilla's larynx.

"Daddy, please! Please stop, Daddy!" she begged and pleaded with her father.

Kafis removed his hand from around Camilla's neck. He tossed her backward like a rag doll. He picked Kafisa up and hugged her.

"It's all right, baby girl. Everything is all right," he said to Kafisa as he began rocking her the way he did when she was just a baby. "Daddy's sorry," he continued. "I didn't mean to hurt Mommy. I didn't mean to scare you. I love you and Mommy." He wiped her tears.

"You don't love me, nigga!" Camilla shouted. She had just regained her breath. "You gonna put your fuckin' hands on me for doing what's right for my daughter? Oh, hell no! You must be out yo' rabbit-ass mind if you think I'm havin' that shit."

Keeping his composure, Kafis put Kafisa down. "Fee, go to your room. I need to talk to Mommy," he told his daughter.

"You not gonna hurt Mommy, are you, Daddy?" Kafisa asked.

"No, I'm not going to hurt Mommy. I promise," he assured her. "Now, go on in your room."

"You damn right you ain't gonna hurt me, muthafucka!" Camilla bellowed.

Camilla had been brought to tears, not because of what Kafis had done to her, but rather from how her daughter had chosen sides without even realizing it. For the past eight years, she had watched the little girl she'd carried for nine months and given birth to grow attached to her father and pull away from her. She had tried to be the best mother that she could possibly be, especially since she herself had never had a mother who cared for her, but from day one, Kafis had interrupted her parenting methods. When she told her daughter no, Kafis would go over her head and tell her yes. When she tried to reprimand her, Kafis would go behind her back and tell her not to worry. From the day Kafisa was brought home from the hospital, Kafis had let her have her way.

*In his eyes, she can do no wrong*, Camilla thought as she wiped her face.

She noticed her daughter staring at her. The look was so hateful that it caused Camilla to lose control. "You little bitch! Who you think you lookin' at like that?" she shouted at Kafisa. "I'll kill you in here, you little black-ass heifer! You mean nothing to me!"

Kafisa's eyes widened at the sound of her mother's words. Her mother made her regret coming to her defense. She wished she had never stopped her father from choking her. Kafisa shot her mother a look that cut deep into Camilla's heart. At that very moment, Kafisa decided that she hated her mother.

"Go to your room, baby girl," Kafis instructed Kafisa again.

Kafisa did as she was told without a care about her mother's fate.

Once Kafis thought she was out of earshot and in her room, he started back up. "Yo, I don't know what the fuck your problem is, but if you ever talk to my daughter like that, put yo' hands on her, or threaten her again, you'll be the one that'll be dead up in this muthafucka. You hear me?" Kafis spoke with conviction in his tone. It was more of a promise than it was a threat.

Camilla could see the rage in Kafis's eyes. She thought better than to challenge him, but she was determined to address the issue that had caused her to put her hands on her daughter for the first time.

"Yeah, I hear you, Kafis! But you want to know what the fuck my problem is? Huh?" she yelled, lashing out. "My problem is, you have our ten-year-old damn daughter in here countin' your damn drug money, exposing her to all this shit, like it's cute," she began. "Did you ever stop to think what type of effect all of this will have on her in the future, Kafis? What do you think you are teaching our daughter? That it's okay to have a man that sells drugs and has guns and money laying around his family? Is that what you want to teach her? So it's okay for her to see all this shit you're doing?"

"You don't know what the fuck you talkin' about," Kafis interjected dryly.

Camilla rolled her eyes. "I sure do." She wiped her face for a second time. "I watch how you are with her. I hear the things that you say to her, quotin' those fake-ass rules of the streets and shit, but I haven't heard you tell her that money is the root of all evil. I thought our reason for moving out of the ghetto and putting our daughter in private school was so she can have a better life than the one we had when we were kids. You still teaching her things with your ghetto mentality, though." Camilla let out a light chuckle. "I guess it's true when they say, 'You can take the nigga out of the hood, but you can't take the hood out of the nigga.'" She shook her head in disgust. "Kafis, our daughter is not from the streets. We are. That doesn't mean that we have to instill them in her."

Kafisa listened to her mother as she hid behind the wall. She was surprised to hear some of the things she heard her mother say to her father. It was the first time she had heard her mother talk like that to him. From what her little ten-year-old mind could compute, based on what her mother was saying, Kafisa drew the conclusion that her dad was someone who made his money by selling drugs. This was something she was taught in school to stay away from, say no to, and she believed that drug dealers were bad guys.

She didn't want to believe her father was one of those people. After all, those kinds of people didn't have a family. After hearing her mother refer to her father as one of those types of people, she knew that there had to be some type of exception to the rule, because her father was not a bad person. She had no idea about the lifestyle her father lived. Had Kafisa known, though, there was no doubt that she would have loved him just the same. She continued to listen as her father began to speak.

"All that shit you talkin', save it." Kafis jumped closer toward her. "Don't ever question my methods as a father or as a man. I know what the fuck's best for my daughter." His words were stern and uncompromising.

"Nigga, please! You don't know shit about raisin' no damn kid, especially not no girl." She rolled her eyes at Kafis and dismissed him with a wave of her hand.

"I know I can do a better fuckin' job than you," Kafis shot back. He tore into Camilla like hot slugs. "You think I have her around all this shit because I want her to turn out like yo' money-hungry ass? Not at all. I have her around it so she'll be used to seeing it. So she won't be impressed when she gets older by some nigga who pulls up on her in a new truck or coupe, flashing money in her face to manipulate her into whatever. You never had nobody to teach you about the power of the dollar. That's why you don't respect it," Kafis said, pointing out Camilla's shortcomings. "And that's why you reckless when it comes to handlin' it, and I would never let you run things as you want to."

He paused. "A lot of that is my fault, though, because I could've taught you, and I should've taught you, but I didn't. My daughter, on the other hand, she's going to know everything that I know. She ain't gonna be no square. She's going to be both book smart and street smart, the best of both worlds. Whatever she wants to do or be in life, she'll be able to do. The choice will be hers, and hers alone, so don't come at me with all this bullshit, 'cause I ain't tryin'a hear it."

Camilla let out an insane laugh. "Save that shit for them other bitches that don't know no better," she snapped. "Just like her father, she ain't gonna be shit if you raisin' her!"

Kafis shook his head. He couldn't believe Camilla had just said that with a straight face about their daughter. It took all his strength not to wrap his hands around her thin neck and choke the life out of her. Instead, he went a different route. "If you don't like the way I'm raising my daughter, then you can get the fuck out and take yo' ass back to the projects, where you belong! If you can't handle this life, then get off the muthafuckin' pot, bitch!" Kafis told her. "Matter of fact, that's exactly what your dumb ass gonna do." He made Camilla's decision for her without any compassion or empathy.

A big lump formed in Camilla's throat. She tried to clear it in an attempt to speak. This was not the first time Kafis had proposed that she return to her old neighborhood, the one he had moved her out of, when they got into an argument, but this time his words hurt her. He had made it perfectly clear numerous times before that he believed that without him, she would not be able to survive. He seemed to believe that she would feel the need to crawl and beg her way back into his world. For a while, she had believed this herself, but as her pride and her ego had grown stronger with the passage of time, she'd reached the conclusion that there was no truth in what Kafis Jackson implied. She was determined to prove him wrong.

"Nigga, you think I need you? Tsk! Please! You ain't make me, Kafis. If anything, I made you, Big Fis!" she said in a mocking tone, letting his street name drag. "Ain't nobody know who you was until you started fuckin' with me." She chuckled. "You was just little dirty-ass Kafis from the projects. Now you done made a few dollars and think you the shit. Whatever! Nigga, it's a million of you out there, and you best believe you can be replaced!" Camilla's words were strong. As the words rolled off her tongue, it crossed her mind that she might regret them, but she was hurt and was determined to say what she thought would hurt him. If it worked, she couldn't tell, because Kafis had little, if any, reaction to what she had said. He just stood there, expressionless, as she went on, trying to convince him of her powers of self-preservation.

Kafis had had an idea that Camilla felt this way, but he had ignored it because she was his child's mother. Now, to actually hear her come out and say it to his face was a different story. Her words had pierced his heart like a poisonous dagger. There was no way that he was going to give her the satisfaction of knowing this. He remained calm.

"I'm glad you told me all that. Now I'll be able to sleep better at night when I put yo' ass out and send you back to where I found you." He knew he was officially done with Camilla. "By the time I leave here, you better be gone, or you ain't gonna be able to go nowhere ever again!" Kafis told her. His tone had changed from calm to deadly. "Think I'm playing, then be here and see what happens."

Camilla was unfazed by his threat, thinking they were just having an overheated argument. "You ain't said nothing. I'll leave. Let me just pack my shit and get my daughter. Then you'll never have to worry about hearing from us again!" she replied. She, too, was ready to put an end to what she knew had been stale for quite some time.

Without blinking, Kafis corrected her. "You ain't got shit to pack. Everything in this muthafucka I paid for. You don't own shit in here. All you can do is call you a cab and tell 'em where to come pick you up at. As for my daughter, she ain't goin' nowhere! She stayin' with me." He let his words register in Camilla's mind. The widening of her eyes let him know she had heard him loud and clear. "Like you said, she ain't from the hood, so ain't no need for her to go there," Kafis added without a shift in his tone.

You could see the tears forming in Camilla's eyes all over again as Kafis's words set in. In the midst of all that was going on and being said, she had never given any thought to the possibility that Kafis wouldn't let her leave with their daughter. However, she was not surprised. She knew how he felt when it came to his daughter.

Kafisa was in tears due to her parents' argument, but she knew that there wasn't anything she could do about it. She was not at all surprised by what her mother had said to her father, because she had heard Camilla on the phone many times, telling one of her girlfriends the same exact things, when her father wasn't home. She was surprised to hear her mother say that she would leave and she was going to take her with her. There was no doubt in her mind that her father would never allow it. His words confirmed this, and she was relieved because she did not want to leave her dad. She continued to listen, curious as to what her mother's response would be.

"What? Kafis, you can't be serious!" Camilla cried out.

"As a heart attack," Kafis replied. "My daughter is staying with me. She ain't goin' nowhere!"

Camilla shook her head in disagreement. "I'm taking Kafisa with me one way or another," she spat back, calling his bluff.

Before she even knew what was happening or had a chance to react, Kafis's backhand sent her crashing to the floor. "You better not ever threaten me in your mutha-fuckin' life!" Kafis shouted. He stood over her, looking down at her. He knew what she was implying. "If the police even look at me funny, I'll come and kill yo' dumb ass, you hear me?"

He pulled his .40 caliber out of his waistband and pointed it at Camilla's head. Camilla held her hand up, as if she could actually prevent a bullet from penetrating her hand and going into her face if Kafis were to pull the trigger. His reputation preceded him in the streets, and although he had never gone to such extremes in their fights, she knew that Kafis was crazy enough to shoot her.

"Fis, I'm sorry. I didn't mean . . . ," she said, starting to retract all that she had previously said.

"Shut the fuck up! I don't wanna hear that 'I'm sorry' bullshit. Just get up and get the fuck out my house. You better be thankful you Kafisa's mother, 'cause on the strength of that, you still alive. Trust me, if you wasn't, your ass would have been dealt with accordingly. Believe me!" He glanced down at his Rolex watch, then back at Camilla. "You got thirty minutes to get up outta this muthafucka," he informed her.

Without waiting for her to leave, he spun back around to make his way back to the kitchen. When he turned around suddenly to see what was happening behind his back, his heart began to melt. Kafisa stood there, in the middle of the living room, in tears. Realizing that he still had his gun out, Kafis tucked it behind his back, out of Kafisa's view. He wondered how much she had seen or heard. The look in her eyes told it all. Instantly, shame overcame him at the thought of his daughter witnessing what had just taken place.

"Kafisa, go to your room, like I asked you to do before. Daddy'll be in there in a minute to talk to you." It was all he could say to delay the inevitable conversation he would have to have with her so that she understood why he did what he did and said.

Kafisa wiped her eyes. She looked over at her mother. Her eyes locked with Camilla's pain-filled eyes. She knew she was the cause of her mother's pain, but she didn't care. She watched as a tear dropped out of her mother's left eye. Kafisa broke her stare with her mother to avoid shedding her own tears. She then turned and made her way toward her bedroom.

The yellow taxi pulled up in front of the luxurious Brooklyn home three minutes before the thirty minutes Kafis had given Camilla were over. Kafis was just finishing up counting and rubber banding the rest of the five-dollar bills when he saw Camilla walk toward the front door with nothing but the clothes on her back. He shook his head. Overall, he loved her, but he knew she was not healthy for him. He wondered if he had been too hard on her.

Camilla stopped at the front door and looked back at him. He wanted to say something, but his pride would not allow him to. She had crossed the line and had said something that was a deal breaker for him. He could take and handle anything, but what he wouldn't tolerate was someone threatening to send him to jail. Kafis strongly believed that anybody who could get another person locked up deliberately was not to be trusted. Because of his belief, he stuck to his guns. He stood and stared at Camilla in silence.

Camilla let out a light chuckle and rolled her eyes. She turned and reached for the door handle. She, too, wanted to say something but couldn't bring herself to do so. She wanted to apologize and beg for another chance. Instead, she opened the door, stepped outside, and closed the door behind her, then made a beeline for the taxi.

She turned and took one last look at the place she had known as home for the past twelve years. *So many memories*, she thought. She peered up at Kafisa's bedroom window. Her eyes instantly became misty. She saw Kafisa standing at her window, looking down at her. She waved and blew Kafisa a kiss for the last time.

Kafisa had been waiting for her mother to come out of the house. As soon as she saw her, she began to weep. Her emotions were running wild. She was mad at her mother, but she loved her and didn't want her to go. The thought of not knowing when she'd ever see her again saddened Kafisa. She wanted to open her window and cry out and tell Camilla not to go, but didn't want her father to be mad at her. She watched as her mother climbed into the taxi. Kafisa could not hold back the flood of tears that threatened her eyes. As she watched the taxi disappear up the block, she realized that Camilla hadn't even told her she loved her.

As Camilla got into the taxi, she wondered when Kafis would tell her to come back. She knew that leaving her only child was wrong, but she had to stand her ground. Once the taxi was heading up the street, Camilla thought about making the taxi driver turn back, but she didn't.

Kafis needed to swallow his words and live with the fact that he had kicked out the mother of his child.

She thought about how she would have to stay in the filthy projects until Kafis's temper had cooled down enough for him to let her come back. Thinking back on her life in the projects, she realized that she had only bad memories: a mother who didn't care about her whereabouts, a father she never knew, and the large number of her mother's boyfriends who had had their way with her starting when she was age ten.

Now she was going back to her mother's house, but not by choice. She only hoped she still had a room there when she showed up. The last time she actually saw her mother, she was fifteen years old. When Camilla informed her mother back then of what those boyfriends had done to her, her mother kicked her out. Her mother thought that Camilla was the aggressor and that she had been trying to seduce her boyfriends to get special treats, which she often got because of their guilty feelings.

Camilla hated to return empty-handed. She had no clothes, no money, not even a second pair of underwear. She only hoped her mother would take her back in.

The taxi pulled up to Marcy Projects. "That will be twelve dollars, please," the driver said as he turned his head to look at her.

Camilla was calm, cool, and collected when she spoke. "I'll be right back with the money." Her hand was on the door handle.

"Wait. Hold up. You didn't have the fare when you got in here?" He instantly locked the doors.

She contemplated telling the driver that she had just been kicked out of her home and ejected from her only child's life. She looked at the dashboard, where pictures were posted of the driver's family. *Maybe he'll understand*, she thought. Camilla started to cry and told the driver her situation through her sobs. She didn't know if it would work, but with him being a family man and all, she had fifty-fifty chance.

"Do you believe in God?" he asked.

"Yes," she answered, not knowing where this question would lead.

The driver stared at her and was silent for a few minutes. All that was heard was Camilla crying for a pass. "Go ahead," he finally said. "One good deed will be paid by another, and hopefully, you'll make God the first priority in your life so that you'll have the strength to carry on. God bless you, young lady, for He is putting you through the ultimate test."

"Thank you. Thank you so much." She heard the doors unlock, and she got out of the taxi.

The driver rolled down the passenger-side window. "Young lady, don't you forget He will be the only one to get you through this struggle."

"I won't. Thank you again for your kindness." Camilla wiped her face and started toward her mother's building.

It was a walk she had never thought she would have to do, since she was with Kafis. Camilla was thankful that the taxi driver had let her off the hook when it came to the fare, but if the driver hadn't let her out of the taxi, she would've cried rape, and he himself would have needed God to get him through his test. She chuckled. Camilla reached her mother's building and pushed the apartment buzzer.

"Who this?" a harsh voice answered.

"It's Camilla, Yvonne's daughter. Let me in."

"Cam? What you doing here?" The last time Camilla had been called by that name was over fifteen years ago.

"Can you let me in so I can tell you, Mama?" She waited, not knowing if her mother would buzz her in. After waiting in silence for a minute, she figured her mother was not going to let her in. As she turned around to leave, the door buzzed, surprising Camilla. "Thank God," she mumbled to herself. She still didn't know what to expect when she reached her mother's door.

She stepped into the elevator and tried to hold her breath all the way up to the fifth floor. The urine smell was something she would never forget. When the elevator chimed on the designated floor, she rushed out into the hallway, gasping for air. Unfortunately, she had forgotten that the stench was even worse on the fifth floor. Camilla quickly walked to her mother's apartment and noticed that the door was already open.

"Mama?" she called out as she tapped on the door.

"Come on in and shut the door," Yvonne instructed, sucking her teeth in the process.

Camilla did as she was told. After all, she was there on the humble.

"Now, come have a seat over here and tell me why you have abruptly shown up here after all this time." Yvonne lit one of her Newport 100s.

Camilla was surprised to see what her mother looked like after all these years. Her face looked older than sixty, and she was far from sixty. Camilla didn't know what to think when she spotted her mother's needle works on the stained coffee table. When she was younger, she had never noticed her mother's drug habit. Yvonne had hid it very well. She anticipated the conversation she was about to have with her obviously drug-addicted mother, who had no shame.

"So what happened? He done left you? He caught you with someone else? You married that wannabe nigga, didn't you? Where my grandchild at? I would like to see her before I die." Yvonne blew smoke into the air.

Camilla tried not to blow up at her mother for her blatant verbal assault. She sat down but remained silent.

"What? You can't talk now? I want to know why you're here, Cam." Yvonne puffed away on her cigarette.

"Mama, I need a place to stay until I can return to Kafis. If you want, I will give you a couple of hundred dollars once I return home. That's on my word. I just need a place to stay until everything settles down." She hated to beg her mother.

"You left one thing out. Where is my grandchild?"

"I left her with Kafis."

"You did what? You stupid little bitch. Are you out yo' mind? It don't matter what that man has done. You always take yo' child. How else you gonna get benefits?"

Camilla wanted to pose those very same questions to her mother, but she knew she wouldn't get an honest answer. Instead, she closed her eyes and tilted her head back, questioning why she had ever thought of coming back here. This was a mistake she was going to pay for with her life, she feared, as she was unaware of her new surroundings. Much had changed in the projects. The hustlers, pimps, and hoes were now only an arm's length away, with no shame to their game. They flaunted their products for sale out in the open. There was no hiding them anymore. Suddenly everybody was now a money-maker and shaker, no matter what the hustle was.

"Are you gonna answer my question, Cam, or have you zoned out on some other shit?"

Camilla opened her eyes and looked at her mother. "Can I stay here or what, Mama?"

"You got money?"

"No."

Yvonne shook her head. "Stupid, just stupid. Of course you would leave without a plan and leave your only responsibility in life."

Camilla had had enough of her mother's hurtful words. It was time for her to answer the same questions. "Mama, was I not *your* only responsibility in *your* life? What did you allow to happen to me? Why did I leave, Mama? Why?" Camilla stood up.

Yvonne looked at her with the nastiest stink eye ever. Camilla's questions went unanswered, mostly out of shame.

"Are you gonna let me stay or not?" Camilla folded her arms across her chest, fuming with anger.

"Yeah, but you better find yourself down at social services bright and early tomorrow morning, 'cause ain't no way I'ma let you stay here for free. You better tell them yo' baby father done left you alone to care for your child and he set all your shit on fire. They should give you emergency benefits if you say the right words, and you better, 'cause if you show back up here with no money, you gonna have to sell yo' ass to get some, just like what you did with my old boyfriends."

Camilla wanted to smack fire out her own mother's mouth, but she held back and started walking toward her old room.

"Where you think you going?" Yvonne asked.

"My old room," Camilla snapped.

"Bitch, that ain't yo' room no more. You gave that shit up when you walked up out this house. You can sleep right on that sofa."

Camilla looked at the stained, ripped-up old sofa. It was amazing that Yvonne had not purchased a new one in all this time. The cushions were so flat, it was as if she would be sleeping on plywood. She shrugged her shoulders and shook her head. "I need a key."

"No, you don't. I'm always home." Yvonne lit another Newport 100.

"So you gonna make me give you money and not give me a key to go and come as I please?"

"Yup!" Yvonne was quick to answer.

"Well, if you expect money to support yo' habit, then I expect a key and my old room back."

"Really?"

"Think about it." Camilla walked toward the front door. She thought if she sat out front, she would be able to see what was going down in the hood. Once she was outside, she sat on the bench that was nearest to the building, scoping out the scenery before her.

Before long a cute young man approached. "Hey, ma. You tryin' to holla? I got that mean green."

She smiled at the fact that he had approached her, giving her the feeling that she still had it. She knew it wasn't because he wanted to sell to her.

"You smoking with me?" she asked, trying her charm.

"If you rolling, I am smokin' fo' sho', sweetie."

"You is if you stayin'," she cooed. "Where the wrap?"

"I got one right here. Here you go." The young man pulled a pack of Backwoods out of his back jeans pocket.

After she rolled the blunt, they both sat, talked, and smoked. After a while she knew he was feeling her. Now was the chance to see what Marcy had turned into after she left.

# Chapter Two

*Two years later . . .*

The blue and yellow flames of the stove's eye caused the pot of water to reach a boil. Twelve-year-old Kafisa Jackson watched as her father lowered the Gerber baby food jar into the pot of boiling water. The jar contained fourteen grams of some of Colombia's purest cocaine mixed with Arm & Hammer baking soda and seven grams of lactose.

"You see that?" Her father pointed to the little bit of residue that floated atop the water in the Gerber jar. "That's no good. If it floats to the top, it's not coke." He grabbed hold of the Gerber jar with an oven mitt and began making a circular motion with his wrist. "Hand me two ice cubes."

Kafisa did as she was told. She scurried over to the sink. She snatched up two pieces of ice from the bag sitting in the kitchen sink and handed them to him. She watched as her father dropped one of the ice cubes into the Gerber jar.

"Look." He gestured for Kafisa to come closer to see what was taking place in the jar as he continued to shake it. "All of that is the coke. You see how it's coming together?"

Kafisa nodded. She peered into the jar. She saw that what had once been liquid was becoming a solid piece.

"Come on, baby. Come together for Daddy," her father said to the drugs. "Listen to this," he told her.

Kafis dropped the second ice cube. The motion in her father's wrist increased. Kafisa turned her head to the side. She listened attentively, even though she had no idea what she was listening for. Then she heard and witnessed the solid piece of cocaine clinking against the inside of the jar.

"There she goes!" her father exclaimed, referring to the drug. "Yeah, this a good batch right here."

He went over to the sink and drained the water out of the Gerber jar, then walked over to the kitchen table, where the remainder of the half kilo sat. Kafisa watched as he dumped the powdered-cocaine-turned-rock onto the newspaper on the kitchen table. Once it had dried out, Kafis put the grams of base on the triple beam scale. A grin appeared on his face. His initial fourteen grams of powdered cocaine had turned into twenty-one grams of rock cocaine.

He turned to Kafisa and said, "They gonna love this in the streets, baby girl."

Kafisa smiled.

"Were you watching?" Kafis asked his daughter.

Kafisa shook her head.

It was Kafis's turn to smile. "Good." He pulled out the chair from underneath the table. "Come here," he instructed Kafisa. He patted the chair's cushion. "Sit."

Kafisa sat in the chair. Kafis pushed her closer to the table. This was the first time her father had allowed her to sit at his worktable. Kafisa stared at the items before her. She had seen them many times, but they looked different now that she was sitting in front of them and not looking at them from her father's lap. Since her mother had left, her father had been introducing her to a lot of his street business and teaching her more about the game. She was eager to learn whatever her father was willing to show her. Kafis placed his hands on Kafisa's shoulders.

"Put one of those masks and the gloves on."

Kafisa did as she was told.

"I don't want you catching a contact from the fumes or getting it in your pores through your fingers. This shit is dangerous!" Kafis warned. "Promise me, you'll never try this. I don't ever wanna hear you're using this junk. You hear me?" His tone was stern.

Kafisa nodded to indicate she understood. She could tell her dad meant what he had said. His eyebrows always turned into a unibrow whenever he was serious about something.

"Okay." Kafis returned to his calm self. "What I'm about to show you, people pay for. Hopefully, you'll never have to use any of the things I've shown you, but in this cruel world, you never know." He kissed her on top of her head. "Now, I want you to take one of those pieces out of that bag and put it on that plate." Kafis pointed to the Ziploc bag containing chunks of powdered cocaine.

Kafisa unzipped the plastic bag. She grabbed a chunk of the drug and removed it from the bag.

"Now put it on there," Kafis instructed.

Kafisa took the coke and put it on the scale. She watched as the needle on the triple beam fluttered from left to right until it stopped.

"Okay, take the razor and shave off the extra grams," Kafis continued. "Make sure you—"

"I got it, Daddy," Kafisa said, cutting her father off.

Kafis smiled proudly. He threw up his hands in submission.

Kafisa removed the seventeen-gram chunk of powdered cocaine from the scale and then picked up the Gemstar single-edge razor. She angled the razor over top of the chunk of coke. She pressed the razor gently into the product, then angled it back and pressed down harder. A small piece of the coke detached from the compressed chunk. Kafisa took the main chunk and put it back on the scale. The needle repeated itself. It fluctuated between the numbers thirteen and fourteen until it finally stopped.

"Good girl." Kafis rubbed the top of Kafisa's head.

Kafis felt like she had just scored an A+ on a major test. Her father's reaction to her weighing up the half ounce of coke fueled her eagerness to please him. She retrieved one of the small Ziploc bags from the box to the right of her. Kafisa put the chunk of coke in the bag and set it on the table. She closed her eyes and sat there for a second. She envisioned her father doing what she had watched him do so many times. Once she saw in her mind's eye what she needed to see, Kafisa snatched up the bag with the half ounce of coke and pushed the kitchen chair back. She made her way over to the stove.

Kafis watched in admiration as Kafisa poured the coke into the water inside the Gerber jar, followed by the baking soda and lactose. Kafisa set the Gerber jar in the pot of boiling water. She peered into the boiling pot and watched as particles began to float to the top of the jar and most of the powdered mixture dissolved and became liquid.

"Daddy, hand me two ice cubes," Kafisa requested without bothering to look back. She was focused on the Gerber jar.

Kafis smiled. "Yes, ma'am."

Seconds later, Kafisa was moving her wrist in a circular fashion, just as she had seen her father do. She began to nod as the second ice cube she dropped into the jar caused the liquid to solidify. Kafisa's wrist motion increased. A huge grin appeared on her face when she heard the rock cocaine clink against the jar.

"I did it, Daddy!" she exclaimed.

Kafis stood there with his arms folded and nodded proudly. "Yes, you did, baby. But you're not done yet," he reminded her.

Kafisa made her way over to the sink and drained the water out of the jar. She then dumped the rock, which resembled a white chocolate cookie, on the newspaper on the table. She looked from the drugs to her father. She could tell she was impressing him. She was eager to find out how well she'd done. *Did I bring the cocaine back to its original weight or gain additional grams?* she thought. She knew that if she'd done everything correctly, there would be additional grams. She wanted to make her father proud.

Satisfied with the amount of time she had let the product dry, Kafisa made sure the triple beam scale was level before placing the rock cocaine on it. The needle began to glide across the top of the numbers. Both Kafisa and Kafis watched as it passed the line that represented fourteen. Kafisa beamed as the needle approached the twenty line. Kafis smirked as it passed twenty-one and landed on twenty-two.

Kafisa realized immediately that the drugs she had just cooked up for the first time weighed more than the grams her father had cooked up. "I beat you, Daddy." She flashed a cheesy grin.

"Yes, you beat me, baby." Kafis shook his head.

The average person would consider him a monster and an unfit parent for what he had just shown Kafisa, but in his eyes, he had just given his daughter a gift that would and could take care of her for the rest of her life if anything were ever to happen to him or if they ever lost everything. For the past two years, he had taken on the role of both parents in the absence of Camilla. He had raised Kafisa the way he felt she needed to be raised, and no one could tell him different. She was getting older, and Kafis knew that pretty soon he would have to let her leave the nest and spread her wings. He wanted to make sure that her wings were the strongest they could be, in case of an emergency.

"Come here." Kafis opened his arms.

Kafisa fell into her father's embrace. She never felt safer than she did when she was in her father's arms.

"Never forget what I taught you." He kissed Kafisa on the top of her head.

"I won't," she promised.

She knew she wouldn't. Everything he had ever taught her was embedded in her young memory bank. There was no doubt in her mind that someday she would have to utilize some, if not all, of the things her father had shown her, and when the time came, she would be ready.

She looked up at her father. "I love you, Daddy." She smiled.

"I know. I love you too, baby." Kafis Jackson returned his daughter's smile.

That was all Kafisa needed to see and hear. She hugged her father as tight as she could, then closed her eyes, knowing he was the only parent she had. Her mother had been out of her life now for two years without a word, and she hadn't even shown up to visit. *How could a mother stay away from her only child*? Kafisa wondered. After questioning her mother's actions for only a minute or so, Kafisa concentrated on the only real parent she had. Her father meant more to her more now than he did when her mother was around.

# Chapter Three

On any other beautiful day, Kafisa would be out enjoying the Columbia, South Carolina, weather, but instead, she stood in a Brooklyn cemetery and watched as the pallbearers lowered a casket containing what was left of her mother's toxic body into the open hole in the ground. Kafisa took the white rose given to her by one of the caretakers and tossed it onto the coffin. She watched as it slowly traveled downward. She stood among thirty or so sobbing strangers, who offered their condolences to her every chance they got during the funeral services. Some had introduced themselves as relatives, but she felt no family connection to any of them. As far as she was concerned, they were all foreigners to her.

While everybody was filled with grief and sorrow over her mother's demise, Kafisa was emotionless. She felt nothing, or at least that was what she displayed. She did not shed one tear. She was in attendance only because her father had ordered her to go, despite the fact that he did not attend. It was because of his reason for not attending that Kafisa was present. He had expressed to her how he felt somewhat responsible for the death of her mother and couldn't bear seeing her looking any different than she had the day he had put her out. Kafis's guilt and shame were the reasons he had paid for her mother's entire funeral. Kafisa didn't blame her father, though. She blamed and resented her mother for what she had become.

When she found out her mother had started using the very same drugs her father sold, she had tried to convince her father that it was not his fault she had fallen in love with crack cocaine and heroin. When she graduated high school a year early, her father had informed her of her mother's whereabouts and the conditions of her lifestyle. He had given her the opportunity to decide whether she wanted to be a part of her mother's life or not for the first time since her mother left. Kafisa had chosen not to, not because of what her father had told her about her mother's lifestyle, but because her mother had never asked about her only child's whereabouts or sent word that she missed Kafisa or even wanted to see her.

Kafisa had, however, seen to it that her mother knew she had graduated high school one year earlier than she was supposed to, due to skipping ninth grade. Kafisa had made a copy of her diploma and had mailed it to the address her father had given for her mother, not because she'd wanted her mother to be proud of her, but because she'd wanted to prove Camilla wrong. Kafisa had never forgotten the words her mother had spoken that day to her father about how their child was never going to be anything in life as long as he was raising her. It was Camilla's words that had motivated Kafisa to excel in school and in life. They were the motivational fuel Kafisa had used to succeed in any and everything she set out to do. Now the woman who had given her a reason to strive for perfection was gone.

When the graveside service was over, some people stood around, while others made their way to their respective vehicles. Kafisa lingered at her mother's burial site. She had one last thing to do before she could leave. Just before the grave diggers began to toss dirt onto

Camilla's casket, Kafisa reached into her Gucci bag. She pulled out a folded-up sheet of paper. *This will be the last time I prove anything to you*, Kafisa said to herself. She tossed the sheet of paper onto the coffin, just as she had done the rose. She couldn't help but think how ironic it was that the day of her mother's funeral was the same day she received her college degree. *I have turned out better than you thought I would, bitch*, she thought to herself. *With no thanks to you.* Kafisa had a blank expression on her face.

Everyone who was standing around was curious about what she had just thrown into her mother's grave site. Kafisa paid the whispers and murmurs no mind. None of them knew her, and she didn't know any of them, and that was the way she wanted to keep it. Kafisa left them all wondering as she hopped in her father's limo and instructed the driver to take her home.

A smile came across Kafisa's face as soon as she saw the matching black Suburban and Mercedes-Benz CLS500 sitting in her father's driveway. It had been nearly three years since she had last stepped foot in the all too familiar house. It had been just as long since she had seen her dad. Although she did not agree with his wishes for her to stay as far away as possible from New York, she understood. She knew the life her father lived, and for as long as she could remember, he had never told her anything that wasn't the best for her.

The thought of their reunion excited Kafisa as her limo pulled up behind the super-white Benz CLK at the curb, which was a graduation present from her father. He had been unable to attend the graduation ceremony, for reasons that he would not discuss with Kafisa over the phone. He didn't have to, because she already knew why.

It was the same reason he had ordered her to stay out of Brooklyn all these years. She could always tell by his tone when she spoke to him whether things were peaceful or turbulent.

It saddened her that at the age of forty-eight, her father was still in the game. She had expressed her feelings about this to him on many occasions, with no results. She always received the "This is who I am" speech and the "This is all I know" answer whenever she suggested that he choose another profession or just retire as an OG. For now, she would let it go . . . or at least until the next time. She hoped that her words would one day seep in and that the bullheaded man she knew and loved as her father would make a change. She hoped it would be sooner rather than later.

Kafisa knew how stubborn he was. There was nothing in the world he wouldn't do for her. It had been proven time and time again that Kafis Jackson would not only take a life but would also give his own to protect her, but getting him to give up the game was like asking him to commit suicide, if you let him tell it.

Kafisa couldn't help but think about the one incident she had thought would make her father give it all up. It was then that she had realized the power of the game. Back then she had been too young and had not been fully educated about the rules, laws, and codes of the streets. Knowing what she knew now, though, convinced her that if what happened that day had not been enough to cause her dad to give it up, then nothing else would. For the past four years, both the scar on her forehead and the scar on her left inner thigh had been a reminder of just how dangerous her father's lifestyle was. Her thoughts began to slip into the past, and she traveled back in time to when she was just thirteen years old.

"Fee, you know you the only one I can trust, right, baby girl?"

"Yeah, I know that, Daddy," Kafisa answered, trying not to reveal just how nervous she actually was.

Ever since her mother had left and gotten strung out on drugs at the hands of her new boyfriend, Kafis had been juggling being a parent and running an operation. More times than he would have liked, he had taken Kafisa along with him when he conducted his business. She remembered how on those occasions, he would pull up on the street corners. A bunch of guys, both young and old, and wearing the latest hip-hop fashion and flashy jewelry, would one by one come up to his car. Kafisa would watch Kafis hand them the wrapped-up packages she had seen him put together at home. Sometimes they would go to the same areas, and he wouldn't give them anything. Instead, he would only collect money from them. He would always place it in the drawstring bag that Kafisa had become familiar with, then hand the bag to her once they had pulled off.

Once she got a little older, her father always tried to handle most of his transporting affairs while she was in school. It didn't always pan out that way. There were still times when he would have to take her along with him, like on this particular day. Normally, he would have taken care of the bulk of his weight sales by the time Kafisa's private school let out at 2:45 p.m., but his last deal had been pushed ahead from 2:00 p.m. to 3:00 p.m. With the way that Kafis handled business, being prompt was everything. Anyone who dealt with him knew that. At the same time, as a father, he also had an obligation to his daughter, so rather than neglect one or the other, he decided to kill two birds with one stone. He knew that killing those two birds came with many hidden consequences.

*It was twelve minutes to three by the time he pulled away from Kafisa's school, and he explained the situation to her as he drove to his destination. From the private school, Kafis knew that it would take him only ten minutes to get to where he was going, so he was confident that he would make the scheduled time, providing he didn't run into any traffic jams along the way. Out of force of habit, he checked to make sure that he had his driving credentials on him, and to his surprise, not only was he traveling without a license, but he also had no identification on him whatsoever. It dawned on him that back at the house he had changed his pants without transferring his wallet, which he was sure was lying on his nightstand.*

*The thought of traveling illegally with both drugs and guns in his SUV made Kafis leery and unsure of his decision. He knew that if he was to get pulled over right about now, it would be over for him, and his daughter would be alone in this cruel world he lived in. He couldn't take that chance. All he could think about was what would happen to his little girl if he were to go to jail. That alone was enough to convince him that he had to do the one thing that he thought was best at the time in order to safeguard both his and Kafisa's future in the event that he was unlucky enough to get pulled over.*

*He pulled over, reached in the backseat, and retrieved a duffel bag containing ten bricks of coke. He then reached up under the driver's seat and pulled two .40-caliber Glocks from under his seat.*

*"Well, I know you trust me. That's why I need you to take everything out of that duffel bag and put it in your book bag, and hold on to these for Daddy, okay?" he said, referring to the drugs in the bag and the guns he had just handed her. This was the first time that he had ever asked her to handle anything other than his money outside the house. Although she was not afraid, she*

*was nervous about this particular exchange. No matter what, she knew that she would always have his back, not only because that was what she thought he expected, but because she loved him.*

*Kafisa did as she was told. Moments later they were back on the road, en route to his destination. She rode shotgun as Kafis pulled his gold Denali into the Red Hook section of Brooklyn and drove to the designated meeting spot. He looked over at Kafisa, who now sat calmly across from him, despite what she held in her possession. For the average thirteen-year-old it might have been too much to endure, but Kafisa had been taught earlier on that she was not your average thirteen-year-old kid. While growing up, she had accumulated firsthand experience of the game through watching her father, so this was just another learning experience for her.*

*As they drove, Kafis's words resonated in her mind. "You're a brave girl. I know niggas in this game that would have been sweatin' bullets and shittin' bricks, being in the truck with all of this. You definitely got my blood in you. You a born thoroughbred Jackson, and I wouldn't trade my baby girl for nothing or no one in the world."*

*With one minute remaining before the meeting, Kafisa noticed the parked vehicle as her father turned into a parking lot by a tennis court. He pulled along-side the gold, four-door Acura Legend. Kafisa noticed the funny-colored front license plate on the Acura. The license was blue. Kafis saw that one of the indi-viduals he intended to do business with was from out of town. This would be the fourth time he was selling them something after meeting them at the Black Expo at the Jacob Javits Center in Manhattan. They were from New Jersey, but from the Brick City, which had triggered their conversation.*

*One thing had led to another, and before they knew it,
they were doing business together. Their first buy was
a key, and then they bought two, then two and a half.
Each time their money was correct, and they left as satisfied customers. Kafis had no problem with conducting
business with the two individuals, other than the fact
that they toted their guns whenever they copped from
him, which was understandable, being that they were
out-of-towners. Kafis had been in the game a long time,
and the two Newark dwellers seemed more like stickup
kids than actual ballers, but he knew that looks could be
deceiving, so he brushed the notion off, especially since
they had money to cop bricks. As long as their money
was correct and there was no funny business, there was
no reason to be leery.*

*After Kafis parked next to the Legend, the dark-
skinned kid who called himself Bo hopped out of the
driver's side, but the brown-skinned one, who went by
the name of Hub, was nowhere in sight. That was the
first sign that something was fishy, and it should have
made Kafis cautious. Bo came over to the driver's side of
Kafis's Denali.*

"What's up, Dinero?" *he said, greeting Kafis with a
pound and calling him by his street name.*

"Where ya man at?" *asked Kafis, wondering whether
Bo had come alone.*

"He up in this bathroom. He should be out in a minute,"
*replied Bo.* "Who this?" *he asked in reference to Kafisa.*

"This my daughter," *Kafis stated firmly, seeing the lust
in Bo's eyes. He couldn't believe this young nigga had the
audacity to blatantly disrespect him by checking out his
teenage daughter right in front of his face. He had killed
people for less, but apparently, this little nigga was not
aware of that, judging by the way he was looking at
Kafisa. What little respect Kafis had had for the kid was*

now gone and had been replaced with dislike. Were it not for all he had to go through to see to it that he made it to the checkpoint with the material he was traveling with, he would have called off the deal, but despite his personal feelings, business was business, so he changed his mind about reneging. He knew that this would be the last time he did business with these two Newark cats.

"Yo, go get ya manz so we can do this," Kafis told him, putting emphasis on his words, and the kid named Bo smirked.

"He already here," replied Bo.

"Where at?" asked Kafis, not seeing his partner, Hub.

"I'm right here, motherfucka!" barked Hub.

He revealed himself on the passenger's side of the Denali, where Kafisa sat. Startled by his sudden presence, Kafisa jumped. Before Kafis could react, Bo got the drop on him.

"You know what it is, nigga!" Bo yelled, with his .38 revolver drawn. He had it aimed at Kafis's head.

"Please don't hurt my dad," Kafisa pleaded.

"Shut the fuck up, you little bitch," Hub spit out, with no remorse.

Instant rage swept across Kafis's body, and he lashed out at Hub, despite the gun that was being held to his head. "You punk-ass muthafucka, don't talk to my daughter like that!"

"Nigga, fuck all that! Where that shit at!" Bo yelled. He delivered a blow upside Kafis's head with his pistol to show how serious he was.

Unfazed by the blow and more mad about it than anything, Kafis refused to cooperate, knowing that he was not dealing with professionals. He disregarded the blood trickling down the side of his face. He himself had robbed enough dudes when he was on his grind to know that when you were dealing with someone who posed a threat, you had to make an example out of them first before you did anything else, to show them you meant business. Knowing that these two individuals were amateurs, he intended to stall them for as long as he could, until he could figure out a way for him and Kafisa to come up out of this situation alive. Then he realized there was no way that he could predict their next move. He cursed himself for not cooperating sooner, knowing that this could all turn out badly.

"Get the fuck out of the truck!" Hub shouted through clenched teeth. He snatched open the Denali door and grabbed Kafisa roughly by the arm.

"No! Get off me! Get off me!" Kafisa screamed as she resisted.

Hub silenced Kafisa with a smack upside the head with his pistol. Her body went limp. He pulled her out of the SUV.

Kafis made an attempt to rise up in his seat, but Bo pointed his .38 at his head just as Kafis was about to launch himself at him. He gave him his best Dirty Harry impression. "Go ahead. Make my day, motherfucka!" he said with a grin on his face. "Yo, we ain't gonna ask you twice, nigga. Where them motherfuckin' bricks at?"

Kafis told them that they were in the backseat. Hub sprang into action, leaning into the back of the car in search of them.

"Where at? I don't see 'em. Oh! This nigga think it's a game!" shouted Hub. "That's what you think? Huh?" he growled at Kafis. He cocked his revolver back, threatening to pull the trigger.

Kafis said nothing.

Bo nodded. He cocked the hammer on his revolver. "See if we motherfuckin' playing when I blow ya fuckin' brains out, bitch, before I give your daughter her first taste of dick!"

*The three shots came out of nowhere.* Boom! Boom! Boom!

"*Ah, fuck!*" *Hub screamed.*

"*What the fuck! Oh, shit! Hub . . . Hub!*" *Bo yelled out.*

*That was the opportunity Kafis had needed. He opened the door to his Denali and banged it into Bo's midsection. Those unexpected shots that rang out had caught Kafis by surprise as well. The blow from the door caused Bo's gun to go off before he went crashing to the ground. Kafis hopped out of his truck and snatched up Bo's .38 before he could fully regain his composure and retrieve his gun. When Bo looked up, he saw Kafis standing over him, with his own pistol pointed in his face.*

"*Yo, Big Fis . . . man! Please! We wasn't gonna hurt you or your kid! You know the game, man!*" *Bo said with pleading eyes, trying to reason with Kafis.*

"*I don't want to hear that shit, muthafucka. You tried to play me like I'm some joke! Nigga, you should've played lotto. You would've had a better chance of winning! Now your greedy ass will never know how good you had it, muthafucka!*"

*Kafis emptied the revolver into Bo's face with no remorse.*

*In the midst of all the commotion, he didn't realize until the shots had ceased ringing in his ears that Kafisa had been calling him. Kafis ran over to the passenger's side of the Denali, where she lay on the ground. Blood dripped from her inner thigh. She still had the .40-caliber gun in her hand that she had just used to kill Hub.*

"*Daddy, he shot me!*" *Kafisa cried out. Tears rolled down her face. One of the wild shots Bo had fired when the car door hit him had struck Kafisa.*

"*Don't worry, baby girl. You gonna be a'ight,*" *Kafis assured his daughter. He got up and began pulling Hub out of his truck. Once he had thrown Hub's lifeless body* on the ground, he picked Kafisa up. She was shaking uncontrollably.

"Daddy, it burns!" she told him.

"I know, baby girl. Just hold on. I got you," Kafis told her as he too began to shed tears.

He could not believe what had just happened. He and his pride and joy had just escaped death. Had it not been for Kafisa and her instincts, he knew that it could have easily been the two of them who were laid out in the park, instead of Bo and Hub. He knew he had to get up out of the area before the police arrived, and he had to get his daughter medical attention immediately, because she was losing a lot of blood. Kafis jumped in the driver's seat after placing Kafisa on the backseat of his truck and headed to the house of a friend who was an ex-army veteran and specialized in gunshot wounds, because a hospital was out of the question.

Kafisa lay in the back of her father's Denali, in pain, traumatized by the whole ordeal she had just experienced. When she closed her eyes, flashes and images of what she had just done flooded her mind as the sounds of the guns going off still rang in her ears. She had no idea what had possessed her to go into her book bag and pull out one of her father's .40 calibers, nor could she recall even going into the bag, let alone pulling the trigger. When her father had pulled the body out of the truck and had let it fall to the pavement, she'd known that this was not just some nightmare that would go away in time. This was real, and someone had just died by her hands.

The thought of her taking someone's life was enough to send chills through her entire body. She envisioned Hub's body lying there, his eyes still open. As the reality of the whole situation began to set in and she was able to play it back, Kafisa felt no remorse or regret for what *she had done. She reasoned with herself that if it were not the assailants lying out there back in the parking lot, it would be her own father, and she would have never known that, because she would have been raped, then killed, too. Thus, it was because of her actions that she was still alive to see her father survive, and she was content with what she had done.*

Kafisa's thoughts returned to the present as she entered the domain that she knew to be her home. A warm feeling greeted her and swept through her body. For her, this was a place filled with many memories from the past, mostly good ones, and a few bad ones to go along with them, but overall, she had no real complaints about her upbringing, despite her mother's beliefs. To become the young woman that she had become, after being raised the way she had been raised and by whom, said a lot about Kafisa as a female. She was proud of herself. She knew that she fell into the small, exceptional percentage of people in the world who would succeed in life when they reached adulthood, despite their parents' lack of parental skills.

Despite the fact that her mother and father had never married and had not been together for most of her life, that her mother had fallen victim to drugs, that her father had been a notorious drug dealer and gangster from the time she was born, and that she had grown up around drugs, Kafisa believed that she had turned out pretty well. Given that her father had both educated her about and exposed her to the streets, she knew that instead of going off to college and getting her degree, she could have easily chosen to spend the next four to six years of her life in the family business. Kafisa strongly believed that if she got into the drug game, she would become just as successful at it as her father. She was convinced it was in her blood.

Kafis wouldn't hear of it. So, she had chosen the academic route instead. Kafisa was determined to continue to work hard in school and to obtain her law degree. Her father had plans for her the moment she got her law degree. He had a job awaiting her in New York City, at a well-known law firm. The thought alone motivated Kafisa. She figured if she couldn't represent her father and his crew in the streets, at least she could represent them in the courtroom if they ever needed it. Kafisa smiled at the irony of it all.

Kafis thought he had heard his name being called, but he wasn't sure due to the surround sound in his theater room blaring through the speakers. He paused the *Black Caesar* DVD he was enjoying on his built-in flat-screen plasma TV. He heard his name being called again. He immediately recognized the voice. A smile spread across his face as the voice drew near. By the time Kafis turned around, Kafisa was standing in the doorway of the plush theater room. As quickly as he could, Kafis got up out of his seat and met his daughter in the middle of the room.

"Hey, baby girl!" he said, holding out his arms to hug his only child.

"Hey, yourself, old man," Kafisa replied, welcoming her father's arms. She embraced him and returned his hug.

A grin covered Kafis's face at his daughter's reference to him being old. He didn't look or feel a day older than thirty. Kafis considered himself to be somewhat of a health nut. He was on a strict no-meat diet and exercised daily. He also believed that all the young females he surrounded himself with kept him feeling and looking young and healthy, but for the past few years, ever since he had passed the forty-five mark, Kafisa had joked about him getting up there in age.

"I see you still got jokes," he replied with a little sarcasm.

Kafisa detected the sarcasm in Kafis's tone. She knew that her father did not like to be reminded of his age, but she deliberately teased him about it every opportunity she got, to remind him of just how long he had been in the game. Kafisa knew, however, that the reality of the matter was that for his age, her father looked exceptionally good and was able to stand next to the best of the best youngsters in the game who had it going on both in the appearance department and in the financial department.

Oftentimes when they went out together, he was mistaken for her man rather than her dad. Despite the fact that Kafis appeared young in her eyes and everyone else's, Kafisa felt that her father was just too old to still be living the life, playing the game. Technically, she was not from the streets, but because she had been raised by someone who was, she knew what the streets were about and what the rules, both old and new, that governed them were, which was why she worried so much about her father.

Kafis was from what would be considered the old school, which meant that the individuals who played the game respected it and the rules by which it was played. Back in Kafis's glory days, everyone knew their position and played it, whatever it might be, and if you were the type who could play different positions, then you were one of the elite, a ghetto superstar in the game, so to speak. Kafis had told Kafisa stories about how it was growing up, how you had to know how to fight, and how you *would* fight if necessary, if you wanted to hold on to your girl, your money, or establish a credible reputation. Back then everybody simply respected the game, which was why rats and snitches didn't get any love. There was a unique way during Kafis's era of marking those who took the cowardly way out in the game, making it easy for those who played by the rules to identify them on sight, compliments of spots like Trenton State Prison and Rahway State Prison in New Jersey, along with Rikers Island and Sing Sing in New York, and numerous other prisons keeping it gangsta around the globe.

Kafisa remembered when her father had shared with her his first experience of prison at the young age of nineteen, long before she was even a sperm cell and an egg. He had been sentenced to a five-year bid after copping out to a conspiracy to possess CDS and taking a plea bargain to avoid going to trial after finding out that the state's key witness against him was a close friend of his at the time. While waiting to be shipped upstate, he came across the state's key witness on Rikers Island. It was then that he was schooled in the popular saying "Snitches get stitches," and that was exactly what he gave the kid: a buck fifty from his temple all the way down the side of his cheek, a lifetime scar to remember his disrespect.

Nowadays snitches didn't get stitches. They got trips and vacations, and that was exactly why Kafisa feared for her father. Under the new-school rules, you had participants getting into the game who were not representing the positions that they were playing. For instance, the ballers who stacked chips and had never been to jail, or had been to jail and didn't want to go back, they caught diarrhea of the mouth about those who professed to keep it gangsta, put that work in, and their guns went off. When retaliation came into play, they knew who had shot 'em, according to the police report. Then there were those who simply hated on you because they weren't you, so they dropped a dime on you.

Kafisa was well aware of how her father carried it in the streets, and she knew that any of these three scenarios could easily pertain to him if he continued to outthink and outdo the new breed of money getters, who were finding it somewhat difficult to come up in the game due to Kafis's and his team's existence in the streets. Sometimes she wished that she could have just had a normal childhood and normal parents with a normal life. Then again, what was normal for two individuals who had grown up in poverty-stricken households? she wondered.

Kafisa knew it was going to be what it was going to be. She reasoned with herself, like she had so many other times before, and was grateful for what she had and what she had learned from her father. A smile came across her face. "I'm just messin' with you, Dad. You look nice. It's good to see you doing well. I've missed you," she said, her words sentimental.

"I missed you too, baby girl, but don't be getting all soft on me now," replied Kafis, with half of a smirk on his face.

"I'm not!" she answered defensively, still smiling.

Kafis was as tough as they came, but when it came to his daughter, he melted like fried ice cream whenever she showed her emotional side to him. He had raised her to be just as tough and emotionless as he was, but at times her mother's side of her would come out and get the best of her, and him too.

Kafisa reminded Kafis so much of her mother before the drugs got to her. She was a lighter version of her mother. Each time he looked at her, it made him realize just how much he really did miss Camilla. Kafisa had inherited her long, silky jet-black hair, along with Camilla's light brown, slanted Asian eyes and her deep dimples when she smiled. She was at least three inches taller than her deceased mother, who had stood at five feet eight, but they were both built similarly. Camilla had had the shape of a supermodel, with the posture to match. She had been in between the size of Naomi Campbell and Tyra Banks, and hands down, she would have given them both a run for their money if she had been a model. Kafisa possessed that same build, but that was where it stopped. Physically, Kafisa bore a resemblance to her mother as an adult, but internally, she was her father's daughter all the way.

"What are you still doing in New York, and why didn't you call and tell me?" questioned Kafis. His tone and demeanor had become more serious. He remembered that he had given Kafisa specific instructions not to stay in New York after her mother's funeral, out of concern for her safety. There was a territorial beef between his team and some young and upcoming gunners, who were wild enough to send a message to him by doing something to her.

"I didn't call, because I wanted it to be a surprise. Besides, I wanted to see you," Kafisa replied innocently, seeing the seriousness on her father's face. She grimaced. She hated when he made her feel like a little girl. She locked eyes with him until he broke his stare.

Kafis shook his head and let out a gust of hot air in frustration. He had expected Kafisa to give him the answer that she had. He knew how dangerous it was for her to be in town, but he understood why she had to come. A vast amount of time had passed since he had last seen his daughter, and her arrival was a nice surprise. Only she could make him feel the way he was feeling now. Since the day she was born, Kafisa had been her father's kryptonite. It was at times like this when he thought strongly about getting out of the game and just living an ordinary life, but he knew that right now this was impossible.

"I know, baby girl, and it's good to see you too." He smiled. "What's left of you, anyway," he added, making a joke about the weight she had recently lost.

Kafisa rolled her eyes. She was actually proud of herself for the pounds she had shed. "What's that supposed to mean?" she asked, with her hands on her hips, already knowing what it was that he was insinuating.

"That means you need some meat on those bones of yours. What? You don't like the food in South Carolina? Them women love to eat down there in the South. Don't tell me you goin' Hollywood on me," Kafis teased.

"Dad, please!" She paused, waving at him with her hand. "You so corny, and so old school, I might add."

Kafis laughed. He always got a kick out of Kafisa referring to his style as old school, although in reality he was, and he was proud of it. Being old school was what kept money in his pockets, a roof over his head, and it was what had enabled him to live as long as he had in the game. He smiled at the thought.

"What?" asked Kafisa, catching his smile.

"Nothing. It's just good to have you back home," he answered, his eyes wet with tears, as he leaned in and hugged her. "Now, can an old-school dad take his old- and new-school daughter out to eat?" Kafis asked jokingly.

"Of course you can, sir." Kafisa lit up like the Fourth of July.

It was good to be back home, regardless of the reason that had brought her back. Above all, it was good to see her dad.

# Chapter Four

"Kafis, what's doing, my friend? It's always a pleasure." The maître d' greeted Kafis with a handshake and a hug.

"Same ole, same ole, Fran," replied Kafis, embracing the short Italian man with a small build.

Francis Costillo, whom he called Fran, was as connected as they got. Ever since Kafis saved his life at Fort Dix, a federal prison, the two had been as thick as thieves. Under any other circumstances, Fran's family would have had a problem with their association, but Kafis's reputation spoke for itself. He was respected by all, no matter their gender or the color of their skin.

"And I see you brought your beautiful princess along with you this time." Fran directed his attention to Kafisa. "Fee, it's been a while, sweetheart. Come here."

Kafisa didn't budge.

"What? You don't remember Uncle Fran no more?" he asked her, then planted a kiss on each side of her face.

That caused Kafisa to blush instantly. She had known the maître d' for almost her entire life, since long before the Village Café opened up six years ago. When she first met Fran, she had been just a little girl. At least once a week she and her father would travel out to Staten Island, New York, for dinner in the evening and cookouts during the summer. Going to Fran's house was one of the most memorable highlights of Kafisa's childhood because it entailed riding the Staten Island Ferry, and she had always enjoyed getting on the ferry. It was then that she fell in love with boats and the ocean, causing her to persuade her dad to buy a boat when she got older.

In a way, Fran was like an uncle to her, because he had always been there for her the way any uncle would be there for his niece. Kafis had no sisters or brothers, but because the two people he trusted the most and some of his other comrades had kids, it was as though she had a bunch of cousins to play with. Other than Kafis's right-hand man, Fran was the closest thing her dad had to a brother. Fran had a son, Francis III, who was two years younger than Kafisa, and a daughter, named Francine, who was two years her senior. They both treated Kafisa like a sibling.

Kafisa knew her dad trusted Fran and had the utmost respect for him. She could recall the countless nights Fran had babysat her in Staten Island while her dad took care of business. He was the only man Kafis had trusted enough to leave her alone with. That had made it easy for her to embrace Fran's kids. Kafisa and Francine would stay up all night and talk about what they wanted to do and be when they got older, while Francine's little brother would help his dad count money, the same way Kafisa helped her dad. Ironically, she and Francine both wanted to be attorneys so that they could represent their families, if need be, whereas Francis III was being prepped to carry the family torch someday. Francine had been a friend and a big sister for Kafisa all throughout her childhood.

The love between her father and the Italian man had always been readily apparent. Kafisa had seen the two of them lend each other money and cars, something that she had never seen Kafis do with anyone else. It wasn't until she was older that she realized what that was all about. She remembered being in Fran's wedding, alongside Francis III and Francine. She also remembered when Fran opened the full restaurant with a bar up on Richmond Hill Road, a restaurant that had an Italian ice stand outside. To her, there was no Italian food restaurant that could compare to her uncle Fran's Village Café.

"Uncle Fran, now you know it's not even like that," Kafisa replied. "You know how much I love you. You're my favorite uncle," she added, flattering him.

"I'm your *only* uncle, sweetheart," he shot back, with a smile and a wink to go with it.

Everyone smiled.

"Fran, how's your wife Concetta, li'l Fran, and Francine?" asked Kafis.

"You know, Concetta is still Concetta, and my boy, well . . . he's still trying to find his way," Fran replied with his Sicilian accent, keeping his same smile. "Now, Francine, my pride and joy . . ." He beamed. "She's a hotshot lawyer now. Works for a one of the top law firms in Manhattan."

Kafisa smiled. "Nice. Please let 'em know I send my love." She paused for a moment. "And I'd like to get Francine's number before I go, if you don't mind."

"Absolutely. No bother at all. Let me just get you guys squared away."

Both Kafis and Kafisa nodded.

"My apologies, Fran," Kafis said. "I know we just popped up on you, but this one here just popped up and surprised me after Camilla's funeral."

Fran's look switched to serious. "First, my condolences . . . Where's my manners?" He placed his hand on his chest and bowed in Kafisa's direction. "It slipped my mind completely," he said apologetically.

"Thanks, Uncle Fran." Kafisa's words were low and dry. She couldn't care less about the death of her mother.

Fran eyed Kafis.

Kafis grimaced.

Fran immediately picked up on it and changed the subject. He knew the history and the reason for Kafisa's coldness about the entire matter. "As for you . . ." He directed his attention to Kafis. "Please don't insult me like that, brother. Where there's no room for others, there is always room for you. As we speak, your table awaits," Fran stated sincerely.

"My bad, brother. Thank you."

"Come on. Forget about it! Don't make me cry. Enjoy your meals. Everything is on the house. Ralphie will show you to your table," Fran said as a young Italian waiter appeared with two menus in hand.

"Thanks, Uncle Fran. It's good to see you too," Kafisa offered with a smile before they parted.

"Great to see you, sweetheart. Keep making us proud. We're over here rooting for you." Fran winked for a second time and waved good-bye. Seconds later he was gone.

"Good afternoon, Mr. Jackson," greeted the young waiter named Ralphie. "Ma'am." He nodded to Kafisa.

Kafisa returned his nod.

Ralphie led them to their table, and once they were seated, he handed them the menus. "Are you ready to order, or do you need some time?" he asked, knowing full well that they had their favorite dishes memorized.

"No, we're ready, Ralphie," answered Kafis for both himself and Kafisa.

"Okay. Will you be having the usual, sir?" asked Ralphie, remembering that he had served Kafis baked ziti on several occasions when he had dined at the establishment.

"Not today, son. Today I think I'll go with the linguini with clams. I haven't had that in a minute," answered Kafis.

"Excellent choice, sir. And for you, ma'am?" Ralphie said, directing his attention to Kafisa.

She smiled, doing her best to hold in her laughter at being called ma'am, especially by someone only a few years younger than she was, give or take. She knew that the young waiter had to be fairly new, because she had not seen him at the restaurant when she last visited almost three years ago, and besides, he would have known who she was if he had he been here for a while. After all, anyone who had worked at the Village Café for a while knew that she was one of Fran's nieces and Kafis's daughter.

"Yes, she'll have the veal Parmesan," Kafis said. "And can you bring us a bottle of white wine?" he added, looking up.

"Yes, sir," replied Ralphie, collecting the menus.

After a fulfilling meal and a beautiful conversation between father and daughter to cap it off, it was time to call it a night. The two of them had spent hours just reminiscing about some of their better days in the past and discussing politics and world events. Kafis was so impressed by his daughter's intellect. He was gloating and was proud to be her father. *If only Camilla could see her now*, thought Kafis, knowing that Kafisa's mother would also be proud of her daughter, despite her personal views about him as a parent.

A slight sense of sadness fell over Kafis. It was no secret that he missed Camilla and wished that she could be there, sharing such moments with him and Kafisa. He still felt somewhat responsible for Camilla's death. He had invited Kafisa out to tell her all she needed to know in case anything ever happened to him, but the evening had been going so well without him discussing his business, and so he had put the subject on the back burner for now.

Night had fallen, and Kafis was exhausted both physically and mentally. "Let's go home, baby girl," he suggested, rising from the dinner table. "Your old man is getting tired," he added as he let out a yawn.

Kafisa smiled and rose from her seat as well. "Yeah, it is way past your bedtime, ole man," she joked.

That made Kafis smile. His mood instantly changed from down back to up. His daughter had managed to pull him out of his funk without even knowing how he had just been feeling. It had been an enjoyable evening between father and daughter. Kafis was tempted to bring up what was on his mind but decided again to save it for the next day.

# Chapter Five

Kafisa was awakened out of her sleep. She thought she had heard a noise. Throughout her childhood, because of the lifestyle her father had led, she had always been a light sleeper. She had been taught to be alert at all times. At a young age, Kafis had schooled her on the importance of being on point no matter where she was or what she was doing. Even when she was asleep, she had to be alert, he had told her. She remembered his words clearly, as if it was yesterday. "Never sleep. Only rest!" And later on in life this advice had proven to be very valuable.

Her wits had saved her from a situation during her sophomore year of college. A guy she was dating got tired of taking no for an answer. One night, after leaving a party intoxicated, he broke into her off-campus apartment, with the intention of forcing himself on her. Luckily for Kafisa, she heard the living-room-window glass hit the floor, alerting her to danger. When she hopped out of bed and made it to her bedroom door, she could hear tip-toed footsteps and heavy breathing outside her bedroom.

As soon as the guy eased the door open and stepped inside the room, he was met with a Louisville Slugger baseball bat upside the head. Had she not recognized his voice as he called out her name in a drunken stupor, Kafisa knew that she would have beaten him to death with the bat. Instead, she threw him out. She vowed never to tell a soul what had happened, especially not her dad.

She knew if she had, the kid's life would have ended for real.

Not sure about what she had heard, Kafisa climbed out of bed to go check on her father. When she reached his door and entered his bedroom, he was already awake. It was obvious that he, too, had heard a noise, given that he was standing there with a gun in one hand and a finger up to his lips, gesturing for Kafisa to be silent. At the sight of her father, her suspicions were confirmed. Someone unknown to them was in the house.

"Stay there," Kafis whispered. He quietly walked over to where Kafisa stood. "There's another gun in my top drawer. Get it out and use it if you have to. I'll be right back," he instructed, still whispering.

Kafisa just nodded her head. She was not afraid, not of the gun or the situation. She was familiar with them both. She was no stranger to danger, nor was she a slouch when it came to a pistol, and her father knew that.

"Lock the door behind me," said Kafis as he crept out of his bedroom.

"Be careful," whispered Kafisa.

Once her father was gone, Kafisa did as she was told. She locked the door and retrieved the .38 revolver from Kafis's dresser drawer. Now, with the gun in her hand, she contemplated going downstairs to assist her father, but then she easily dismissed the idea. If he had wanted her to back him up, he would have said so, Kafisa reasoned. That was the type of man her father was, and all her life he had been that way. He was someone who knew what he wanted and how to go about obtaining it, and he wouldn't hesitate to ask for a person's help if that was what the situation required, no matter who or what it was. She didn't want to go against his orders, so she stayed put, without fear.

She waited impatiently with gun in hand. She placed her ear to the door. She was unable to hear anything.

Minutes went by, but still nothing. Then, just when she thought her patience had run out, she heard someone coming up the steps, or rather more than one *someone*, because she heard more than one set of footsteps, she was sure. Not knowing what to expect, and not having any time to think, Kafisa cocked the hammer of the revolver, stepped away from the door, and took aim.

The sound of the knob on her father's bedroom door shaking caused her to tense up. *Whoever at this door, tryin'a get in, is in for a rude awakening*, thought Kafisa as she held her finger steady on the trigger. She believed that if someone was able to make it upstairs, then that could mean only one thing: they had to have gotten the drop on her father. With that thought in mind, Kafisa was ready, willing, and able to lay her life on the line and make whoever was on the other side of the bedroom door pay for her father's demise.

The rapid knocks on the door startled Kafisa but did not scare her. The knocks almost caused her to squeeze the trigger of the .38 out of reflex. She gripped the gun tighter. She still had it cocked and aimed at the would-be target on the other side of the door.

*Bam! Bam! Bam! Bam!* "Ms. Jackson, we know you're in there. This is the FBI. We need you to open the door immediately!" shouted an unknown man from the hallway.

The words that had come from the other side of the door did not move Kafisa the way they might have the average female. *Average* was hardly a word that could be used to describe her. Kafisa was, in fact, a rare breed, possessing the best of both worlds when it came to perception. She was just as sharp street-wise as she was textbook-wise, which was why she wasn't impressed by the shouts that came from the unidentified man. She had been taught by one of the best.

For all she knew, the words spoken on the opposite side of the door could have come from a potential stickup kid, thought Kafisa. He and his partners could easily be posing as federal agents in an attempt to get her to let her guard down so they could enter the room to complete their robbery. She could hear her father's voice in her head. *Trust no one.* This was the conclusion she drew, and there was no way that she was going to let that happen.

A million thoughts raced through Kafisa's mind as she tried to determine the best way to handle the predicament she was now in. She felt tears begin to form in her eyes at the thought of what the perpetrators who had invaded their home could have done to her father, but she fought them back, knowing that now was not the time for her to be falling apart. She had to remain strong for both her and her father's sake, because there was a good possibility that he was still alive, and he would be counting on her to use what he had instilled in her to get them through this situation.

*Bam! Bam! Bam!*

The repeated knocks on the door broke Kafisa's train of thought. The same voice called out to her once again. "Ma'am, this is your final warning. Open the door now, or we'll be forced to kick it in!" the so-called FBI man threatened.

This time, his words were spoken with more conviction. Something about them made Kafisa question her initial thoughts. Whoever stood on the other side of the door did not sound like any regular street thug pretending to be the police. She was almost positive, but not 100 percent sure, and so she was still hesitant about opening the door. *What would my father do? Come on, Fee. Think,* she said to herself. She could not process her thoughts quickly enough. A sudden disturbing noise shattered her concentration.

*Boom!* That was the sound the door made as it burst open from the impact of the battering ram. Kafisa's heart skipped a beat. She watched the door break off its hinges and fall on the right side of the bedroom. Had it not been for the badge that she spotted instantly when the door flung open, she would have surely squeezed the trigger of the gun she still had in her hand and possibly shot one of the officers dressed in plain clothes. Federal agents began filling the room.

*Confusion* would be the best word to describe Kafisa's reaction to the scene. As instructed, she dropped the .38 she held tightly in her hand and kneeled on the floor. She placed her hands behind her head, and one of the agents roughly lowered her arms and cuffed her hands behind her back. By now the room was filled with a dozen or so federal agents. The only thing on Kafisa's mind was the whereabouts of her father. Her question was answered when she was escorted downstairs. Other law enforcement officers, wearing blue and yellow FBI jackets, were leading Kafis toward the front door.

The sight of his only child in handcuffs stabbed Kafis like a dagger to his heart. Shame fell upon him. All her life, he had put her through so much, without hearing so much as an ounce of complaining. He loved and respected her for that. Now he had placed her in a degrading position. He knew what was in store for her once they reached the local county jail, and he cringed at the thought that she would be subjected to this. There was no doubt in his mind that she was her father's daughter and possessed his strength, but this was not a part of the game that she had been exposed to, and he wondered for a second how she would hold up through it all.

Her facial expression assured him that she was all right, but there was no telling how she was mentally. Like him, she had the ability to maintain a convincing poker face, even when she actually had a losing hand. He knew that her biggest concern would be his well-being and not her own, and he felt it was imperative that he let her know that he was good. Just before they whisked him away, Kafis looked at his daughter. He simultaneously shot her a wink and flashed her his famous "Daddy's little girl" smile. Seeing that, Kafisa's whole demeanor changed. She returned her father's smile right before the two agents led him out the door.

When Kafisa arrived at the local FBI office for questioning, it was obvious that the agents thought that holding her on suspicion of conspiring with her father in his illegal activities would make her spill his entire operation, as if she were a scared little girl. That was far from the truth. She held her ground. Her father would be proud if he saw her resilience.

"Now, Kafisa is it? We have a sticky situation here, and I think you already know the outcome, so coming clean now may help your case. What can you tell us to put some leverage out there for you?" asked the FBI agent who had placed the handcuffs on her. He sat at a table across from her.

"I don't know shit. Where's my lawyer?"

"So you need a lawyer?" the agent asked, knowing the interview was over before it had even started.

"Yes, I do."

"Okay. I guess you are entitled to a lawyer. It may be a while before we can get one. Sit back and relax. Can I get you anything?"

"No. Again, I want my lawyer, you fat fuck."

Just then a knock was heard on the door. One of the FBI agents got up to open the door. A well-dressed, six-foot-two, dark-haired man entered the room and stood before them.

"Good morning, gentlemen. My name is Andrew Parker. I'm Ms. Jackson's attorney. Now, if my client is under arrest, please let me have a word with my client."

The FBI agents looked at each other in surprise.

"Can you guys get the fuck out now? I need to talk to my lawyer," Kafisa demanded.

"Sure thing, Mr. Parker, but I have one question for you," said the agent who had addressed Kafisa.

"And what would that be, sir?" Andrew asked.

"Who contacted you?"

Kafisa only prayed that this lawyer was on her side and wouldn't let these bastards railroad her into selling out her father.

"Sorry, but that is privileged. Now please, I would like a word with my client."

A smile appeared on Kafisa's face. She knew exactly who had sent the lawyer. Her uncle Fran was always looking out for those close to him. After the agents left the room, she immediately asked about her father. "What's going on with my father? Is he okay? Is he in this building?"

Andrew took a seat vacated by one of the agents. "Hello, Ms. Jackson. I know you want to know about your father, but at this time it looks like they had him under surveillance for the past year. A confidential informant even infiltrated his crew. In this business there's always a snake lurking around the corner, waiting to take everything, even if that means sleeping with the enemy."

"Someone in his crew snitched on him?" Kafisa let out a deep breath.

"But you, young lady, have a small problem. They want to charge you with some trumped-up charges. Since they needed to break into the room where you were, the first charge will be resisting arrest. Second, attempted murder of a federal agent, because you were holding a loaded weapon and aiming it at them. Third, conspiracy, because you were seen with your father all day yesterday. Now, most of these charges won't stick, and since this is your first offense, you have a good chance of walking after seeing the judge."

"Conspiracy, attempted murder, resisting arrest! This is some real bullshit. What's my uncle Fran saying?" Kafisa was confused about where these charges had come from. The only charge she thought would be accurate was a weapons charge, since she had no permit and the gun was used only for protection. She only hoped that her father had no bodies on that gun, or else she would definitely be facing some jail time, no matter how good a lawyer she had.

"Your uncle is very confident of my legal abilities, or else I wouldn't have been on retainer for the past ten years." Andrew smiled.

"Okay, since it was one o'clock in the morning when they broke into my father's home, when do I go in front of a judge?" Kafisa asked, hoping to get the answer she was looking for.

"You should be seeing the judge no later than ten this morning. I have already put in all the necessary motions for you."

"And my father?"

"He, on the other hand, will have to take it to trial to reduce his time," Andrew answered truthfully.

"Well, we all know he won't take any deals. He would have no remorse or regrets if he had to do his time for the crime." Kafisa lowered her voice a bit, knowing her father might be facing some serous time, far greater than his previous five-year bid.

"Okay, Ms. Jackson, I will be in court, doing what I have to do so you can be released on bail. You keep your head up and say nothing to any agent. I don't care if they ask you how you are doing." Andrew stood up to leave.

"Thank you," Kafisa said as he headed for the door.

"No need to thank me. This is what I'm paid to do." He smiled before he walked out the door.

Kafisa wanted to cry, but she knew that would be the last thing her father would expect. For now she was going to sit back and relax, because everything was being handled.

A few hours later Kafisa found herself before a judge. Her hands were sweaty. She was nervous because she did not know what the outcome would be. Andrew didn't look worried at all. He was smiling at Kafisa to assure her that they would prevail.

"All rise for the Honorable Judy Weinberg," the bailiff announced. "We have docket number two-eight-five-zero-five before you."

The judge entered the room and took her seat on the bench. She got down to business straightaway. "You may be seated. State, what are your remarks?"

"Good morning, Your Honor. Ms. Jackson is charged with conspiracy with a known criminal, the attempted murder of federal agents, and resisting arrest. We are asking that bail be denied."

Kafisa wasn't shocked to hear the charges, because her lawyer had already told her what to expect, but hearing them delivered out loud by the state's attorney added an intensity to the whole matter and made her a little wary about whether or not she would be walking out of the courtroom a free person.

Andrew stood and faced the judge. "Good morning, Your Honor. My client has no prior offenses. Matter of fact, she was visiting her father for the first time in three years at the time of this incident. She picked up a gun for protection because as far as she knew, unknown assailants had broken into the house she called home. These charges are far-fetched, and the state's attorney is grasping at straws for a conviction."

"Ms. Jackson, where do you reside?" the judge asked.

Kafisa looked at her lawyer first, and he gave her a nod, indicating she should answer the question.

"I reside in South Carolina." She kept it brief. Kafisa provided no extra information.

"Why are you in New York?"

"Visiting my father."

"I see. Now, when you grabbed a weapon, were you in fear for your life? Did federal agents announce their presence?"

Kafisa looked at her lawyer again for permission to speak. Again, he nodded his head.

"Yes, I was in fear for my life. No, the agents did not announce themselves until they broke through my father's bedroom door."

"Your Honor, the agents did announce themselves before entering the house," the state's attorney asserted.

"I think if they had properly announced that they were federal agents, Ms. Jackson would not have been in fear for her life. Also, she aimed the weapon, not knowing there were—"

"Your Honor, the agents announced themselves *before* breaking through the door," said the state's attorney.

"Did the agents announce themselves at the front door or *after* they broke into the house?"

"Your Honor, Ms. Jackson did not know that federal agents were in her father's house," Andrew declared, then looked at Kafisa with a glowing smile.

"I believe I asked the state a question." The judge did not like the fact that her question had gone unanswered.

"I will have to acquire the report from the warrant," said the state's attorney.

"Did they have a no-knock warrant?"

"Your Honor, I will have to get the warrant they acted on."

"Why don't you have it now? I think I am ready to rule."

"Your Honor, I ask for a recess to acquire more documents," the state's attorney pleaded.

"Your request is denied. Being unprepared is not something I can overlook. Ms. Jackson, I believe that you were in fear for your life and that the federal agents did not announce themselves before entering the house. Your bail is set at twenty thousand dollars, with a six-month probation sentence. After your probation is up, your record will be cleared and sealed. You cannot leave the state for the next six months. If you are arrested on any charges between now and when the six months have elapsed, your bail will be revoked, and the charges will be reinstated."

"Your Honor, Ms. Jackson has conspired with a known criminal, her father, Mr. Kafis Jackson, who has been under—"

"State, I have ruled. Defense, will you be posting bail?"

"Yes, Your Honor." Andrew flashed another smile.

"Your Honor—"

"State, again, I have ruled. Next time be prepared." The judge looked at the bailiff. "Next case."

An hour later Kafisa was walking out of the courthouse, with the assurance that nothing would be on her record after six months. She was pleased with the judge's ruling and extremely satisfied with her lawyer's success in reducing her charges to a mere probationary period. Now she had to see her father to understand what had really gone down and why.

# Chapter Six

*One month later . . .*

"Please step through the metal detector," the steroid-talking white officer said.

Kafisa sucked her teeth and did as she was told. Out of all the places where she could be visiting her father, this was the last place she had expected to be or wanted to be. She had driven for two hours to get to the Philadelphia Federal Detention Center.

"Stop right there," a butch-looking white female officer commanded in an authoritative tone.

Kafisa came to an abrupt halt. She rolled her eyes as the butch-looking female officer waved a metal wand up and down her body. She started at the front, then made her way to the back and then to the front again. Once she thought the officer was done, Kafisa proceeded to move forward.

"Just a minute, ma'am." The female officer put the metal wand in front of Kafisa to block her path. The wand landed right in front of Kafisa's breasts. She could feel the metal touching her nipples. Kafisa knocked down the black-and-yellow wand in front of her. "Is there a problem?" the female officer asked aggressively.

"Yes, there is," Kafisa shot back. "I don't appreciate you trying to fondle me on the sly," she spat angrily.

Her words caught the attention of other visitors waiting in line to visit their loved ones. They also caught the attention of a sergeant posted up on the jail wall, observing the conduct of his fellow officers. Before the butch-looking officer could react, the sergeant intervened.

"I got it, Johnson." The sergeant placed his hand on the shoulder of the female officer whom he had called Johnson.

Johnson shot daggers at Kafisa, who met and matched her stare, before she sidestepped her and posted up for the next female visitor. Kafisa chuckled lightly under her breath at the female officer. *This bitch don't know how close she was to getting fucked up*, thought Kafisa.

"My apologies," Sergeant Davis offered.

His words calmed Kafisa's confrontational demeanor. She nodded solemnly. "Thank you."

"Don't mention it," the sergeant replied. "You're Kafis's daughter, right?" It was more of a statement than a question.

"Yes." She was surprised by the sergeant's comment.

"He's been expecting you," Seargeant Davis informed her. "Right this way."

As she followed the sergeant, all she could think about was what it had taken for her to even find out where her father was being held. She had gone through hell getting information on where and why they were holding him. As high profile an attorney as he was, and despite all the money her father had been paying him, his own lawyer had been having difficulties finding out anything. It was actually Francine who had tracked Kafis down. After a few phone calls Kafisa had been informed that he was actually being held in FDC Philadelphia. After receiving the information about his whereabouts, she had stopped by the post office to check her P.O. box, which she'd had since she was a junior in high school, and she had found a letter from him telling her that he needed her to come visit him.

Ever since she had been released from FBI custody, Kafisa had been staying in a penthouse suite in Times Square, courtesy of her uncle Fran. The FBI had seized the place she had called home for most of her life, along with all the rest of her father's assets. When she had returned to the house, they hadn't even allowed her to get any of her things. Aside from what she had on during her arrest, Kafisa's only belongings were back in South Carolina, where she attended school. She wondered if her father was aware of all that was going on out in the real world while he sat in the Philadelphia penitentiary.

Just then, as if on cue, Kafis Jackson came strutting through a metal door. Kafisa had to do a double take when he appeared in front of the Plexiglas. He was bigger than he had been the last time she saw him, which was nearly a month ago. She hadn't seen him this size since she was a kid. He had muscles popping out in places she didn't know muscles existed. His brush cut had turned into a miniature Afro, and his chin-strap beard was now a long, fluffy, full-size one. He also sported a pair of what seemed to be reading glasses. Kafisa just stared at him like it was the first time she had ever laid her eyes on him. He sat down and grabbed the phone. She picked up the phone on her side.

"Hey," he greeted her.

"Hey, you." Her excitement showed in her voice. It was good to see him, and she told him so.

Kafis smiled.

"How's everything?" she asked.

"As good as it can be under the circumstances," he replied.

"That's good to hear. I'm sorry for—" She didn't get a chance to finish. Kafis held his hand up to stop her from continuing.

"No need for apologies or regrets. The important thing is that you're here."

"You're right," she agreed. Even now, Kafis was schooling her.

"How are you holding up?" he asked, lowering his volume.

Kafisa nodded. "I'm fine. Just been worried about you," she confessed. "They were giving me the runaround, not giving me any information."

"That's all a part of the game, baby girl." His tone was nonchalant.

Kafisa could tell he had given his current predicament some thought. Whenever he sounded the way he did now, his mind was already made up about something.

"So, is everything good? In your letter you said you had something important to talk to me about."

Kafis ran his hand down his face, then stroked his beard. Kafisa could tell he was collecting his thoughts. "Yeah, I do." Kafis cleared his throat. "I wanna tell you a story," he said.

Kafisa gave him a confused look.

"Just listen," he told her.

"You know I am." She told herself not to interrupt him.

That made Kafis smile. A lump formed in his throat. Only she could make him feel the way he was feeling now. Kafis cleared his throat. "When I was eight years old, your grandmother sat me down and schooled me to the game. One day, after coming home from a half a day of school, I accidentally walked in on her while she was mixing up some drugs in her bedroom. When she saw me, she stood up. She escorted me into the kitchen. There she taught me what she was doing and everything else she knew. By the time I turned thirteen, I knew everything about the drug game there was to know.

"Even though she taught me all of that, she always made me promise to stay in school and get an education. My senior year I came home to find my mother in tears.

When I asked her what was wrong, she told me that her connect had gotten arrested and no one else would sell to her. Shortly thereafter, things began to get rough for my mother and me. So, one night I caught the train over to New York City and arrived at One Hundred Forty-Fifth Street in Harlem and posted up. I watched as jokers who looked like drug dealers approached Spanish dudes.

"Within minutes, I witnessed drug and money transactions between the black and Spanish hustlers. I waited until I thought I had found the right hustler, and then I followed him. I followed him all the way to the subway station, and then right before he made it to the steps, I made my move. He never saw it coming. I crept up from behind, yoked him up, and put the knife I had hidden behind my back up to his throat. I told him to run his pockets, or I would slit his throat, and I meant it.

"He reached into his pocket and gave me a small brown paper bag with a piece of tape on it to conceal it. I took the package with my left hand, while holding the blade firmly up against his neck with my right hand. Everything was going smooth until he made the fatal mistake of reacting. To this day, I don't know what he was trying to do, but he never got the chance to do it, because without hesitation, I slit his throat from ear to ear with the Rambo knife I had. I remember being scared to death, and I ran for my life. I nearly ran all the way down to One Hundred Twenty-Fifth Street nonstop. I made my way to the One Hundred Twenty-Fifth Street train station to head back to Brooklyn. I was paranoid the whole while.

"When I got home, I tore open the brown bag. Based on the color, I knew it was coke. I went and got the scale I knew your grandmother kept in the house. When I placed the package on there, it read fifty-six grams. That was the day I became a drug dealer. A year later I moved us out of Marcy and into a brownstone. That following year your grandmother died. Before she died, she told me to make sure I used what she had taught me to get ahead in life and never forgot that." Kafis paused for a moment. "Do you know why I'm telling you this story?" he asked his daughter.

Kafisa didn't have a clue, but she was glad he had shared that piece of his life with her. She shook her head no. Instead of speaking, she waited for him to tell her why.

"The reason I told you that story is that"—he took a deep breath—"the something your grandmother told me is the something I'm telling you now."

His statement caught her by surprise.

Kafis picked up on it. "Listen, I know what I laid on you is a hard pill to swallow, but with all that has happened and is going on right now in them streets, we needed to have this talk," he began. "At the end of the day, it doesn't matter what I made in them streets. When the smoke clears and the dust settles, there will be nothing. These people are gonna take it all, and there's nothing you or I can do about it."

She listened attentively to her father. The more he talked, the more a weird feeling swept through her body. "Dad, don't say that." Kafisa scowled.

"Baby girl, just hear me out please," he insisted. "These crackers ain't playing fair. They got somebody playing for 'em that used to be on my team. Just don't know who, though."

Kafis had been charged with conspiracy, with the intent to distribute cocaine, and now they were trying to throw the book at him. He was a man with money, power, and influence that was so far reaching, nobody had even known how high up he was until now. Based on information provided to the Feds about murders and drug trafficking over state lines, they had enough evidence to charge him under the CCE Statute, also known as the Kingpin Statute. He had officially become one of the FBI's Ten Most Wanted, and now they had captured him. According to them, at his command, his team had been responsible for a slew of murders of rival drug dealers, had had ties to the Italian mob, and had engaged in drug trafficking and transport in over fifty cities and states. The government was trying to make sure he went away for the rest of his life and never saw daylight again. They had even tried to get his daughter on similar charges.

"This may be the last time you see your ole . . ." Kafis inhaled, then exhaled. "Yeah, this is where it ends for me."

"Dad, why are you talkin' like this?" she asked.

"Look, don't question me." His tone switched from calm to strong. "Sooner or later, everything is going to get crazy back home, and I want to make sure you're prepared and can handle what comes behind it. I've already sent letters to your uncle Fran and Corey. Those are the two people you can turn to if need be." He paused and shook his head. "I'm sorry, honey. I should've done better. Could've prepared better." Kafis lowered his gaze and dropped his head in shame.

"Hey, ole man. Hold your head up," Kafisa thundered into the phone.

That caused Kafis to chuckle into the receiver even before he raised his head back up.

"No apologies, no regrets, remember?" Kafisa shot her father's words back at him.

The irony made him smile. "You're right," he agreed.

"And no getting soft," she added with a smile.

"Only for you, baby girl." Kafis smiled with his eyes. "Regardless of that, though, you'll always be in my heart and in my mind. You're my only real blood family, you understand me?"

"Absolutely!" Kafisa replied in a stern tone. "We're family for life!" Kafisa looked her father square in the eyes and repeated her words again.

A tear managed to escape Kafis's left eye. He wiped it away quickly, then put his fist up to the Plexiglas. "I love you, baby girl."

Kafisa placed her palm on the Plexiglas. "I love you too, Daddy." At that moment, an unspoken connection had been made between father and daughter.

Kafis stood up. "One last thing," he said.

Kafisa noticed the change in his demeanor again. She waited for him to tell her what was on his mind.

"The game is officially over for me." Kafisa watched as her father's nostrils flared. He began to fidget with his hands. "I know I can't stop you, so I'm not even going to try." He took another deep breath. "Just promise me one thing."

Kafisa locked eyes with the man who was responsible for her being the woman she was today. "Anything." The respect was undeniable in her tone.

"If you gonna play it, play it to the fullest!" Kafis slammed his right fist into the palm of his left hand. "Don't take no shorts from nobody, and make sure you surround yourself with people who don't, either."

Kafisa had heard him loud and clear. She nodded in agreement. So many thoughts and questions invaded her mind, but she held back from expressing them. She knew that if her father was saying all this to her, then things had to really be serious. She also knew that if he had just given her his blessing to step into the world he had taught her about—something he had wanted her to do only in case of an emergency—then things were really bad. Words her father had said to her when she was a little girl now resonated in her mind. *If I ever give you my blessing to play this game, then we've hit rock bottom.* So Kafis had just told her that they had hit rock bottom. It was now her turn to wipe away a tear that had managed to escape her right eye. She quickly wiped it away and maintained her composure.

Kafis stared at his daughter long and hard before he spoke. He knew he had just opened Pandora's box, but he felt no remorse about any of it. He knew what Kafisa's decision would be. "That's my baby girl." He smiled. "Believe none of what you hear and less than half of what you see." His demeanor turned serious. "Normally, I would tell you that if you're the smartest person in the room, then you're in the wrong room, but in this case, always make sure you're the smartest person in the room."

Kafisa nodded. She was all too familiar with her father's "smartest person in the room" quote. She knew it was his way of telling her to always stay on point and three steps ahead of everybody else.

Kafis shook his head and grimaced before he spoke again. "I don't want you coming down here anymore to see me, either. This will be the last time you see me like this," he stated. Before Kafisa could rebut or put up a fight, Kafis hung up the phone, spun around, and walked off.

Kafisa watched as the officer held the door for her father. Her mind was racing a million miles a minute. It took everything in her power not to break down in tears and scream for her father to return. She fought all those feelings off. It wasn't until she heard the officer on her side of the Plexiglas announce that visiting time was over that she snapped back to reality.

After visiting her father, Kafisa hopped back on the road. She played her father's words back in her head over and over as she cruised up the Pennsylvania Turnpike, heading back to New York. *If you gonna play it, play it to the fullest*, replayed over and over in her mind, but what stood out the most was something else he had said. *Believe none of what you hear and less than half of what you see*. She had no clue what that statement meant, but she had a funny feeling she would find out soon enough once she returned to New York.

# Chapter Seven

Kafisa awakened suddenly. She had managed to fall asleep a couple of hours ago. She instinctively reached under her pillow and grabbed her .380 caliber handgun. Explosive knocks on the door to her hotel suite had broken her sleep, and they rang out again now. Kafisa hopped out of bed and cocked her weapon. She scurried out of the bedroom and made her way over to the suite's double doors. She wondered who could be at the door. Only one person knew where she was, and that was Uncle Fran. She had told no one else where she was staying.

All types of thoughts raced through her mind. After all, her father had told her not to trust anybody. Her thoughts were interrupted by the rapid knocks again. She jumped back as the thunderous knocks echoed in her ears. Kafisa's heart rate rose as her pointer finger rested on the trigger of the chrome semiautomatic. Her jaw clenched. She took a deep breath, then exhaled. She tiptoed closer toward the door to look through the peephole. She was all too ready to use her weapon if she had to. Her gun was now pointed chest level at the door. *Better them than me*, she thought, remembering what her father had taught her about enemies and beef. Kafisa eased up and peered through the peephole. She let out a sigh of relief when she saw who it was.

Kafisa flung the door open just as Francine Costillo was about to continue her assault on it with her pale white knuckles. She was met with a smile as soon as her childhood friend looked up and noticed her standing in the doorway.

"Girl, you scared the hell out of me!" Kafisa exclaimed.

"Yeah, right!" Francine let out a light chuckle. She stepped toward Kafisa and threw her arms around her. "You're not scared of anything," she added. She kissed Kafisa on both cheeks.

Kafisa welcomed her embrace. It was her turn to laugh at Francine's comment. She broke free of Francine's hug. "Come in." Francine accepted the invitation. Kafisa stood there and held the door open as Francine strutted into the room like a supermodel. "How did you know I was here?" Kafisa asked, letting the door to the suite close.

"Do you really have to ask that?" A twisted look appeared on Francine's face.

Kafisa let out another chuckle. "You're absolutely right. You are your father's child."

Francine beamed. "I missed you!" she bellowed.

"Me too," Kafisa returned.

The two exchanged another hug.

Francine broke the hug this time. "I heard about Uncle Kafis." Her mood turned serious.

Kafisa batted her eyes and nodded.

"That's one of the reasons why I'm here," Francine continued.

"What's wrong? Has something happened?" Kafisa now had a concerned look on her face.

"No. No. I'm sorry for making you think that," Francine offered apologetically. "Everything's fine. At least as fine as can be expected," she added.

Kafisa gave a sigh of relief. "I'm sorry for even thinking the worst," she said, apologizing for jumping to conclusions.

Francine waved the apology off. "It's okay." She walked across the suite to the bedroom and sat on the bed. "My father sent me." Francine got down to why she hadn't taken no for an answer at Kafisa's hotel room door. "He wanted me to come and tell you that your dad wrote him a letter, and that from this day forward you are a daughter to him, as well as a sister to me. He was instructed by your father to see to it that you returned to school and got your law degree. These are the keys to the CLK your father bought you." Francine removed the Mercedes-Benz keys from her Louis clutch, along with a stub from the parking garage where the car was located. "It was the only thing my father could get back for your dad without jeopardizing the family."

Kafisa nodded repeatedly. "Give Uncle Fran my deepest love and appreciation. Let him know I totally understand."

Francine smiled. "He knows."

"You said that was one of the reasons you tracked me down. What are the others?" Kafisa wanted to know.

"Yes, but everything ties in with my initial reason for coming," Francine announced. "According to your father's letter, once you are finished with school, he has given you his blessing to enter into his business affairs as a representative of the Jackson family, and he asks that my father vouch for you."

Kafisa could not believe her ears. Even now, from behind bars, her father was protecting her and had her back. Never in a million years would she have thought that he would even consider letting her in the game, let alone try to put her in the position he was once in. She had had no idea he even thought she was capable of playing the game on his level. The conversation was starting to make a little bit more sense now. In two days Kafis had managed to surprise her with his actions. She was still trying to take it all in.

"I remember when my dad first asked me to join him at the table." Francine gave her a confident look. She had an idea what was going on in Kafisa's mind.

Kafisa stared at her oddly. "What do you mean?"

"What do you think I mean, silly?" Francine chuckled. "Don't let the business suit and the big office fool you. I, too, am my father's daughter, just as you are Uncle Kafis's." She smiled.

"Wow!" was all Kafisa could conjure up.

"Wow is right. And that's the final reason why I am here."

A look of confusion appeared on Kafisa's face. "I don't understand," she admitted.

"Your father started his legacy in Brooklyn," Francine began. "Based on what my father told me, Uncle Kafis built an empire that was invincible and indestructible, up until recently. Our fathers' relationship was built on trust, love, respect, and loyalty. Our fathers will still have that same relationship built on the same principles until time ends. Even from the inside, your father has proven to be the man that my father has always admired and respected on the highest level. Although a weak link has jeopardized your father's empire, your dad has done everything in his power to maintain his reputation and credibility. Because of that, you will receive the same courtesy and will be offered the opportunity to rebuild and reclaim what Uncle Kafis once governed."

Kafisa asked Francine a dumb question. "Brooklyn?" She was still trying to put it all together.

Francine could tell Kafisa needed a clearer picture. "Yes, Brooklyn," Francine replied. "But there are some conditions to it, and you have to be fully committed to restoring your legacy," Francine added.

"It doesn't matter! Whatever it takes, I will be fully dedicated," Kafisa asserted. A new burst of energy seemed to enter her body.

Francine smiled. "Your father said you'd say that in the letter he wrote to my dad, which is why he specifically told my father to let you find your own way in your own familiar territory before we offer any assistance."

This was the third time in two days that Kafisa was surprised by something her father had said or done. She couldn't help but laugh. It reminded her of something her father used to say. "Help the bear," were the words he would spew whenever someone asked if he needed help with anything. *Still teaching me lessons, huh, ole man?* she said to herself silently.

"So, he wants me to set up shop in Brooklyn if I get in this game?" Kafisa asked, making sure she was clear about what Francine was saying her father had requested.

"No. His specific words were, 'I want her to make everybody in Brooklyn respect her. Let her figure out how.'"

Kafisa nodded her head. "I wouldn't have it any other way."

"Good. Then once you achieve that, the doors will be open, and you will have access to an unlimited supply of Colombia's purest cocaine and China's purest heroin." Francine rose from the bed. "I will be your connect." She handed Kafisa a business card with a number handwritten on the back. "This is the only number you should ever use to reach me at concerning this conversation. Please rip it up after you store the number in your phone, under something only you can remember, other than my name, and flush it down the toilet." Francine leaned in to Kafisa and hugged her. "It was great seeing you, my sister. I look forward to what the future holds for us. Welcome to the family."

"Thank you." Kafisa returned the hug.

Francine looked down at her gold, limited edition, female Presidential Rolex. "Well, I have to run. I'm meeting a client in this area." Francine made a proud face and then made her way toward the door to the suite. Kafisa trailed behind her and then opened the door.

Francine paused in the doorway. "By the way, this conversation never took place," she said. Then she made a beeline for the elevators.

Kafisa let the suite door close behind her. Francine had just given her some food for thought, and now she was hungry. She had no clue how she intended to capitalize on the position her father had put her in. What she did know was that she had a few years to think about it. *You haven't heard the last of the Jacksons*, she thought to herself as she made her way back to the bedroom. She was going to make her father proud. She would come back with the force of a true scholar to get the family's empire back.

# Chapter Eight

Kafisa went to bed early that night. Between her father being locked up, her switching hotels every day for her own safety, and her thinking about being the head of the table, a position she was destined for, Kafisa was mentally and physically drained. It had been a long and tiring day, but at the end of the day, things were looking up for her. Fortunately for her, she had been cleared of all charges and her probation was suspended, thanks to the help of an attorney friend of her uncle Fran. They continued to show that they had her back.

Now that she was free of all charges, she was finally going to get out of New York and return to South Carolina, as promised. After her visit with Francine, she was more than motivated to return to South Carolina. Kafisa had contacted her and her father's travel agent and had had her book her on the earliest flight possible out of JFK tomorrow. She was all too eager to put distance between herself and the Big Apple. After she had finished up her packing, exhaustion had finally caught up to her and settled in. Kafisa had peeled off her clothes and had made her way to the shower. After showering and grooming herself, she'd lain across the king-size bed. In no time she'd slipped into a deep sleep. She started dreaming about being in the car with her father on the highway.

*They were being chased. Not only by state troopers, but by the DEA, the ATF, the county police, and the Feds. There were helicopters hovering overhead.*

*Kafisa peered over at her father, who was driving and mumbling to himself at the same time. She could hear him saying, "The game is dead," over and over again. Kafisa became nervous from her father's crazy New York driving. She tried to tell him to slow down, but he wouldn't listen. The more she asked him to slow down, the faster he drove.*

*Kafisa began to perspire profusely. For the first time, her father was scaring her. Then, out of nowhere, they hit a divider. Kafisa cried out as the truck started flipping. As it flipped, she looked over at her father. Blood was dripping from his head on down to his face.*

Kafisa's eyes immediately shot open. She was breathing uncontrollably and wheezing. Goose bumps covered her arms from the chills she had. She had soaked her sheets and pillows with sweat, and the dampness, combined with the cold air from the air conditioner in the hotel room, had her nearly freezing. She peered over at the digital radio alarm clock. It was a little after six in the morning. She realized she had slept for seven hours.

She climbed out of bed and made her way back into the bathroom. When she looked in the mirror, she noticed that her eyes were bloodshot. The nightmare she had awakened from had freaked her out. She turned on the shower. Only this time, instead of taking a hot, steamy shower, Kafisa adjusted the water so that the temperature was cool. Still nude from her previous shower, she stepped under the cool spray. She placed her head under the showerhead and let the cool water blanket her entire body. Images from her nightmare tried to invade her thoughts each time she closed her eyes. She shook them off and sided against closing her eyes again. She remained in the shower a little while longer, then got out.

Something didn't feel right to Kafisa. The nightmare she had just awakened from seemed so real, despite the fact that she knew it wasn't. She couldn't stop thinking about her father. At that moment, she wished she could pick up the phone, like she was used to doing, and check on him, but that was not possible. There weren't too many times in her life when Kafisa had defied instructions or requests given by her father, but the way she was feeling, she just might have to, and she was not concerned about the fact that he would probably be mad at her.

She remembered his last words before their visit at the detention center had ended. *I don't want you coming down here anymore to see me, either*. She knew it would eat her up inside and kill her if she didn't check on Kafis before she left New York. Kafisa grabbed a towel from the bathroom's metal rack and wrapped it around her dripping wet body. She wasted no time in retrieving her phone. She scrolled through her recent calls until she found the number she was looking for, then dialed.

"Hey, it's me again. I'm sorry, but I need you to reschedule my flight for later on tonight. An emergency came up," she informed her travel agent.

Seconds later she was thanking the travel agent and ending the call. Kafisa had decided that today she was going to check on her father. It had been nearly a month since she had last seen him or heard from him. The nightmare had really disturbed her. Kafisa glanced over at the room's radio alarm clock. It was approaching the seventh hour. She knew she didn't have much time if she wanted to make the visit. She quickly dried off and dressed.

An hour and a half later, she was exiting the highway in Philadelphia as she made her way to the detention center where her father was being held. Kafisa dreaded the process she knew she had to go through to get to see her father, but it was a price she knew she had to pay to see him. The entire drive down, she couldn't stop thinking about her dream.

When she entered the main building at the detention center, an eerie feeling swept through her entire body. *I hate this place. I'll die before I end up in here*, she thought to herself as she made her way to the window to register for her visit with her father. She got in line, and as the line moved forward, her thoughts and her attention were drawn elsewhere. She made eye contact with the dyke officer she had had a problem with the first time she came down to the facility. She noticed the officer looking at her oddly. She was not in the mood for another confrontation with this officer. Rather than playing the staring game with her, Kafisa rolled her eyes and turned her head in the other direction.

"Next!" bellowed the officer at the window.

Kafisa approached the window with her ID in hand.

"Name of visitor?" the officer asked. He never bothered to look up at Kafisa. His eyes were focused on the computer screen he sat in front of.

"Kafis Jackson."

The officer glanced up at Kafisa as soon as he heard who she was visiting. Kafisa noticed the peculiar look on the officer's face. It was the same type of look the butch officer had plastered across her face when she and Kafisa had made eye contact.

"Is there a problem?" Kafisa asked. The irritation in her tone was unmistakable.

"Just a moment, ma'am," the officer replied.

Kafisa could tell something was wrong. She watched as the officer picked up the phone. She couldn't make out what he was saying through the glass, but the way he kept looking at her and back at the computer screen while he talked on the phone was all the confirmation she needed that something was not right.

"Something must've happened," she heard someone a few bodies behind her say.

Kafisa's patience started to grow thin. "Excuse me!" she exclaimed.

"Someone will be right with you," the officer informed her as soon as he hung up the phone.

"Be right with me?" she said. "Be right with me for what? What's the fuckin' problem?" she demanded to know.

Just then, a metal door could be heard buzzing, and out walked the sergeant who had assisted her the last time she had visited. Kafisa was all too ready to cause a scene, until she heard the metal door buzz again and saw another man walk out. He was dressed in a two-piece suit that appeared to have been tailored just for him. Judging by his beard and kufi, she assumed the Middle Eastern–looking man was Muslim. It wasn't until she saw the *dhikr* beads and the Koran in his hand that she knew her assumption was accurate.

"Can somebody tell me what the hell is going on?" she asked the sergeant. As she spoke, her eyes cut back and forth from him to the Muslim brother, who stood a short distance behind the sergeant. "I'm getting tired of being harass—"

"I'm sorry," the sergeant said, cutting her off. The look on his face was one of compassion.

"Sorry for what? Just let me see my father. Don't give me the runaround. Tell me why it is taking so long to see my father!" Kafisa barked, misreading the sergeant's demeanor.

"You don't understand, Ms. Jackson."

Before Kafisa could ask the sergeant to explain what he meant, the Muslim man intervened, extending to Kafisa the Islamic greeting of peace. "*As-Salaam-Alaikum,* sister."

"*Wa-Alaikum-Salaam,*" Kafisa replied, directing her attention to the Muslim man.

Although she had never practiced Islam, her father had made it perfectly clear to her that she was a Muslim and that she must always greet other Muslims when in their presence or when greetings were offered to her. She was curious to know why the Muslim brother was intervening in her issue with the facility.

"I am Imam Abdus Samad, the imam for the detention center."

His introduction meant nothing to Kafisa. All she cared about was seeing her father and finding out why they were not allowing her to do so. She could hear the frustration and anger in the voices of the people behind her, who had grown tired of waiting. She was tempted to turn around and say something but decided against it. Instead, she stayed focused on the situation.

"I was asked to come out here and speak with you," Imam Abdus Samad explained.

A confused look appeared on Kafisa's face. "Talk to me about what?"

"Can you just step over here right quick?" The sergeant used his hands to direct her out of the line of visitors waiting to get in to see their loved ones.

"Here goes the bullshit." Kafisa let out hot air in frustration. She shook her head as she stood off to the side with the sergeant and the imam. "Okay, so what's the problem?" Her tolerance level was almost at zero, and it was apparent in her tone.

"Again, my apologies," the sergeant offered for a second time. "Imam Abdus-Samad will explain everything to you if you'd just go with him."

"Why do you keep fuckin' apologizing to me? Explain what? Go where? Why am I being asked to leave without seeing my father?" Kafisa's tolerance level had fallen to zero in a matter of seconds. "Somebody needs to tell me what the fuck is going on! Do I need to get my father's attorney involved?" she said, her booming voice echoing throughout the lobby. All eyes were now on her.

"Sister Kafisa, please calm down. I will explain." The imam's tone was calm and humble.

"Well, get to it, 'cause I need to see my father immediately. If you think I'm getting back on that long-ass line, you are surely mistaken."

"Sister Kafisa, as believers, we are taught that there are only two things that Allah promises us—life and death."

Kafisa stood and listened as the imam spoke. She had no clue about what he was saying and why he was saying it. Still, she knew not to interrupt him, for she had already disrespected him by cursing in his presence.

"Your *abi* was a believer," Imam Abdus Samad continued.

A look of frustration appeared on Kafisa's face. "Imam, no disrespect but—"

"My beloved sister," the imam said, cutting her off. "Allah has called your *abi* home." He could tell she didn't understand what he was trying to tell her.

The sergeant picked up on this as well. "I'm sorry, Ms. Jackson," he said, joining in.

"Why do you keep fuckin' apologizing to me?" She looked at the sergeant, then at the imam. "I'm sorry, Imam. I'm feeling this is all intentional. I just want to see my father." Kafisa spoke in a softer tone now, hoping to get an answer. She had grown tired of the delay and the riddles she felt she had been receiving. "Look, all I want is for someone to tell me what the fuckin' problem is and to let me in to see my father. Is that a crime? Maybe I should get his lawyer on the phone." The irritation in her tone intensified and was apparent in her demeanor.

The sergeant grimaced. He knew there was no getting around what needed to be said to Kafisa. He removed his sergeant's hat. "There was an incident in the facility." The sergeant cleared his throat. "Your father was the victim of a vicious attack. We're sorry. He didn't make it."

The sergeant's words went from Kafisa's ears straight to the pit of her stomach. She thought her ears were deceiving her, but her gut confirmed what she had just been told. Kafisa tried to conjure up a response, but no words would come out. She began to feel light-headed. She reached out for something to lean on. The imam stepped closer to her, just in time for her to grab hold of his right shoulder.

"Are you okay, sister?" he asked.

Kafisa heard the question but couldn't respond verbally. Instead she nodded. Her stomach was repeatedly doing somersaults and twisting into knots. Her heart seemed to be beating up against her chest at an abnormal pace. She closed her eyes in an attempt to regain what little composure she could have after hearing the disturbing news, but it only made matters worse. Out of nowhere, vomit spewed out of her mouth and onto the imam's pant leg. She was doubled over as she continued to regurgitate her breakfast in the lobby of the detention center.

The sergeant was the first to assist her. "Are you okay, Ms. Jackson?" He kneeled down to help her stand upright.

"Don't touch me!" Her words were laced with venom. She shook the sergeant's hand off of her back. "Don't fucking touch me! Don't nobody touch me!" she screamed.

The sergeant backed away. He understood and didn't want to make matters worse.

Uncontrollable tears began to spill out of Kafisa's eyes. Images of some of her most memorable moments with her father began to run through her mind. She still didn't want to accept the news. A million and one questions invaded her thoughts. How could this happen? Who could've gotten that close that he couldn't see it coming?

Kafisa became dizzy. The room seemed to start spinning. It felt as if she couldn't breathe. Her chest began to tighten. She tried to open her mouth to say something, but nothing came out. Her vision was blurry. She blinked once, then twice, in an attempt to focus. Instead, where it was once blurry, Kafisa saw nothing. Total darkness fell upon her right before she passed out.

The sergeant spoke into his radio. "We need a medic in the lobby immediately. A visitor has passed out."

"They done gave her a heart attack," said one person toward the end of the line.

"That's fucked up," yelled another person in the line.

"I'm recording y'all," someone else yelled out.

"You should stop recording before your phone gets confiscated," the sergeant said calmly to the person who was recording them.

"Should we move her to the bench, Sergeant?" the imam asked, concerned.

"I don't want to until the medic gets here. We don't want to get sued for something. You know she wouldn't want anything more, since we couldn't save her father."

"Well, at least let me put my blazer under her head." The imam removed his blazer, folded it, and placed it under Kafisa's head.

"Where is this damn medic?" the sergeant asked no one in particular after five minutes had passed.

After two additional minutes had passed, the medic finally showed up, casually walking toward the scene and laughing.

The sergeant's face turned red with anger. "Get over here now, God damn it!" he shouted.

"Sergeant, she just passed out. That's not a medical emergency. Some smelling salts will do the trick," the medic explained. The medic removed a bottle of smelling salts from a pocket in her white coat. She twisted the top off the bottle and waved the smelling salts under Kafisa's nostrils as the sergeant and the imam hovered. "Can you guys give me some room here?" the medic demanded.

In an instant Kafisa came out of the darkness and opened her eyes. "What is that awful smell?" She pushed the medic's hand away. "Get it away from me!" She started to cough.

"Can someone go into the bathroom and retrieve some paper towels?" said the medic.

The sergeant quickly headed toward the men's bathroom. A minute later he returned with a handful of paper towels. "Here you go."

"I'm going to clean myself up. I'll be out in a minute to talk to her a little more," said the imam.

"I don't need to talk to you, Imam," Kafisa said as she tried to get up. She felt dizzy all over again.

"Whoa! Hold on, little missy. You need to let the spell pass. Can I put the smelling salts under your nose? It will make you feel better." The medic put the smelling salts under her nose without waiting for Kafisa's response.

"I told you to get that shit away from me!" Kafisa pushed the medic's hand away and eased herself up to a standing position. She no longer felt the dizziness that had besieged her. She snatched her purse from the floor, then bolted toward the door without another word.

"Ms. Jackson!" the sergeant yelled out.

When Kafisa reached the door, she turned and yelled, "Fuck you, you bald-headed bastard! You'll pay for letting my father die!"

Kafisa stormed out of the building and headed for the parking lot. When she reached her car, she got in and sat quietly, trying to catch her breath. When she finally did, tears started streaming down her face. She knew her father wouldn't want her to cry, but she couldn't help it.

Kafisa had just lost the person she most admired in her life. Her mind raced with questions. *What do I do now? Who do I turn to now? Uncle Fran? Although he has always treated me like family, will this continue with my father's death?*

# Chapter Nine

The next day, Kafisa sat at the gate in JFK with her Dior shades on and a fistful of napkins in hand. She refused to go through the airport while revealing her bloodshot eyes. She had been up practically the entire night, pondering the bomb Francine Costillo had dropped in her lap and the death of her father. She honestly couldn't believe he was gone for good.

When she woke this morning, she had to make one of the hardest decisions she had ever had to make in her life. When she recovered from her blackout down in Philadelphia and returned to New York, she had not expected to receive the call she had. Last night Francine had come by and shown her her father's will, and ever since then Kafisa had been fighting the decision to honor the dying wishes of the only man she had ever loved. Honoring his wishes was a hard pill to swallow, but she knew that if she disregarded them, she would disrespect his memory. She still had a bad taste in her mouth after sitting on the sofa in her hotel room and listening to Francine read her father's will. A few tears managed to escape from under Kafisa's Dior sunglasses as she played her father's words back in her head.

*My beloved daughter,*
*I greet you with the highest form of peace,*
Assalamu alaikum wa rahmatullahi wa barakatuh. *If my words are reaching your ears, then Allah, the*

*Most Merciful, has called me back home,* insha'Al-lah. *If this is the case, then I know you're not going to like what I say, but you are immediately to leave Brooklyn, actually New York as a whole.*

*Do not concern yourself with my burial. All my arrangements have been made, and within twenty-four hours my flesh will be no more. I want you to leave as soon as my will has been read in its entirety. If you do anything other than that, you will be dishonoring both my name and my reputation, as well as the Jackson brand.*

*I'm sure all that I have worked so hard for has been taken away, so I have nothing to leave you. It is one of my biggest regrets. But I will leave you with something far more valuable than any dollar amount I could have left you. If you respect my wishes, then upon your completion of your degree, academically speaking as well as street wise, any and all doors will be opened for you. The choice is yours. Choose wisely.*

*Either way, I love you no matter what.*

"Flight five-two-four to Columbia, South Carolina, is now boarding," were the words that brought Kafisa back to the present.

She stood and grabbed hold of her roller bag. She glanced over at the board that had the Columbia, South Carolina, departure information listed on it and then back in the direction from which she had entered the airport terminal. So many thoughts flashed through her mind. Her emotions were running wild. *Should I disrespect my father by ignoring his request and going to his funeral, or should I go forth with my education, as requested? I fear the worst. Will our family name be restored and regain its honorable standing?*

"All first-class and elite passengers may board now." The gate agent's words blared from the speakers at the gate.

Although Kafisa had a first-class ticket, she did not make her way to the gate. She just sat back down as the other first-class ticket holders boarded. Minutes passed, and other groups were called to board the South Carolina flight. Kafisa still remained seated. She was still battling the fact that she was about to hop on a plane the day after finding out her father had been killed. Kafisa shook her head. *This can't be happening*, she thought to herself.

"Last call for flight five-two-four," the gate agent announced.

Kafisa continued to sit there, shaking her head. *Why you doing this to me?* Her question was directed to her father. Kafisa closed her eyes, but they immediately shot back open. She could have sworn she had heard her father's voice. *It'll make you stronger.* The words echoed in Kafisa's head. She stood up and grabbed hold of her Louis Vuitton roller bag.

"Wait!" she called out just as the gate agent was about to close out her computer screen.

"Are you on this flight?" the agent asked. She had seen Kafisa sitting there the entire time.

"Yes," Kafisa replied. She handed the agent her ticket.

The agent looked down at the ticket as she scanned it. "This says first class. I saw you sitting over there for the longest time. Why are you just boarding now?" The agent was curious to know.

Kafisa took a deep breath, then exhaled. "Because I wasn't sure whether I was going to board or not," she responded as she took her ticket.

Kafisa made her way down the ramp. She had only one thought on her mind as she boarded the flight. The next time she returned to Brooklyn, New York, it would be to carry out her father's instructions to the fullest.

# Chapter Ten

*2012*

"You sure you ready for this?" thirty-two-year-old Corey Davis, aka C-Dub, asked the passenger in the Ford Taurus rental.

They sat parked on the corner of Schenectady Avenue and Sterling Place, with the car running. C-Dub had the heat on high to keep the winter chill out. They rotated a blunt of Orangina back and forth as they sat outside a smoke shop, observing the flow of human traffic. The passenger nodded in rapid succession while taking two pulls of the drug, then passed it back to C-Dub. The neighborhood was semi quiet on this particular Sunday evening.

C-Dub stared at his passenger. He could see the hunger in those eyes. He was all too familiar with that look. He could spot it anywhere. It was a universal look that only those who were truly hungry and would stop at nothing to eat possessed, he believed. It was the same look he himself had possessed twenty years ago, when he was trying to get on and find his way in the game.

It was because of the way he had gotten on his feet that he had agreed to even consider what was being asked of him. It was actually the passenger's father who had put C-Dub on. He had received his first kilo of coke from Kafis Jackson. C-Dub couldn't help but shake his head and smile to himself over the irony of it all. To some, it would seem wrong, but to him, it was an honor. Before his mentor's demise, C-Dub had stopped at nothing to try to repay Kafis Jackson every chance he got, so this would be no different for him. Still, he had mixed feelings about what he had agreed to do.

He could have gotten anybody to take care of what he was handling, but he felt this was the perfect opportunity to kill two birds with one stone. One, he'd be eliminating one of his most threatening competitors and rivals in the Brooklyn borough, and two, he'd be helping someone who was the offspring of the man who had helped him.

"Like I said before, this is on the strength of your pops." C-Dub paused. "But you fuck this up, and there is no second chance. You pull it off, you'll be set for life. Understand? I have to know you will honor his name at any cost necessary."

Again, the passenger nodded.

A grin appeared across C-Dub's face. "Yo, you act just like Big Fis." C-Dub let out a light chuckle. He had referred to the passenger's father by his street moniker. *If only I had such a successor to keep my legacy going*, he thought to himself. "That's a good thing, though, because your pops was a man of few words and much action. Let's see how strong his bloodline is," he added as a sinister grin appeared on his face.

Just then, the reason why they were parked a safe distance up the street emerged from one of the brownstones in the middle of the Crown Heights block.

"That's him right there." C-Dub pointed.

The passenger rose up, eyes low, and zeroed in on the intended target. It was either now or never. If the passenger couldn't handle this, there would be no reason to show up in Brooklyn ever again.

C-Dub reached into his waistband. "Time to shit or get off the pot." He handed her the .380 semiautomatic, followed by the blunt.

She accepted the chrome piece and the marijuana, then did a quick inspection of the gun while puffing on the weed cigar, before removing the safety on the weapon. She then put the .380 up under a goose-down jacket.

"I'll be waiting for you at the end of the block, by the projects," C-Dub noted.

The young passenger made eye contact with him and nodded for a third time. After pulling a black skullcap down low, just above the eyes, she passed the blunt back to C-Dub.

"Nah, I'm straight." C-Dub waved off the potent substance.

The young passenger took another pull of the blunt, this time taking a long drag. Smoke exited her mouth and nose, creating just the right high. All she could think about was what stood in the way of destiny. She cracked open the car window and flicked the small blunt out and rolled the window back up.

*Shit or get off the pot.* C-Dub's words resonated in the passenger's young mind. C-Dub was right. She had waited a long time for this. Two long years, to be exact, for the first opportunity to showcase her talent. The passenger had finally reached the age C-Dub had designated to come back and see him. Coincidentally, it was the anniversary of the death of her father.

Taking a deep breath, she said, "Time to go take a shit," just loud enough for C-Dub to hear, before grabbing the door handle and exiting the rental.

Thirty-three-year-old Drew Myrie stepped onto the porch of his two-story, half-million-dollar brownstone. "*Bumbaclot!*" he cursed in his Jamaican native tongue.

He removed the hair tie from his locks, then blew into his hands to take some of the chill off. He reached into the front pocket of his black leather trench coat and pulled out a pack of Newport 100s. He popped one of the cigarettes in his mouth. He then reached into the inside pocket of his trench coat to retrieve his lighter. Coming up empty-handed, Drew began to conduct a pat search on himself. "Tsk! *Ras clot!*" He sulked.

He usually never left the house without some sort of light on him. He was a chain smoker. He smoked cigarettes just as much as he smoked weed, and he smoked weed practically all day, every day, which was why he was fiending for a cigarette. He had run out of smoke. It was up in Brownsville where his stash spot was located.

He glanced at his gold nugget watch. "Where da *bumbaclot* taxi boy dem?" he asked aloud. He was pissed off that he had to run back upstairs for a light, but his irritation came from the lateness of the taxi he had called. He had a five-kilo deal set up for later that evening and was on a strict time schedule. He needed to shoot over to Brownsville and get back in time to take three kilos and stretch them to five with cut before he met with the buyer.

Drew looked left, then right. To his right, he saw a young-looking girl walking in his direction. To his left, a young-looking boy was traveling his way as well, coming from the opposite end of the block. Rather than running back in the house and risking missing his taxi, Drew opted to ask one of the two young people who would soon pass him for a light. *Mi know di likkle young gal or my youth dem smoke*, he thought.

The girl was the first to reach Drew. "Excuse me, sweetheart," Drew began.

Before he could ask his question, the girl scurried past him, with a look of disdain plastered across her face. She never even looked Drew's way.

"Pussy hole!" Drew muttered, cursing the girl.

He didn't pay the silver Ford Taurus any mind as it cruised past his brownstone. He was more focused on his own ride. He peered up the block in search of his taxi, hoping it would buck the corner at any moment, but there was nothing in sight. The young-looking boy had just reached the brownstone before Drew's.

"My youth, ya got a light?" Drew asked.

"Sure, dread," was the response he received.

"Oh, excuse me, sweetie," Drew said, correcting himself. "Mi don't know ya a young girl and not a young lad," he explained. He realized the person he had thought was a boy was actually a girl. Her attire had deceived him.

"Come." He waved the girl into the area inside the gate of his brownstone. He started down from the porch at the top of the steps to meet her halfway. "Shit!" Drew cursed. He had nearly tripped and stumbled off his porch. He had caught himself just in time, but the cigarette was not so lucky.

The Newport 100 had dropped out of his mouth. He bent down to retrieve it. Had he gone into his pocket and pulled out another one, things might have turned out different.

Drew's eyes grew unforgettably wide as he stopped in mid-motion.

The impact of the explosion on his skull knocked him backward after the shot rang out in the air. He lay stretched out at the bottom of the steps of his brownstone, choking on his own blood. The shot to the head did not kill him instantly, but the additional two shots from the .380 into his heart ended what little life he was holding on to. Drew would never know he was part of a test and a strategic street move.

\*\*\*

Twenty-seven-year-old Kafisa Jackson shoved the .380 semiautomatic C-Dub had given her into her goose-down jacket pocket. She pulled her skullcap down farther to mask her face, then walked back through Drew Myrie's brownstone gate. She took a quick survey of the neighborhood, just the way she had seen her father do whenever he had stalked someone who owed him money. She noticed curtains closing and lights being turned off in the windows of other brownstones. She wasted no time taking flight down Schenectady Avenue. Moments later she was hopping back into the Ford Taurus rental, now parked on Albany Avenue, a distance from the front building of the Albany Houses projects.

C-Dub had unlocked the passenger-side door as soon as he saw Kafisa turn the corner. He had never turned off the engine of the rental. "You get him?"

Kafisa nodded rapidly. "Yeah, I got him," she replied in a calm tone.

"Good." C-Dub smiled. He whipped the steering wheel to the left and pulled into ongoing traffic, nearly causing an accident. He shot down Albany Avenue until he reached Fulton Street. Once he was on Fulton, he slowed down.

Kafisa sat in the passenger seat in deep thought. She had just taken a life. She told herself it was for a good reason. *I took a life so I could live a better one*, she told herself as they cruised through downtown Brooklyn. An image of Drew Myrie's eyes appeared in Kafisa's head. She knew she'd never forget them. She wondered what he could have possibly done for C-Dub to have chosen him as her come up. Kafisa knew it had to be something serious. Remorse was a trait her father had trained her to eliminate in her mind as a little girl, so she felt nothing for the victim. Still, she was curious. She peered over at C-Dub.

He felt Kafisa staring at him. "What's up?" His eyes went from the road to her and back to the road again.

"Who was that?" she asked abruptly.

C-Dub hooked a right onto Flatbush Avenue. "Who?" he replied, confused.

"The dread."

C-Dub grimaced. He had known there was a possibility this question would come up. He had hoped it wouldn't, though. "Why you wanna know?" he asked, evading her question.

"My father told me, you should always know the lives you take. Never know when somebody might seek revenge."

C-Dub let out a light chuckle. "You're definitely Kafis's kid." He looked over at Kafisa for a second time. "You really wanna know?"

Kafisa nodded.

"That was the bitch-ass nigga that killed your pops."

At first Kafisa thought she had misheard him. Once she realized she hadn't, she thought C-Dub was joking, but the look on his face confirmed that he was serious. Kafisa's chocolate complexion was replaced with an ash-gray one. She couldn't believe her ears. A world of emotions began to stir within her. She couldn't believe C-Dub hadn't told her the target's identity before.

All this time she had thought her father's murder was a mystery, but the reality was that his killer had been just mere miles away from where she resided. A tear came from out of nowhere and managed to escape her right eye. In an instant, Kafisa shook off the feeling. She dried the one tear and held back the others that tried to break free. Her father had raised her to be strong at all times, and that was exactly what she intended to do. Now that the initial shock had faded, Kafisa understood why C-Dub had done it the way he had. *He had to see if I was really built like that,* Kafisa thought.

"You good?" C-Dub asked.

She cleared her throat and peered over at C-Dub for a second time. "I'm more than good," she responded. "Fuck him. I did what you asked. Now, let's get this money," Kafisa added to ensure that he knew she meant business.

C-Dub began to shake his head. "Yeah, let's do that. Tomorrow's your official training day," he said as he crossed the Manhattan Bridge and entered Chinatown.

Kafisa stared out into the distance. Her father's face appeared in her head. She smiled as he gave her his signature wink and smile. *Rest in peace now, Dad. I swear on my life, I'ma pick up where you left off and get it all back, if it's the last thing I do in life,* she silently promised the man responsible for her being the woman she was today.

# Chapter Eleven

*One year later . . .*

"Who?" The voice came over the intercom.

"Fuck you mean, who? Buzz me in!" Kafisa stared up at the mini camera in the upper far left corner of the apartment building.

"My bad," the voice said.

A second later, a buzzing sound could be heard, followed by a clicking sound. Kafisa grabbed hold of the door handle, pulled the door open, and entered the building. She thought of how proud her father would be. She had gotten her law degree in South Carolina and then came back to reclaim her father's crown on the streets.

She climbed on the elevator, and after the elevator doors closed, she peered up and silently counted the numbers as they lit up. The elevator stopped on three. She stepped off the elevator and walked to the guarded apartment door. When the door opened, everybody in the apartment stopped what they were doing and turned their attention to Kafisa. A nod of approval from Kafisa caused them all to resume what they had been doing prior to her arrival.

Kafisa scanned the room as she made her way toward the back. She couldn't help but crack half of a smile. She had some of Brooklyn's baddest chicks bottling up vials of coke, all of them nude with the exception of the masks they wore. Nearly every chick in BK who had a pretty face and a fat ass and was looking for a come up wanted a job or position in Kafisa's operation, but only the elite were handpicked. Kafisa was really particular about who she let in and put on her team. She was also very funny about who she did business with. For the past two years, she had made her way up through the ranks on her own strength. She had managed to put together a team of hungry wolves, goons, and hustlers to make her presence felt in the BK borough. With a strong crew and a great coke connect, she had built an empire. Now at age twenty-eight, Kafisa Jackson was on top of her game.

"Wassup, sis?" Halimah said, greeting her boss and friend.

"Business as usual." Kafisa waved her hand in the air and shook her head. She had been making her rounds all morning, picking up and doing inventory for her total weekly flip. The spot Halimah ran for her was her final stop. She always saved the best earner for last, because she knew the count would take longer. Besides, Halimah was the closest thing to a friend she had, so she enjoyed her company.

She favored Halimah over the other females on her team not only because she was the best earner, but also because she had known her the longest. Aside from that, she knew what type of stock Halimah came from. Her father had actually worked for Kafisa's dad as an enforcer before his demise. She remembered the times her father had pointed out members of his team to her and had run down their rap sheets, and Halimah's father had always received high remarks from her father for being straight up and loyal. Kafisa had learned years later with Halimah that the apple didn't fall too far from the tree.

"You wouldn't be you if it weren't," Halimah replied, bringing Kafisa back to the present.

Kafisa smiled and nodded. "True."

"Well, you'll be happy to know we had a great week." Halimah beamed.

"When don't you?" Kafisa returned her grin.

"True!" Halimah replied, trying to imitate Kafisa. That caused the two women to share a laugh.

"So, what's the count?" Kafisa asked abruptly. She was ready to be done with the work aspect of things so she and Halimah could do their usual politicking about other things.

"Last I checked, we were at forty-two grand."

"Oh, yeah, you weren't bullshittin'. Y'all had a great week. That's a little over seventeen more than what you usually bring in."

"Exactly," Halimah answered. She gloated at her intake. "And that was a couple hours ago," she added.

Kafisa could see how proud Halimah was. She appreciated how Halimah always tried to impress her with her hustle and lieutenant skills. She liked how Halimah was humble rather than cocky, despite the fact that she brought in the most money. Her father had always told her that if a person could be humble around a lot of money, then they were used to being around money. That was the best way Kafisa could describe Halimah.

"We gotta get that up out of here. That's too much money in the crib," Kafisa said. "Let's tally up the rest and get this over with."

"Okay." Halimah nodded.

Moments later, Kafisa watched as Halimah ran the bills through the money machine. After all the bills had gone through, Kafisa was pleased with the total count.

"I'ma take most of that and flip just for this house alone," Kafisa stated. "Keep the other five."

Halimah nodded. She was still reveling in her weekly intake. "Thanks, sis. I appreciate that."

"You know I got you. You my dawg." Kafisa put her hand on Halimah's shoulder. "After that we can be out and do what we do. Going to the club tonight is going to be fun."

The thunderous music could be heard the moment Kafisa and Halimah exited the elevator and entered the rooftop club. The private affair was lit, like something straight out of a rap video. The Loft was a modern yet plush space that attracted musical artists and celebrities from every aspect of entertainment. There was no telling who they'd see inside the club.

They were escorted to the VIP table that was reserved for Kafisa. The booming music made Halimah want to dance. Her wide hips swayed from side to side as she whopped all the way to their section. Men and women couldn't help but eye Halimah's voluptuous, round ass. She was used to the attention she was receiving on behalf of her ass. At five-eight and 160 pounds of pure thickness, she couldn't help but bust out of any pair of designer jeans she wore, and tonight was no different as she trailed behind Kafisa.

"Welcome back, Ms. Jackson. Ms. Ford," the server greeted. He poured them their usual shots of Cîroc.

Neither of them wasted any time tossing the drinks back. Halimah's face twisted from the sting of the alcohol before transitioning into a relaxed smile. Kafisa let out a light chuckle. She was used to Halimah's theatrics whenever she drank the popular vodka. It was a step outside of her normal sangria, which she preferred to drink.

For the first forty-five minutes they relaxed in their VIP section. They watched more and more guests enter the club. Halimah sipped on her drink and danced in her seat as she watched Kafisa exchange hugs and handshakes with the local street celebrities and the other famous people housed in the VIP booths next to them.

The DJ catered to every kind of person's musical needs, spinning hip-hop tracks into house music, bumping the best pop dance hits, and throwing a rock song in every now and then. As the night progressed, so did Kafisa's and Halimah's partying. After polishing off nearly half a bottle of peach Cîroc, they were feeling it. They exited their VIP section and made their way onto the dance floor. Even though they were surrounded by bodies, they felt as if they were the only two in the room. They took over the dance floor and rocked to whatever it was the DJ was playing. Kafisa did her two-step with her remix to it, while Halimah gyrated every inch of her curvaceous body. All eyes were definitely on them.

Kafisa scanned the crowd. She could see that she and Halimah had even grabbed the attention of other ballers and money getters occupying the VIP sections. She smiled on the inside. *Yeah, muthafuckas, bitches run shit too*, she said to herself. She recognized the majority of the crews who were in the VIP sections. She knew who really had it and who was just frontin'. Above all, she knew that everybody knew who she was. In the game she played, male kingpins came a dime a dozen, but in the five boroughs combined, there were only a few female kingpins, and Kafisa was in the top five, dead or alive.

Kafisa's mood changed as soon as the DJ changed the song he had just been spinning. She bounced to the track as the words "Young niggas move that dope" blared out of the club speakers. Any gangster music about trapping always amped her up. She was a huge fan of Meek Mill, Young Jeezy, and D-Block, to name just a few. Kafisa pivoted and busted her infamous spin move. Blame it on the alcohol, but Kafisa stumbled as she spun.

Were it not for the extended arms that caught her in mid-fall, she would have had an embarrassing moment. She immediately sobered up and withdrew from whoever had broken her fall.

"Thanks," she offered as she raised her head to look up at the man responsible for her not giving the haters something to laugh about at her expense.

"No problem, Confessa."

The name instantly caught her attention. She hadn't heard it since her sophomore year in college, when it was given to her. For the first time she focused on the person standing before her. Her heart nearly melted when she saw hiding behind his beard that smirk she had once looked forward to seeing. She noticed how long he wore his beard now. It was apparent he had never stopped working out. His shoulders were much broader than she remembered, and she could see he had more girth in his chest by the way it protruded through his multicolored polo shirt, complimenting his massive arms.

"Jersey Jay?" Kafisa asked, referring to him by the nickname she had given him. She was almost sure it was him, but she wanted him to confirm it.

"Yup!" He flashed his perfect teeth.

Kafisa stared at him hard. She nearly got lost in his light brown eyes, the way she used to. There was no mistaking them. Kafisa traveled back in time for a split second, until her inner self gave her a dose of reality. *Bitch, get your shit together*! she told herself. *You're a boss now, not some young college chick involved in some puppy love shit*. She shook her head and returned his smile.

"Oh my God. I can't believe it," Kafisa chirped, amazed that she had bumped into him after all these years.

"Man! Come here and give me a hug!"

Kafisa's heart fluttered. She watched his eyes grow low, the way they always did when he meant business, as he spoke with the arrogance and confidence she was drawn to. He extended his arms and attempted to give her a "Long time no see you" bear hug.

Jersey stopped abruptly in his tracks. "Unless your dude in here."

"There you go!" Kafisa rolled her eyes. In that moment she realized why they had ended. "Same ole cocky-ass Jameel. If I had a dude, he would've been whose arms I would've slipped into, not yours."

"Say less." Jameel smiled. He extended his arms for a second time. Kafisa stepped into his welcoming embrace. *Damn, this brother still smells delicious,* she thought as he enveloped her in his Black Butter fragrance oil. The hug brought back so many memories. Kafisa immediately broke the hug.

Jameel laughed. "So, who you with?" he asked.

"My homegirl." Kafisa pointed behind her to Halimah.

Halimah had long ago stopped dancing, but she resumed when she realized her boss knew the guy who had just saved her from falling; only this time she kept her dance moves to a minimum.

Kafisa and Jameel were oblivious to what was going on around them. Nor did they care. They continued to stand in the middle of the dance floor, conversing.

"What about you? No lady? Rider? Boo? Side pieces with you tonight?" Kafisa asked.

Jameel chuckled. "Nah. 'Em days been over. That was then. This is now." He flashed his smirk again. It was the third time Kafisa had noticed it. She started to think he was doing it on purpose because he knew she liked it.

"I hear that hot shit," Kafisa remarked mockingly.

"I'm dead ass. That's my section over there." He pointed over at the last VIP section to the right. "Those my peoples," he continued. "Some of my manz from my hood in Plainfield, out in Jersey, and some of my manz from down in the dirty."

"You still down South?" Kafisa asked.

"Definitely!" he exclaimed. "All through there like it's the tristate area."

Kafisa read him loud and clear. She did a quick scan of Jameel's VIP section. She had noticed it before but then had paid it no mind, because there was nothing of any interest to her there. She never came to the club and gave the impression that she had come out to meet dudes. She was positive Jameel had not been in that section when she looked over there earlier. What stood out to her was the fact that they had two dozen twelve-hundred-dollar bottles of champagne and only five dudes and three females in their section. Jameel would make a party of nine for twenty-four bottles of the best. She was slightly impressed but didn't want to give any credit just yet.

Kafisa was no ghetto genius, but it didn't take a rocket scientist to figure out that either Jameel or somebody else over in that section was doing something in a major way. She wondered why she didn't recognize anybody in his crew. She also wondered how they had come to be in attendance at the upscale club, and as an exclusive party at that. *Maybe one of them females thots from New York and brought them out*, she concluded silently.

"So, none of those chicks ain't your New York piece?" Kafisa shot at him.

Jameel did a quick glance back. "I don't know 'em broads," he then replied. "I was in the restroom and had to make a call. They weren't there when I left. You know how it go, though. My dudes doin' 'em."

"Uh-huh!" Kafisa snickered. "So y'all just stumbled across this spot?" she asked.

"Twenty-one questions, geesh." Jameel laughed. "Nah, my manz, Kamil, from my town. He used to live out here before they moved out my way, so he know the area and got folks out here," he explained.

*It makes sense*, Kafisa thought.

"If you're worried about 'em chicks, I'll tell 'em to leave. You and your homegirl are welcome to join me as my guests," Jameel added.

That got a laugh out of her. Apparently, Halimah had heard him say that, because she let out a chuckle too. It dawned on Kafisa then that the only perception Jameel had of her was as a young ride-or-die chick and not as the boss she was. "Thanks, but I'm good." She turned and pointed to her and Halimah's VIP section. "We got our own spot."

Jameel peered over her shoulder and noticed the bottles sitting on the table of the empty VIP section. His infamous smirk broadened. "No doubt." It didn't take him long to figure it out. "Put my number in your phone." Jameel pulled out his iPhone. "You never know when it may come in handy. It's even lovelier than you remember," he noted, referring to the money Kafisa used to see him make when she knew him in Columbia, South Carolina.

*He has no idea*, she thought. She didn't expect him to know her status. After all, he was from Plainfield, New Jersey, and she was a "Bed-Stuy, do or die" Brooklyn boss lady to heart.

"Just shoot me a text letting me know it's you." She handed him one of her business cards.

Jameel took a quick glance at it, smiled, and stuck it in his pocket. "Definitely!" He nodded. He was impressed with the fact that Kafisa had a business card.

"You still say that." Kafisa had noticed that he still favored the word *definitely*.

"Yup! And yup, too, before you ask," he replied.

The two of them shared a laugh. Then there was a familiar silence for a few seconds. It seemed as if the music had stopped and all that existed was Kafisa and Jameel. He was the first to break the silence.

"It was good seeing you, babe." He leaned in and gave Kafisa another hug. "I'ma hit you later," he cooed in her ear.

His words went straight through Kafisa's earlobe and traveled between her inner thighs. She closed her eyes for a split second and smiled on the inside. She had forgotten how sensual he was.

Halimah had already begun to make her way back over to their VIP section as Kafisa and Jameel said their good-byes.

"Still smoo—" Kafisa's words were interrupted by the vibration of her cell phone on her hip. She retrieved it. When she saw who it was, she held up a finger. She read Jameel's lips as he told her he was out, then watched him vanish into the sea of people before answering the call.

"Hold up. I'm in the club!" she shouted into the receiver once Jameel was out of sight. She could barely hear what the person on the other end of the line was saying, so Kafisa walked in the opposite direction of the speakers. She was able to hear him once she got near the club's exit doors. "What's going down?"

"Fee, you got to get back to the borough and quick," an irate C-Dub informed her.

"Why? What the fuck is the problem?" She could tell from his tone that something was wrong.

"Your girl Jazz, the dumb ass, got knocked at JFK while trying to board a plane with something she didn't have no business tryin'a board with, ya dig?" C-Dub spit in code.

"Yeah, I follow you. But to where?" Kafisa was puzzled.

"According to her, headed to Virginia," he said. He knew Kafisa wasn't going to like the news.

"*Fuck!*" Kafisa breathed into the phone.

It had just dawned on her that Jazz had told her she was going to visit her cousins in Virginia and was going to look into how they operated down there. Kafisa found it strange that she was having two conversations in one night about the South. First, she had run into Jameel, who was hustling down there, and now Jazz had gotten caught while trying to get down there. She told Halimah to wait there while she finished talking to C-Dub. She stepped outside of the club's main room to finish the conversation.

"Please tell me you're fucking with me. For real, 'cause if you is, I'ma beat yo' ass on some serious shit!" Kafisa was secretly praying that this was all a joke.

"You must not have been watching the news," he said. "It's all over. She's in custody right now." The seriousness was all too clear now in his tone. "One of my peoples that work at the top of the TSA chain told me they interrogating her now."

Kafisa grimaced. "She didn't say anything, did she?" she asked, hoping for the better of the worst. She wondered if Jazz would rat her out.

"Nah, she holdin' up, according to my peoples," C-Dub replied. "They said she isn't saying a damn thing, other than that she doesn't know how it got there." He let out a light chuckle. "I just thought you should know. I'm pretty sure you don't need this type of heat at your doorstep now that you are free and clear," C-Dub added.

"You right about that shit," Kafisa replied with attitude in her tone.

"Whoa. Don't shoot the messenger," C-Dub shot back.

Kafisa hadn't realized she had just snapped at C-Dub for nothing. She apologized to him immediately, not wanting to ruffle any feathers. "My bad, OG. I didn't mean any disrespect," she said.

"It's cool. I get it," he told her, accepting her apology. "But on another note, based on what she got knocked with, she gonna have to lay down, no matter what lawyer you get her," C-Dub pointed out. "And there's a strong possibility the big boys have stepped in, 'cause that's a federal offense fo' sure."

Kafisa hadn't even thought about that. Jazz had fucked up and had crossed over from local to federal with her dumb-ass move. Kafisa's mind drifted off as she considered the serious consequences of Jazz being in custody.

"Who knows what they might do there?" C-Dub's words brought Kafisa back.

"Tell me what they could do."

"They could search her phone, look at her recent calls. Anything, Fee, really. They in control. But I don't know. . . . Right now it's too early to know. But another thing . . ."

"What's that?" Kafisa was all ears. She had a feeling she was not going to like what C-Dub had to add about the already crazy situation.

"If they do step in, you probably gonna have to lay low too, until this shit blows over."

It was as though C-Dub had just introduced her to spring water. Kafisa hadn't given that scenario any thought, either. She was grateful for how C-Dub had her back. "I understand," Kafisa told him, and she really did. "I'll be there tomorrow, and hopefully, that won't be the case."

"Yeah, hopefully," C-Dub agreed. "See you then."

Kafisa hung up abruptly and made her way back into the main room of the club. She spotted Halimah, who was now back in the VIP section. She had her hands up, as if to ask, "What happened?"

Kafisa made her way over to Halimah. "We have to go!" she told her. Kafisa's mood had just been dampened, and the look on her face demanded that Halimah get on the same page.

"What's going on?" Halimah asked.

"This fuckin' chick Jazz got knocked." Kafisa's irritation was more apparent now. "Tryin'a sneak some shit on the plane." She shook her head in disbelief. "I know she know better than that shit, but it seems she thought her shit was untouchable," Kafisa explained as they scurried to the elevator. She exhaled irately and punched the button to the elevator, as if that was going to make the elevator doors open faster.

"I'm sure it'll be okay," Halimah said, trying her best to calm a heated Kafisa.

Her words hardly calmed Kafisa down; instead, they made her even more furious. "Nah, shit is serious. This bitch knows too fuckin' much about my operation," Kafisa uttered.

"Well, if that's the case, the question is how thorough do you think she really is?" Halimah asked cautiously.

Kafisa nodded. *That's the million-dollar fuckin' question*, she thought. "Time will tell," she replied as they made their way toward one of the building's exits.

Once Kafisa and Halimah were out of the building, Kafisa handed her valet ticket to the attendant. She blew into her hands and rubbed the sides of her arms to minimize the goose bumps that had appeared out of nowhere. The temperature had dropped while they were in the club. If Kafisa weren't freezing, Halimah would've asked the question she had been dying to ask her boss ever since she witnessed the exchange between her and the guy who had caught her on the dance floor.

"That's the price you pay for tryin'a look cute and shit," Halimah teased.

Her comment received half of a smile from Kafisa. Any other time she would've shot back some slick shit in rapid succession at Halimah, but all she could think about now was the disturbing call she had just received. It wasn't until Halimah inquired about Jameel that Kafisa gave the other woman her full attention.

"If you must know, nosy ass," she said with a solemn look on her face, answering Halimah's question, "that was my first love." Kafisa let out a light chuckle. That was all she offered.

Halimah left it at that. The two hopped into Kafisa's Range Rover and drove through the New York City traffic in silence.

Meanwhile, back in the club, all eyes were on Jameel as he made his way back to his VIP section. He didn't noticed everyone's stares. Jameel was still trying to wrap his head around running into Kafisa Jackson. *Damn! She looks even better than I remembered*, he thought to himself. So many memories resurfaced in his mind.

"Nigga!" His homeboy's shout brought him back to the present.

"What's good?" Jameel asked his comrade Kamil. He wondered why he had a distorted look on his face.

"What you mean, what's good?" Kamil questioned. "How you know ole girl?" Kamil was curious not only about how he knew her, but also about their conversation.

Jameel had already jumped to conclusions and answered, "Why? Wassup? You know her dude or something? And let me guess. He some heavy hitter out here in New York." Jameel's words came across as dry and sarcastic.

"Bro—," Kamil began, but Jameel cut him off.

"Before you even say anything, my dude, hear me out."

Kamil shook his head. "Go ahead, bro."

"Man, what, you cool with the nigga or something?" Jameel asked, suggesting the obvious. "Last I checked, I was your manz from the sandbox, so what the fuck is up?" Jameel said, taking offense to Kamil shaking his head.

"Bro, relax!" Kamil told him. "You don't even know who you were talkin' to!"

"Nigga, fuck you mean, I don't know who she is?" The irritation could be heard in his tone.

Kamil's brother, Kamal, approached them and watched as they exchanged words. He just shook his head and laughed, because Kamil had already filled him in on who Kafisa really was. He knew Jameel was clueless about her status in the streets. He didn't even bother to intervene.

"That's one of my exes," Jameel declared, his voice booming. "Nah. Matter of fact," he said, correcting himself, "that was my motherfuckin' heart right there."

Both Kamil's and Kamal's jaw dropped to the floor at Jameel's words.

"That's crazy!" Those were the few words Kamil could conjure up with a straight face.

"What's crazy?" Jameel wanted to know what foolery his boys were busting his chops about.

"It's crazy that your motherfuckin' heart is one of the biggest fuckin' drug connects within the five boroughs, and you need a fuckin' plug so you can get the fuck out of Plainfield and back down South," Kamil told him.

It was Jameel's turn to drop his jaw on the floor. He fell back onto the VIP couch. He couldn't help but laugh to himself. *My ex-babe a boss?* he wondered. He pulled out the business card Kafisa had given him. He hadn't looked at it when she first handed it to him, thinking it was just a regular business card with her information. He smiled as he read it to himself. *Kafisa Jackson, entrepreneur. We provide quality and excellent service.* He smiled wider. *Hell yeah, I'ma definitely call you,* he thought to himself as he put the card back in his pocket and then sat back. He believed he had a slight edge over everyone.

# Chapter Twelve

Kafisa still couldn't believe it. Despite what she had watched on the news when she arrived back home, she still thought her eyes were deceiving her. Just as C-Dub had said, Jazz had been charged with trying to traffic drugs through the airport to another state. Although they had a jacket over her face, when the Feds were whisking her out of the airport, there was no mistaking Jazz's unique pigeon-toed and bowlegged stride. Kafisa had watched as they escorted Jazz to an awaiting black SUV, which reporters had swarmed.

She shook her head in disgust as she sat in Junior's in downtown Brooklyn and waited for C-Dub to arrive. They had agreed to meet up at noon. The news about Jazz was a hard pill to swallow. She didn't want to believe that somebody she had trusted with her life had crossed her and committed the ultimate betrayal. She had taught Jazz nearly everything there was to know about getting money and fending for herself. Kafisa had disclosed some things to Jazz that not even Halimah or Laverne, her second highest earner, knew. This was why the disturbing news C-Dub had later texted her—that her name had come up in the investigation—had her both infuriated and somewhat on edge.

Apparently, C-Dub had been given the information that the Feds had come in and interrogated Jazz at the airport. The news stories on television had confirmed that for Kafisa. C-Dub's inside source had later informed him that Jazz had mentioned the name Kafisa Jackson during the interrogation, but the informant wasn't sure why she had dropped this name. Kafisa was sure it wasn't for selling Girl Scout cookies. She believed that if Jazz had mentioned her to the Feds, then it was crime related.

Kafisa glanced down at her watch. It was quarter after twelve, and C-Dub had still not arrived. Kafisa was antsy, so she pulled out her cell phone, scrolled down to C-Dub's number, and hit the CALL button. He picked up on the first ring.

"I'm right outside," he informed her.

She peered out the front window of the restaurant and saw C-Dub's black-and-silver Maybach. "I see you." Kafisa hung up the phone. She admired the enormous luxury car. It was actually on her bucket list. She had already told herself that by her thirtieth birthday, she would have every chick and nigga on her dick when she pulled off the lot with her Maybach and stunted through the hood with her girls. Her train of thought ceased with the sudden presence of C-Dub.

Kafisa stood and hugged the man who had been her mentor since her father's demise. "So, talk to me." Kafisa wasted no time. "What's good?" she asked.

C-Dub, who now sat across from her, grimaced. "Doesn't look good at all." He shook his head.

That was not the response Kafisa was looking for. "Tsk! Damn!" She cursed under her breath. "This backstabbing bitch!"

C-Dub nodded. "Yeah, I don't know what she tellin' them people, but she sayin' somethin' relevant. I got my peoples on it, but its airtight right now."

"I appreciate it," Kafisa replied. She was riled up to the fullest but didn't want to display how she really felt in front of C-Dub. Her father had always told her, "Never let 'em see you sweat." Although she considered C-Dub family, she knew this was one of those times when she had to heed her father's advice. "So, how you think I should play it?" she asked calmly, wanting to see where his head was at in this sticky situation.

"Honestly?" C-Dub stared into her eyes, grasping her true feelings. "You're going to have to disappear for a minute." He let his words marinate in Kafisa's mind before he spoke again. "At least until we can get more info on this thing. There's too much at stake right now. She was one of your top earners," C-Dub reminded her. "Which means she knows a lot about everythin'." He ended with a stare that Kafisa couldn't misread.

Kafisa was now fuming inside even more, if that was possible. If she could get her hands on Jazz, she knew she would kill her. Everything she had worked so hard for, she could feel slipping through her fingers. In just under two years, she had managed to earn the respect of Brooklyn and had climbed higher up the criminal ladder than the majority of families under C-Dub's umbrella.

A sharp pain jabbed her in the side as she thought about how close she had come to fulfilling her father's last wishes. She had almost been ready to use the number Francine Costillo had given her that day at the hotel three years ago. And now this. She believed that if C-Dub felt this was the best way to handle the circumstances, then she was going to respect that. After all, with his blessings, she had been able to spread her wings and stretch her operation across the entire borough of Brooklyn. Were it not for him and the teachings of her father, she didn't know where she would be, thought Kafisa.

"So, who's gonna run my spots?" Kafisa didn't even try to dispute C-Dub's decision.

C-Dub let out a sigh of relief. "Man, I thought this was going to be harder than you made this." He smiled. "This is the best way. Lay low and come back even stronger, like you never left," C-Dub told her.

Kafisa gave half of a nod.

"As far as your spots, all new crews will be put in there. Your girl Jazz has jeopardized every fuckin' thing you had rollin'," C-Dub informed Kafisa.

You could see the muscles in Kafisa's jaw tighten up. She knew the rules of the game, so she couldn't be mad at anybody but herself and, of course, the bitch-ass rat, Jazz. Because of one bad apple, her entire barrel of goods had been spoiled. "So, where Halimah and Laverne gonna go?" She wanted to know about her two top earners.

"They gotta lay low too," C-Dub announced.

A twisted look appeared on Kafisa's face. "So, how my team supposed to eat, Dub?" She was not feeling that at all.

"Fee, you trippin' right now." C-Dub's tone became low and solid. "This is all a part of the game. They knew what they were signing up for. You, out of all people, should know you gotta take the bitter with the sweet. So, if they ain't put nothing up for a thunderstorm or a rainy day, then they either gonna drown, get soaked, and choke, or you gonna throw 'em a life preserver." C-Dub broke it down clearly. All Kafisa could do was listen attentively as C-Dub went on about the situation.

"You, Limah, Verne, and Jazz were a crew," C-Dub pointed out. He caught the look on Kafisa's face. "What it all boils down to is this." C-Dub took a deep breath and exhaled. "If they were watching Jazz, and the only people she was ever around if she wasn't by herself was y'all, who else do you think they had under surveillance during that time? Huh?" he asked.

As much of a boss as she believed herself to be, at that moment, Kafisa felt like a student getting after-school help, being taught a lesson. All that C-Dub had just said had never crossed her mind. The ironic thing about it was that she had actually gone to school and had learned well the very thing C-Dub had just broken down for her, yet she now seemed clueless about it all. She felt like a rookie, but she refused to come across like one.

"It's cool, Dub. I respect the game. I got Limah and Verne." Her tone was as smooth as baby oil on a baby's bottom. "Shit, I got enough money to float us until this shit blows over," she added, with a little chuckle in her voice, although she was dead serious.

Kafisa's response was commendable. She had managed to put up high six figures off of what she had made off the work she got from C-Dub throughout the years. Thanks to what her father had taught her, Kafisa had been seeing nearly the same thing C-Dub was off of each kilo of coke and the birds of raw dope she got from him. "Shit, maybe we'll travel the country until shit cools," she continued, considering her potential future plans. "Just give me until the end of the week to knock the rest of the shit off I got and then—"

"Nah, you got until the sun comes up tomorrow to tally up your inventory in your three spots," C-Dub said, cutting her off. "Anything you got left in any of the houses, you'll be paid for. This thing is serious, Fee," he added with conviction.

Kafisa grimaced. She had taken the situation more lightly than C-Dub had presented it to her. If she hadn't heard him before, she heard him loud and clear now. Her run in Brooklyn was abruptly coming to a temporary end. It was a hard pill to swallow, but there was nothing Kafisa could do about it. The decision had been made, and she had to abide by it.

"You'll have my numbers by the morning." Kafisa stood up abruptly.

"Whoa!" C-Dub grabbed her by the wrist. He peered up at her. "You good?"

Kafisa rolled her eyes before locking eyes with him. "Yeah, I'm good." She nodded.

"You sure?" C-Dub was not convinced.

"I'm good, Dub. I promise." Kafisa flashed her best smile.

"Just making sure." C-Dub matched her smile. He released Kafisa's wrist. "It's not forever, Fee. Only for now," he assured her, trying to ease what little tension lingered in the air.

"I know." Kafisa flashed the same smile. "Let me get on top of this shit."

C-Dub nodded. Two minutes later he watched as Kafisa hopped into her Range Rover and whipped it wildly into traffic. All he could do was shake his head as he opened the menu at Junior's.

# Chapter Thirteen

"Hello?" an annoyed Kafisa answered. She had tossed and turned all night. She had managed to doze off only an hour ago, and now her sleep had just been broken by the sound of her cell phone ringing in her ear—which was why she sounded so irritated when she answered the phone.

"My bad. Did I wake you?" Jameel asked. He had wondered whether eight in the morning was too early to be calling her, but he had done it anyway.

Kafisa recognized his voice immediately. "Nah, you good. Wassup?" Although she had been fast asleep seconds ago, she was now wide awake.

"Everything's *todo bien*," Jameel replied, partially in his Colombian mother's native language. "I was just being a man of my word."

"That what's up. I'm glad you did."

"You sure I didn't wake you up?" Jameel asked, hearing a lot of movement on Kafisa's end of the phone.

"It's cool." Despite all that was going on in her life right now, she still managed to laugh. She knew she had been busted. "I was supposed to be up anyway," she admitted.

"Since you put it that way." Jameel smiled.

"Can you give me a minute?"

"You wanna just call me back?" he asked. He figured she wanted to get the crust out of her eyes and brush her teeth.

"Ten minutes," she said. "Or less."

"Take your time." He hung up the phone, hoping she didn't wake up on the wrong side of the bed.

After brushing her teeth and washing her face, Kafisa was back on the phone with Jameel in less than ten minutes.

"So where were we?" were the words she was greeted with when he answered the phone.

"Me counting sheep until you woke me up."

The two of them shared a laugh.

"How long you been up?" Kafisa asked.

"Since Fajr," Jameel replied, referring to the Islamic morning prayer.

"Oh. You still practicing?"

"Let me put it this way," he said. "The worst believer is better than the best disbeliever."

Kafisa knew what the phrase meant. It was something she had heard her father say when justifying why he was doing what was not right according to his beliefs. "I get it," Kafisa replied.

"So how was your beauty rest?" Jameel asked, flirting.

"Fine," was all she offered. She didn't want to let him know that she hadn't really been able to sleep at all last night and she hadn't had a good night's rest in weeks. She switched subjects. "I see you're still an early bird, huh?"

"You know what they say. The early bird gets the worm," he replied.

"As does the night owl," Kafisa quipped.

They shared another laugh. Kafisa was enjoying their exchange. *Anything to take my mind off of this bullshit,* she thought.

"So, what made you call?" Kafisa asked, hoping she hadn't sounded like a bitch.

"I'm actually on my way back down bottom, and I didn't want to leave New York without telling you how good it was to see you. And I wanted to say good-bye." Jameel was being genuine, as corny as he sounded.

"You're still in the city?" Kafisa asked. She was surprised to hear that.

"Yeah. Had to handle some things in Harlem right quick before I hopped on the road," Jameel answered. "A little later I'll grab me some lunch from this li'l soul food spot over off One-Twenty-ninth," Jameel told her, secretly hoping she would join him.

"I know the one you're talking about. Jacobs," Kafisa said, enlightening him. "The food there is bangin'. I ate there a few times. It was bangin' every time," Kafisa added, giving the intimate restaurant a rave review.

"Would you like to join me?" Jameel asked, not letting the opportunity pass him by.

Kafisa pondered the offer for a moment. She was not really a phone person. She liked to peer into the eyes of an individual when she conversed with him or her. It was a trait she had inherited from her father. "The eyes never lie," he used to say to her.

"That sounds doable," Kafisa replied. "I'm in Brooklyn. Let's meet up around twelve."

"That's cool. Would you like me to pick you up?" Jameel was being slick. He was trying to see where she was staying.

A few hours later the two of them were sitting across from each other. Jacobs was busy, as usual, with the rush hour lunch crowd.

Jameel had arrived first, and surprisingly, he'd been able to lock down two seats for him and Kafisa. When Kafisa pulled up, he admired her beauty as she stepped out of her 2014 Range Rover. Kafisa stepped inside the soul food spot and looked around, in search of Jameel. She heard someone calling her name from somewhere in the back, and she made her way over to him. She couldn't help but admire how well groomed he was. *He could easily be mistaken for an exotic male dancer*, she thought.

They hugged and exchanged smiles. Kafisa nearly melted in his embrace. He wore the same alluring fragrance that had intoxicated her that evening at the Brooklyn nightclub. The bear hug he gave her made Kafisa feel as if she were being smothered with pure love. For a brief moment, she felt safe, and all her problems were nonexistent, but his beard brushing the side of her face brought her back to reality.

"*Bona bonita*," Jameel said as they sat at the table now, complimenting Kafisa on her beauty with an Italian/Spanish saying.

"Thank you." He used to say that to her so much that she couldn't forget both words meant "pretty."

"So, what made you take me up on my offer?" Jameel wanted to know. "I mean, I'm not complaining, just asking."

"Oh. I . . ." Kafisa smiled again. She couldn't believe that after all these years he still had the same effect on her.

After they ordered lunch, the two of them indulged in general conversation, catching up on current events in their lives. Kafisa shared what life had been like for her after college, though she didn't delve into her current profession. She did, however, disclose how her father had been killed, though she left out the details. Jameel shared how he had gone back to Columbia for a little while to visit with his aunt.

During this intimate conversation, they found they had more in common than they had known back then, such as the fact that both of them were their parents' only child. They exchanged views on what that was like. This was the most the two of them had discussed about themselves personally since they had met each other. Their relationship had been strictly sexually oriented. As they continued to converse, surprisingly, Kafisa discovered that Jameel didn't have any children and was single. Their conversation caused time and their troubles to escape them.

When they finished eating, Jameel glanced at his watch out of force of habit. "Damn. Time definitely be flyin' when you having fun," he blurted out.

Kafisa blushed. "I know you gotta probably go. I appreciate lunch." She then thanked him, but she hated to leave. She wanted to get a little closer, honestly. The feeling he gave her had never been forgotten. She thought she needed that after all she'd been going through.

"My pleasure."

"And the conversation," she added.

"Another pleasure, fo' sure."

"The next one's on me, but you gotta come back to New York for it," Kafisa teased.

"How about the next one be on me and you come to South Carolina?" Jameel rebutted. He had no way of knowing the type of chain reaction the offer he had just presented jokingly would trigger.

His comment caused Kafisa to break out into laughter. It was not humorous laughter, though Jameel mistook it for that.

"What's so funny?" he wondered aloud.

"I'm sorry. I didn't mean to laugh like that," Kafisa said, apologizing. She really hadn't been laughing at Jameel. It was more like she'd been laughing at herself. *Why didn't I think of this before?* she questioned herself.

Jameel stared at her oddly. "Are you okay?" He could see that she was in deep thought.

"Yes, I'm cool," Kafisa assured him.

Jameel continued to stare at her.

"Where are you down there?" Kafisa's question came out of nowhere.

Something about the way she had asked the question caught Jameel's attention. For the first time, she didn't sound like an ex-lover to Jameel. After all, she wanted to know his whereabouts. She sounded more like an opportunist.

"For the most part, I'm based in the Florence, Hartsville, and Darlington area, but I still dip down to the Columbia area. Plus, I'm in and out of North Carolina and Virginia heavy." Jameel had a funny feeling that this was the type of information she was asking for. He remembered what Kamil had told him back at the club last night. It just so happened that he had actually found a coke connect, which was the real reason he was in Harlem, but he was curious to see what was on Kafisa's mind.

Kafisa's wheels were turning. *I'm not tryin'a go nowhere and ride no nigga's coattails*, she thought to herself. *But I know if he's down there, then there's definitely money there, because that's what he's about.* It was apparent she was miles away, although she sat directly across from Jameel.

"Are you sure you okay?" Jameel asked for a second time, breaking Kafisa's train of thought.

"Yeah, I'm straight," Kafisa answered, returning to reality.

"So why'd you ask me that question?" Jameel wasted no time asking, as he wanted to get an edge on where she was coming from. It was a big reach, because if Kafisa was a boss, like everyone said she was, there was no way she would reveal her cards.

Kafisa was still pondering everything. She quickly weighed the pros and cons before she answered Jameel. "Just curious, that's all," she said, downplaying the matter. Were it anybody else, she might have continued to explore her options, but she had too much history with Jameel. Kafisa could tell he still looked at her like she was the young girl he had met at college. For the past two years or so, she had been other people's boss. The last thing she was trying to do was travel backward and become something less. Her father would come back to haunt her for sure if she ever stepped to a lower level.

Jameel nodded. Regardless of how many years had passed, he felt he still knew Kafisa well enough to know she wasn't keeping it one hundred. Not that he really cared; she had her own reasons to keep shit on the low. He had come up top and had found what he was looking for, a connect. So, he didn't need her help anymore, but he felt it would be nice to have Kafisa by his side while he continued to climb to the top.

"Okay," he said. He stood up and extended his arms. "I gotta get on this road."

Kafisa stood and stepped into his inviting arms.

"If you ever change your mind, you got the number now," he said to Kafisa after releasing her from his grip.

Kafisa smiled. "I got you."

Jameel snatched up his Armani jacket from off the back of the chair. Kafisa watched as he slipped it on and then headed toward the front of the restaurant. After four steps, he stopped in his tracks and turned to face Kafisa. "Oh, I meant to tell you. . . . Remember your ex-roommate?"

A confused look appeared on Kafisa's face. She wondered what had made Jameel mention one of her old roommates and ask her such a question. *Please don't tell me someone got a baby by one of them chicks or you fuckin' with her*, thought Kafisa. "Which one?" she asked.

Jameel detected the sarcasm in her tone. "Relax." He flashed his signature smirk. "It's not what you think. I promise. It's more of a message."

"So what is it, then?" Kafisa was now giving him attitude. During her stay on campus she had had two different roommates. She was curious to know which one Jameel was referring to even before she knew why he had brought one of them up.

"I'm talking about your girl Nu-Nu," Jameel shot back. "And picture me fuckin' with her." He laughed, already knowing what Kafisa was thinking.

Even Kafisa had to laugh at that. She knew Nu-Nu wasn't Jameel's type. "You're right," she admitted. "So, what about her?" She was anxious to know.

"If you ran into her now, you wouldn't be laughing," Jameel answered with a straight face.

Kafisa immediately became serious. "What's up with her?"

"What's up with her is that she doin' her numbers down there," Jameel offered. "I remember she used to always say to me, 'If you see Kafisa give her my number' like New York that fuckin' small." Jameel couldn't help but laugh about that. "But who knew?" he added, still laughing.

"Wow!" Kafisa was shocked by the news Jameel had just dropped on her. *Nu-Nu? Gettin' money?* It blew her mind. Never in a million years would she have thought Nu-Nu would be gettin' paper like that. Kafisa found it hard to believe, but she knew anything was possible.

"I know, right?" Jameel said. "I always be messin' with her, tellin' her how I remember she used to be a li'l scary-ass broad, sniffin' up under yo' ass all the time."

Kafisa rolled her eyes. *You have no idea*, she thought to herself. She wondered if Jameel knew just how real his recollection was.

"You want her number?" Jameel asked.

"For what?" Kafisa scowled.

"Hey, where I come from, in this game you can never have too many contacts," Jameel replied, knowing he was right.

"Who says I'm in the game?" Kafisa shot back.

Jameel chuckled. "You want the number or not?"

"Nah. I'm good," Kafisa said, refusing it nonchalantly.

"Okay. Well, take care and be safe out here in the Big Apple."

Jameel had no way of knowing what his words had triggered inside Kafisa's mind. *Take care? Be safe out here in the Big Apple?* Kafisa let Jameel's words dance around in her head. *I can't do shit in the Big Apple. All I know is Brooklyn, and that shit has been shut down over some blabbermouth bitch. How can I take care?* So many thoughts invaded Kafisa's mind, but one particular thought that popped in her head abruptly just then ended the internal battle she was fighting.

Jameel had just reached the counter and was about to pay the bill when she called out to him. "On second thought, yeah, let me get her number."

Jameel flashed half of a smile and asked the lady behind the counter for a pen. He had a funny feeling that he would be seeing Kafisa again, only this time it would be in the South, and sooner than he thought. *It would be my pleasure to show her around*, he thought.

# Chapter Fourteen

"Oh my God! Are you fucking kidding me?"

Kafisa had to remove the phone from her ear because of Nu-Nu's reaction to her screaming her name so loud.

"This better not be no fuckin' joke," Nu-Nu continued.

"You forgot what I sound like?" Kafisa asked. She lamented her choice of words. She was sure Nu-Nu would take them out of context.

"How could I ever forget what you sound like?" Nu-Nu replied. She had calmed down. Nu-Nu had recognized Kafisa's voice. Her reaction had been over the top simply because she was surprised to hear from her after all these years.

"How you been?" Kafisa asked. She had thought long and hard before she picked up the phone and dialed Nu-Nu's number. Now she was ready to cut to the chase.

"A bitch livin'!" Nu-Nu yelled into the phone. "I ain't the same shy girl you remember," she added.

"So I heard," Kafisa responded.

"So you heard?" Nu-Nu said. It hadn't dawned on her to ask Kafisa how she had gotten her number. Her tone became serious. "From who?" Nu-Nu wanted to know.

"From Meel."

"Ooh!" Nu-Nu chuckled. "You had me scared for a minute." Kafisa ignored Nu-Nu's statement. She knew what she was implying. Just like Nu-Nu wasn't the same person Kafisa remembered, Kafisa wasn't the same person anyone in her past remembered.

Where Kafisa came from, if Nu-Nu was in her midst, she would've slapped the taste out of her mouth for even implying that Kafisa might be trying to set her up or might be a snitch. Kafisa was in a predicament due to the fact that somebody couldn't keep her mouth shut, so she didn't appreciate Nu-Nu's remark. Although she knew Nu-Nu meant no harm, it was still disrespectful to a boss with her status.

"I heard you're doing real well for yourself," Kafisa continued. "So am I."

"That's wassup. I always knew you would," Nu-Nu told her. "So, to what do I owe the pleasure?" Nu-Nu had been in the game long enough to recognize street lingo when she heard it.

"I was thinking about coming your way with my two homegirls to see what it looks like down there," Kafisa announced.

"I hear that," Nu-Nu replied. "So, you need a place to crash or something?" Nu-Nu asked, knowing that wasn't the case. She was testing Kafisa.

Kafisa chuckled lightly. "Nah. I'm straight with all of that. I just need some of your time. To catch up on old times and find out what's going on now."

"Absolutely. We can do that!"

Kafisa could tell by the excitement in Nu-Nu's tone that she had read more into her words than what they meant. She sidestepped this and stayed on topic. If anything needed addressing, Kafisa decided she would cross that bridge when she reached it, if and when she got down there.

"Cool. There's a few things I needed to handle up this way before I take my vacation, but I'm almost certain I'm gonna come down," Kafisa told her.

"Okay, just let me know, so I'll be on point," Nu-Nu replied. "It's going to be really good to see you," she added. *Maybe we can get some time alone too*, Nu-Nu thought.

"Yeah, same here," Kafisa shot back, but while she had said those words just to say them, Nu-Nu had meant every word she had said and more. "I'll be in touch," Kafisa said.

"Okay. Until then." Nu-Nu hung up the phone, a wide-eyed smile on her face.

After the call ended, Kafisa had mixed feelings about the conversation she and Nu-Nu had just had, but one thing was for certain: judging by Nu-Nu's reaction to hearing from her, Kafisa knew it wouldn't be hard to find out what Nu-Nu was into. Just like she knew it wasn't going to be hard to get Nu-Nu to follow her lead once she got down to Columbia, South Carolina.

# Chapter Fifteen

Both Halimah and Laverne sat on the living-room sofa in Kafisa's condo with their arms folded, knowing this conversation might lead to a dramatic change in their lives.

"What the hell we know about the South?" Halimah was the first to say. "I'm Brooklyn till I die!" she added with a bit of arrogance. She had been sitting on Kafisa's sofa with a disapproving look plastered on her face while Kafisa filled them in on her meeting with C-Dub and her conversations with Jameel and Nu-Nu.

Laverne, who now had the same disapproving look on her face as Halimah, nodded her head in agreement.

"I feel like fuckin' gettin' locked up just so I can kill that fuckin' bitch Jazz," Halimah spat. She abruptly hopped up off the sofa. "All the shit we busted our ass to establish. All the work you put in out here in these streets, to have it all taken away over some dumb snitch bitch," she ranted as she paced back and forth.

"For real," Laverne muttered, backing her up. "Why the hell we gotta pay for that bitch's disloyalty?"

Kafisa just stood there. If the situation was anything other than what it was, she would've told Halimah to sit her ass back down and watch her tone as she expressed her displeasure. Instead, she let Halimah and Laverne get it all off their chest before she spoke again. She understood their frustration and anger. She felt the same way they did. She couldn't believe the chain of events that had led to her and C-Dub's meeting at Junior's. She knew that Halimah and Laverne wouldn't be feeling the decision C-Dub had handed down, a decision that she had had to accept. Just like she knew that they were not going to be feeling her idea to take their show on the road until things cooled down in Brooklyn. She was fully aware that outside of two of the five New York boroughs, not including BK, they had never been anywhere other than the Brooklyn area.

Kafisa looked from Halimah to Laverne, then back to Halimah. "Limah, sit back down," she said. Her tone was calm. The last thing she needed or wanted was to fall out with her right-hand chick, especially since Halimah would play an intricate part in what she had in mind. She knew that without Halimah and Laverne on board, she couldn't move forward with her plans.

Halimah rolled her eyes and let out a gust of hot air in frustration. "This shit ain't right!" she cursed. She plopped back down on the sofa and folded her arms across her chest. She had the same look that many ten-year-olds did when they were having a tantrum.

"I know," Kafisa offered to ease their emotions. "But this is what it is. These are your options. . . ." She paused for a brief moment. "It's either roll with me or stay in BK and starve, because there's no way you're going to be able to do anything out here without me." Kafisa paused again. "And to respond to one of your issues, you don't have to know anything about the South, because I do. I know the area just as well as I know BK. What I don't know, we can find out together. Overall, we have an opportunity to start all over again, build our own empire, and . . ." Kafisa hesitated. She had thought long and hard before she reached the conclusion she was about to share with her girls. "We won't have to answer or report to anybody other than each other."

Now that they were seeing the big picture, Halimah and Laverne listened attentively. Kafisa had their undivided attention. She was their boss, but she had to answer to someone herself, and that someone had cut off Halimah's and Laverne's life support. Kafisa knew what they were thinking.

"Don't worry about C-Dub," she assured them. "He doesn't have any say-so or anything to do with what we discussing."

"So, where the hell are we supposed to get product from?" Halimah asked dryly.

Kafisa had expected to be asked that question, and she had an answer for it. "Let me worry about that," she told Halimah. "All I need to know is if y'all with me or what? Because I can't do it without you guys."

Halimah and Laverne looked at each other, then back at Kafisa. Halimah shook her head and rolled her eyes. Laverne waited for her to answer. Although they worked for Kafisa, she and Halimah had come up in the trenches together in the Albany Houses projects, and Laverne had had Halimah's back ever since. So, she was down with whatever Halimah was feeling.

Kafisa grimaced. Judging by the look on Halimah's face, she was in for a disappointment. She knew that convincing them to relocate to South Carolina with her was a long shot. Without them, she knew it would be harder and slower to execute what she had in mind. *I've tried,* she thought to herself. *Now I understand what my dad meant when he used to say, "You can lead a horse to water, but you can't make it drink."*

Her thoughts were interrupted by the sound of Halimah's voice. "Okay. I'm in," Halimah declared, agreeing to roll with Kafisa.

A huge smile appeared on Kafisa's face. She was well aware that if Halimah was in, Laverne would be too.

"There better be money down there," Halimah added.

Laverne nodded in agreement, sticking with her girl.

"We'll all see." Kafisa gave pounds to each one of her homegirls. "I promise you, we gonna eat, by any means necessary," she confirmed, as any boss would.

Halimah was the first to speak. "I'm with you." Halimah stood up and hugged Kafisa.

"Ride till we die, right?" Laverne mused, breaking their hug.

"No doubt!" Kafisa smiled.

After exchanging hugs with Laverne, Kafisa walked them to the door.

Before stepping out the door, Halimah turned and asked, "So, when you tryin'a bounce?"

"Before the week is out," Kafisa replied. "I just gotta iron out some more details, but y'all might as well start packing now, though."

Both Halimah and Laverne nodded.

"I'll let y'all know a day in advance," Kafisa assured them.

After the three women exchanged good-byes, Kafisa closed the door behind her two partners in crime. It was as though a heavy load had been lifted off her shoulders. She knew the conversation and the end result could have gone either way. She was glad it had gone the way she had envisioned. Kafisa had successfully accomplished the first step of her plan, and now it was time to tackle the next step. *Now is a better time than any*, she thought.

She scurried to her bedroom and made her way to the place where she had put the missing piece of her puzzle. She stepped into her walk-in closet and retrieved a small metal box she kept up on a shelf in one of the corners. She turned the mini combination lock twice to the right, then once to the left. Once the box was unlocked, Kafisa opened it and then rummaged through the important papers inside it until she reached the bottom. Once she found what she was looking for, she closed the box and put it back in its place on the shelf. With the sought-after item, a business card, in hand, she walked over to her bed and sat down. Kafisa looked at the card. She took a deep breath. *It's now or never*, she thought as she flipped over the card, which Francine Costillo had given her years ago, and then dialed the number on the back.

# Chapter Sixteen

Kafisa waited on pins and needles while C-Dub pondered her idea.

C-Dub cleared his throat. "I think that's a smart move," was the response she received from him.

Kafisa had just informed him of her sudden decision to go back down to South Carolina and to take Halimah and Laverne with her. She had thought C-Dub was actually going to ask her a barrage of questions, so she was surprised when he didn't. She was glad too. She didn't want to lie to him. She had deliberately left out what her intentions were once she arrived in South Carolina and how she planned to execute them. Kafisa had thought long and hard about everything before calling C-Dub. She had reflected on the chain of events that had led her to reach out to him in the first place.

At the time, she had felt it was the only way she could gain access to Brooklyn and carry out her father's wishes. C-Dub controlled nearly 95 percent of the drug flow in the BK borough, which meant he had a lot of say-so when it came to who did and didn't eat in the city. She had been right. After she had proven herself, C-Dub had opened up any lane she wanted to travel in, but now things had changed.

Although the blame for her misfortune fell on her, the fact still remained that C-Dub had temporarily shut down every lane she had had access to over the past two years, which was why Kafisa felt that the less C-Dub knew about her plan for the future, the better it was for everyone. The last thing she needed was him getting on her about not laying low. Besides that, even if she wanted to, she couldn't tell him her plan. Secrecy was a part of her agreement with Francine. One of the unwritten rules that her father had adhered to—and that the people with whom he had done business still adhered to—was to never reveal your connect. With Francine on board, there was no reason why she had to tell C-Dub anything about her upcoming business affairs. Kafisa knew he'd want her to give up her connect. She had proven herself to those who really mattered to her and her future. Although she loved and respected C-Dub for the mentor he had been to her, Kafisa felt she didn't owe him any information other than what she offered.

"I'm going to miss BK." Kafisa sighed.

"Fee, always remember, Brooklyn ain't just where we from. It's who we are. You take BK with you wherever you go," C-Dub said, dropping a heavy fact on her.

"That's some real shit," Kafisa admitted. "BK for life fo' sure," she declared, pledging her allegiance to her home borough.

"BK for life," C-Dub said, following up with the same. "And as far as the girl Jazz goes, I'll keep you posted. I got somebody on it, so no worries about it."

"Thanks for always havin' my back, Dub."

"Don't mention it," C-Dub replied.

"Okay. Well, I gotta go, but I'll be in touch."

"Y'all travel safe, and remember to stay low while you down there. Don't draw any unnecessary attention to yourself. Enjoy all that hot weather until things cool off up here, you dig?"

Kafisa heard him loud and clear. She grimaced because she knew that was not her intent at all. She was a Jackson, and Jacksons were hustlers to the core. That was what she was born and raised to be. It was her destiny. She saw it all now. She knew now would be the perfect time to let C-Dub in on her plans, but she still felt the same as she had before as far as disclosing any of her upcoming plans for the South was concerned—despite C-Dub's mentoring of her in Brooklyn. One had nothing to do with the other, Kafisa believed. Something her father had said often played over and over in her mind. *Always make sure you're the smartest person in the room.*

"I will," was all Kafisa said before ending the call.

*You take BK with you wherever you go*, reverberated in her mind. *Yeah, I'ma take BK to the South*, Kafisa said to herself as she scrolled down to Halimah's name in her phone. She hit the CALL button, and Halimah picked up on the third ring.

"Yo, y'all be ready by five in the morning tomorrow. It's time to make it happen." Kafisa oozed excitement. It was as if she already knew what lay ahead.

"Damn, chick. Why so early?" Halimah asked, not thinking of the obvious.

"I know y'all don't want to be in traffic all the way down there, do you?"

"You right. See you tomorrow morning, bright and early, boss," Halimah said, assuring Kafisa they would be ready.

# Chapter Seventeen

At 5:00 a.m. the highway was nearly empty, and Kafisa, Halimah, and Laverne floated down I-95, heading south. Halimah navigated Kafisa's money-green Range Rover, while Kafisa rode shotgun. Laverne followed them in another car, a Honda, with all their belongings. They had been planning their exit from New York for the past few days. Ever since C-Dub had informed Kalisa that her name had been mentioned in the case against Jazz, allegedly connecting her to drugs, she had been moving like a thief in the night throughout Brooklyn.

After all Kafisa had done for her, she still couldn't believe Jazz had flipped on her. There was no way she was going to jail over somebody else's stupidity. Nor was she going to let her girls go out like that, either. The more time she had had to think about it, the more she had realized that she needed to get the hell out of Brooklyn as fast as possible. She had even realized that no matter how long she stayed away, when and if she came back, there would be problems awaiting her. She had also made up her mind that if she was going to have to go to prison eventually, she had to have enough money put away to last her until she got out.

After speaking to and meeting with Francine recently, Kafisa's confidence was at an all-time high. Francine had gotten the green light from her father to open up the drug pipeline for Kafisa, and Laverne had enough drugs stashed in the secret compartment Kafisa had installed in the whip she was driving behind the Range Rover to get a small country high, thanks to Francine Costillo.

Nearly eleven hours after they set out from Brooklyn, they pulled into the driveway of the best hotel in all of downtown Columbia, South Carolina, and checked in.

"Welcome to the South, ladies." Kafisa smiled. She extended her arms and waved them around, as if she were introducing Halimah and Laverne to a new home.

Two valet attendants immediately rushed over to assist them.

"Welcome to the Hyatt. Y'all checking in?" asked the young African American valet attendant.

His strong Southern drawl made Laverne frown. Halimah held her laughter in when she heard the attendant's Southern accent.

"Yes, we are," Kafisa answered.

"Can I help you with your luggage, ma'am?" the young attendant asked. His coworker, a young Latino male, had already ripped parking receipts off his pad for the two vehicles. Cars were constantly pulling in, and he didn't want to fall behind. He and his fellow attendant had been parking cars nonstop since their shift started.

"Nah, we good," Laverne replied. "We got it."

Kafisa looked at her, then at Halimah. She shrugged her shoulders and let out a light chuckle. She wondered why Laverne was being so dismissive to the valet attendant. She could tell Laverne was not used to Southern hospitality.

"Y'all ain't from round here, are you?" the valet attendant questioned.

"Uh, no," Laverne snapped. "That's why the license plates say New York," she remarked dryly, pointing to the front plate of the Honda and the back plate of Kafisa's Range Rover at the same time.

Kafisa shook her head. She made a mental note to say something to Laverne about her rudeness. She knew that was credited to being not only from New York, but also from Brooklyn, New York. Where they came from, rude was accepted, but since Kafisa had gone to college in the South, she had grown accustomed to everybody waving and being genuinely nice. It was apparent that the valet attendant had not taken offense, nor had he been fazed by Laverne's tone and choice of words.

He let out a loud laugh. "Oh, my bad," he said, apologizing. "But I shoulda knew that, though, 'cause the ladies down here don't act or look the way y'all do."

Laverne didn't know whether to take that as a compliment or as some shade.

"Good looking, brother," Kafisa replied on behalf of the three of them. She pulled out a fifty-dollar bill. "You and your boy have dinner on us tonight." Kafisa handed him the money.

"Appreciate you, ma'am," the valet attendant said, thanking her right before making his way over to the car that had just pulled in.

"Yo, you need to chill the fuck out." Kafisa directed her words to Laverne as soon as the valet attendant was out of earshot.

"What?" Laverne asked innocently.

"Bitch, you know what," Halimah answered for Kafisa. "You know you ain't have to talk to dude like that," she said, reprimanding Laverne without any softness.

"He was in the way." Laverne rolled her eyes, then smirked. "It smells like we're in the country," she continued. She stretched her back and her legs to loosen up her muscles. She had been feeling stiff ever since they hopped on the road.

"How the hell would you know how the South smells if you've never been here before?" Kafisa questioned.

Halimah chuckled.

"Anything that ain't Brooklyn is the South to me, and it don't smell nothing like Brooklyn. That's what I know and am used to," Laverne explained, applying her own logic.

"You sound real stupid." Kafisa shook her head. "Since you said we don't need no help with our luggage, how 'bout you go grab a cart and come get our Brooklyn bags and bring them in this country hotel?" Kafisa shot back in a mocking tone.

By now Halimah was doubled over in laughter. Even Laverne had to laugh at Kafisa's sarcastic yet serious remark. "A'ight. You got that," Laverne said, still laughing.

Minutes later Kafisa, Halimah, and Laverne were all checked in to the biggest three-bedroom, four-bathroom presidential suite the hotel had to offer. The sky-high ceilings were the first thing they noticed. All three of their bedrooms had hot tubs and walk-in showers. The living room area was big enough to host a party with eighty-plus people.

Halimah and Laverne had never stayed in anything of the suite's magnitude, so they were immediately impressed. Kafisa, on the other hand, had been in rooms equally as upscale, and sometimes more so, than the one they now occupied. Her father had made sure she knew what the finer things in life were. When she dated Jameel, he had exhibited the same acquired taste and principles as her father, and he had never stayed in anything other than suites.

"This shit right here, nigga!" Halimah exclaimed, doing her best Katt Williams impression.

"For real," Laverne said, joining in. "This some real boss shit right here."

"Exactly," Kafisa agreed. "And from here on out, that's how it should be carried. We some boss bitches, and that's how we comin' down here." Although she had given them the rundown back in BK, she reiterated to Halimah and Laverne why they were really down there. She wanted it to be clear that they weren't down there for a vacation or to make friends. They were there to infiltrate, monopolize, take over, and get money.

Halimah and Laverne both nodded in agreement.

Just then Kafisa's phone went off. She pulled it out of her pocket and looked at it. She shook her head before answering. She answered yes a few times and then hung up the phone. Kafisa looked at both Halimah and Laverne. "My peoples just said she'll be here in about an hour. That gives us enough time to change and get situated."

The three of them began to go their separate ways.

Kafisa spun around. "Oh, Verne."

Laverne stopped in her tracks. She turned to face Kafisa. "What's up?"

"Make sure you secure the product before you get dressed," Kafisa reminded her.

Laverne shook her head rapidly.

It had just dawned on Kafisa that they hadn't brought in the fifty keys they had stashed in the Honda. She couldn't afford any mishaps. Kafisa knew if anything happened to the bricks Francine had fronted her, both her freedom and her life would be in jeopardy. The last thing she needed was for something to go wrong before she was able to execute her plans. Despite her worrying, Kafisa was predicting a successful time in South Carolina.

# Chapter Eighteen

Kafisa stood outside the hotel with Halimah and Laverne by her side, looking like pit bulls. "Fix yo' faces, 'cause ain't no shade surfacing up in here," Kafisa said under her breath.

Together they watched as the 2008 Lexus with twenty-three-inch chrome rims pulled into the valet area. Halimah and Laverne glanced over at each other and snickered. The Chief Keef track abruptly ended as the four-door car came to a screeching halt. The driver's door swung open, and out stepped Kafisa's ex–college roommate.

"Hey, boo!" Nu-Nu chirped as she hopped out of her charcoal-gray Lexus, wearing an all-white bodysuit one size too small for her natural plus size.

"Wassup, Nu-Nu?" Kafisa smiled at her ex–college roommate.

The two exchanged hugs. You could tell by the hug it had been a long time since they had seen each other.

"Um, I've missed you! Your smell was always good," Nu-Nu cooed. Her words were loud enough for only Kafisa to hear. Kafisa couldn't help but laugh at Nu-Nu, who had wrapped her arms around her as tight as she could. She pressed her body up against Kafisa so hard that you would have thought the two were Siamese twins.

Halimah and Laverne stood in the background, watching the reunion.

"Girl, you lookin' fabulous," Nu-Nu complimented, releasing Kafisa from the long hug. She looked Kafisa up and down as she spoke.

Neither Halimah nor Laverne caught the look, but Kafisa did. Nu-Nu's thoughts were written all in her eyes. She knew what they stemmed from. She wondered whether the issue would get in the way of the plans she had for her enterprise down there in the South. She wondered if it was a bad idea to look Nu-Nu up after Jameel had mentioned he knew what Nu-Nu was into. She brushed off the idea, just as she did Nu-Nu's flirtatious behavior.

"So are you," she said, returning the compliment. She then turned and introduced Halimah and Laverne.

"Hey, y'all." Nu-Nu waved.

"Hey," Halimah and Laverne sang in unison.

"Sooo, waassuuup?" Nu-Nu did her best Martin Lawrence impression, dragging her words out. "You missed me? I missed you," she continued before Kafisa could answer. "I thought I'd never see you again. I mean, I'm happy to see you. It's good to see you. Couldn't believe it was you when you hit me. I'm glad Jameel gave you my number, with his crazy ass. But he gettin' it, though, girl," she said, rambling.

Halimah and Laverne looked at each other. It was apparent they were both thinking the same thing about Nu-Nu, based on their matching facial expressions.

Kafisa just let Nu-Nu ramble on. *Still a chatterbox. Still a hotshot*, she thought to herself. She couldn't help but travel back in time to where it had all begun and the reason why Nu-Nu was acting the way she was.

*"Are you sure you want to do this?" Nu-Nu asked. The word* nervous *might as well have been written across her forehead, because it was the best way to describe her demeanor.*

"Why not?" Kafisa asked, making herself the questioner. "If not with you, who else?"

Kafisa had been bi-curious ever since she had laid eyes on Nu-Nu's track runner's physique. Growing up in Brooklyn, she had been exposed to a lot, so she was no stranger to gay men and women. With what she had seen throughout her younger years, Kafisa wanted better and did not want to be just like her childhood friends, a statistic. She knew hard work and loyalty would get her out of the hood, and she applied those in her academics and found herself in college. Although this was her first time being on her own, she wasn't a dummy, either. She had brains and beauty and used them every chance she could, especially tonight in her dorm room with her naive roommate. The two had been sharing living quarters for a year, and oftentimes her roommate would hint at an attraction, and finally, she was going to get her wish and feed her curiosity.

Kafisa lay across Nu-Nu's bed, admiring her flawless body. Nu-Nu was a plain Jane, but she had a natural beauty about her. She didn't require makeup or weaves. Her skin looked as smooth as butter, but it was often hidden behind her glasses and her long tresses, which were often pulled back in a messy bun or ponytail.

Kafisa removed Nu-Nu's glasses and placed them on the nightstand. She began to touch her face. Startled by her touch, Nu-Nu began to tense up. Her facial expression was now a mix of nervousness and fear.

"You gotta relax and just let it happen," Kafisa assured her, although she too was somewhat nervous. This was actually her first time with the same sex, or with any sex, for that matter. Still, she pretended to be experienced and maintained control. "I got you," she whispered seductively.

*Kafisa ran her finger across Nu-Nu's lips. Nu-Nu sighed and closed her eyes. At that moment, Kafisa took the opportunity to kiss her. She cupped one of Nu-Nu's mounds as she gently pressed her lips up against hers. She started out with small kisses, and this eventually led to her exploring Nu-Nu's mouth with her curious tongue. At first Nu-Nu's lips were tight, but as Kafisa massaged her right nipple and caressed her breast, she began to relax. Kafisa's touch actually felt nice and soothing to her. She parted her mouth and embraced Kafisa's lips and tongue. In no time she began to participate in the exchange.*

*As the two lay in the bed, kissing, Kafisa began to explore Nu-Nu's body some more. She continued to gently rub Nu-Nu's breasts. Her nipples hardened. Their kissing got more intense. Although this was her first time being with a woman, the way she was behaving, no one, including Nu-Nu, would have ever guessed.*

*"Take off your thong," Kafisa said in between the kisses she planted on Nu-Nu's neck.*

*Nu-Nu was turned on. Kafisa could tell she would do anything she told her to at that moment. Kafisa's tongue trailed down Nu-Nu's nakedness. Nu-Nu's body tingled from Kafisa's tongue against her skin. Kafisa continued to shock Nu-Nu's body with her mouth, tongue, and hands. There wasn't anything that Nu-Nu would not do to experience the sexual bliss that she was anticipating as she felt Kafisa travel down toward her love box.*

*The two were in a sexual trance. Nu-Nu felt an explosion of emotions, and out of nowhere, she turned into the aggressor. She grabbed the back of Kafisa's head to bring her back up to her mouth and began to kiss her, but this time with such passion.*

*Kafisa was still fully clothed. "Hold up." She pulled away from Nu-Nu. Kafisa slowly removed all her clothes. That only heightened Nu-Nu's attraction to her. The two lay in the bed in the nude, exploring one another. Without hesitation Kafisa made her way back down between Nu-Nu's inner thighs. Nu-Nu let out small moans of bliss as Kafisa placed her tongue on her rigid clitoris and took the flesh in her mouth. She began an intense rhythm of gyrating.*

*Nu-Nu's legs spread for Kafisa, to take all of her in. Kafisa licked all over her love canal, always paying the most attention to her clit. She took it in her mouth and began to make love to it. Nu-Nu's body shuddered, and her pelvis began to thrust hard. Nu-Nu did not want the feeling to end. She had become wetter than she had ever been in her life from what was being done to her by Kafisa.*

*Kafisa knew at that point that she had the power, and she was not going to stop until Nu-Nu climaxed. She too was heavily aroused and wet as she humped the bed. Kafisa anticipated the attention that her own body would receive. "Is it good?" she asked Nu-Nu.*

*Between heavy breaths, Nu-Nu uttered, "Yes."*

*Her response let Kafisa know she had reached the point of no return. She devoured Nu-Nu's pussy until she begged her to stop. Still, that wasn't enough to make Kafisa end her tongue assault. It wasn't until Nu-Nu had climaxed a few times that Kafisa let up. She swallowed all her nectar like a pro. That was the real reason why she had been interested in having a gay experience. She'd wanted to see what another pussy tasted like to compare it to her own.*

*After she had taken in all of Nu-Nu's love juices, she proceeded to make her way back up to Nu-Nu's mouth and began to kiss her again with passion. She wanted her to taste her own juices, which were all over Kafisa's lips and tongue. Nu-Nu did not hesitate. They held each other in a tight embrace, kissing and grinding on one another.*

*Nu-Nu became aggressive once again. She wanted to return the favor to Kafisa. She slithered her tongue down and past Kafisa's breasts. She proceeded to travel downward toward Kafisa's neatly shaven kitten. She reached the top of Kafisa's kat and peered up at her. "I love you," she cooed before continuing.*

*Kafisa smiled and replied, "I love you too." She chalked Nu-Nu's statement up to the heat of the moment.*

*Nu-Nu lit up like a Christmas tree. She placed wet kisses on Kafisa's clitoris, then attacked her with her tongue. Nu-Nu played with her flesh with her tongue, flicking it back and forth, and consumed all of her in her mouth. Kafisa could not deny the feeling herself as she tried to hold back from reaching another orgasm. She couldn't hold back for long. The feeling was so intense and so good that it was as if she were floating on a soft cloud.*

*After her body went limp, Kafisa stretched out on the bed. Nu-Nu curled up next to her. Kafisa could hear her sniffling.*

*She looked down at Nu-Nu. "What's wrong?"*

*Nu-Nu shifted her body and propped her elbows up on Kafisa's rib cage. "I love you, and I want us to be together." Nu-Nu stared her dead in the eyes.*

*Her response was enough to make Kafisa regret what they had done. Soon after, Kafisa got a room change. After she returned from her mother's funeral, she put distance between herself and Nu-Nu, blaming it on her grieving over her deceased mother, Camilla. After graduation Nu-Nu made one last attempt at confessing her undying love to Kafisa. It was the last time the two women had seen each other. Kafisa returned to New York, leaving Nu-Nu confused and brokenhearted.*

It was now apparent to Kafisa that Nu-Nu still carried a torch for her. She knew she had to nip the shit in the bud before she could go any further.

Nu-Nu could tell Kafisa was reminiscing about their past history. She had been with only two men in her life, and Kafisa was her first sexual experience with a woman, but unlike with Kafisa, it wasn't her last. She had always credited Kafisa for turning her out, but judging by her appearance, Nu-Nu knew that Kafisa was no longer about that life. Nu-Nu felt somewhat sad, because she had thought that she and Kafisa could possibly pick up where they had left off some years ago. She had always felt the safest with Kafisa and had once pictured her being a part of her future—until Kafisa had told her she had to return to Brooklyn and would not be coming back to the South anytime soon.

"My bad, girl." Nu-Nu's words brought Kafisa back to the present. "I'm just goin' on and on about nothing. I'm just glad to see you, is all." Nu-Nu reached out again, catching Kafisa by surprise, and gave her another hug. "We straight," she whispered in Kafisa's ear, just loud enough for her to hear.

Kafisa returned her hug. She let out a sigh of relief. Kafisa was glad Nu-Nu hadn't continued with her innuendos and aroused the suspicion of Halimah and Laverne. Although she had nothing to hide, she didn't feel like explaining the situation to her girls, especially since there were more important things to discuss.

"Y'all get in with me. Let's ride. Let me show you the sweetness of the South," Nu-Nu suggested.

Both Halimah and Laverne looked over at Kafisa. Kafisa nodded and made her way to Nu-Nu's Lexus. Minutes later Nu-Nu was cruising through the city of Columbia, bumping the latest Dirty South music.

"So, give me the lay of the land," Kafisa said. It was time to get down to business. "Let me know how they movin' out here and tell me what you into." She turned toward Nu-Nu.

Nu-Nu glanced over at her, then peered in the rearview mirror at Laverne and Halimah before she spoke. "Well, there's a few locals that be doing their thing, but the real big dope boys are from Miami," she began. "Then you got the Jersey and Philly boys across town, who stay beefing over their areas. That's where Jameel be at when he come into town. There's pretty much a major figure from every borough, including where you from, who out here, gettin' it. Me and my homegirl, Niecy, usually get down together and get our stuff from one of the New Yorkers, anyway, because they seemed to have the best work and be consistent." Nu-Nu flicked her blinker and hooked a right turn.

Kafisa peered out the passenger-side window. She recognized this area, since she had once dwelled here. She drew her attention back to Nu-Nu, not wanting to miss anything.

"We pay twelve hundred an ounce for some good, hard shit and bust it down and make nothing under two bandz and a half. And we buying like four or five ounces a pop a week," Nu-Nu stated proudly. She had no way of knowing that though it was a source of pride for her, what she was accomplishing in the streets did not and could not impress Kafisa and her team. It took everything in Kafisa's power not to laugh at Nu-Nu's proud drug accomplishments, but Halimah and Laverne couldn't hold their chuckles in.

Nu-Nu peered back at them in the rearview mirror for a second time. "What's so funny?" she wanted to know.

"Nothing," Kafisa answered for her girls. She turned around and shot them both disapproving looks, like a mother would her disruptive kids.

"We meant no disrespect, ma," Halimah said, apologizing for her and Laverne's laughter.

"It's cool. Y'all straight," Nu-Nu said. Her Southern drawl was undeniable. "But that ain't what we really wanna do, though," she admitted.

Kafisa listened attentively.

"We want to be able to sell weight," Nu-Nu explained.

Kafisa smiled on the inside. Nu-Nu's words were like music to her ears. "Really?" Kafisa asked.

"Yeah, me and my homegirl wanna sell weight," Nu-Nu repeated. "Bring New York to them. That's where the money's at. I mean, you only gonna get double or something, not even that, but the money is in the quick flip, right?"

Kafisa nodded. "Absolutely."

"Exactly!" Nu-Nu exclaimed. "I already got the numbers in my head too," she added.

Kafisa chuckled. She didn't believe Nu-Nu knew what she was talking about. "What do you mean?" She was curious to know what Nu-Nu was thinking.

"I mean, if I ever get my hands on some birds, I'ma do it like this." Nu-Nu began to break down her game plan. "Say you cop two bricks for twenty-one a piece and sell them for twenty-eight a piece right off the bat. That's a fourteen-thousand-dollar profit right there. Or say you come and sell ounces to the younger kids wholesale, twelve hundred an ounce or a thousand. If you sell thirty-six ounces at a G a whop, that's thirty-six thousand right there. If you sell them for eleven or twelve hundred, that's about forty-three thousand a key."

The way Nu-Nu had broken it down had Kafisa intrigued. Nu-Nu had not only Kafisa's undivided attention. She also had Halimah's and Laverne's ears. Neither Kafisa, Halimah, nor Laverne had ever hustled in the South, or anywhere other than Brooklyn, for that matter, so they were soaking it all up. They all did quick tallies in their head and came to the same conclusion. You could move weight just as quickly as you could move work on the ground level.

"That sounds cool and all, but how many joints you think you could move if you had them?" Kafisa asked.

"Shit!" Nu-Nu let out a light chuckle. "As many as I can get my damn hands on," she remarked.

"Get the fuck out of here." Kafisa matched her chuckle. "So, you mean to tell me, if you had one hundred keys, you could move them?" Kafisa challenged.

"No, that's not what I'm sayin'," Nu-Nu replied.

"Oh, I knew you were buggin'." Kafisa grimaced. She wondered if linking up with Nu-Nu was a bad idea after all.

"What I'm sayin' is that me and my homegirl, Niecy, could move a hundred of them things *if* we could get our hands on them," Nu-Nu explained. A huge smile appeared across her face. "But we'll never know this, because unless them shit fall outta the sky or a motherfucka hit the lottery, a bitch gonna be ouncin' it out here till she die."

Nu-Nu's last remarks caused a thunder of laughter from Kafisa, Halimah, and Laverne.

"Shit. I'm serious! Y'all laughing," Nu-Nu said.

Kafisa was the first to cease her laughter. Her tone turned serious. "What if you could get your hands on that much shit?"

Nu-Nu looked over at her. Something in Kafisa's eyes made Nu-Nu pull over. "What the hell are you talkin' about?" she asked Kafisa. She and Kafisa were now eye to eye.

"First, before I answer your question, let's establish something," Kafisa stated. "One, don't ever talk to me like that again. Okay?" Her stare became sterner.

A sense of inferiority swept through Nu-Nu. Kafisa's words caused her feelings for her to resurface. They took her back to that place when she was cuckoo for Cocoa Puffs for Kafisa. Rather than argue, Nu-Nu shook her head, acquiescing. She had a strong feeling that neither her feelings for Kafisa nor her pride was worth more than the answer she believed she was about to get to her question. "I give you my word. And I apologize for the disrespect," Nu-Nu replied.

Kafisa nodded and smiled. "Apology accepted." She grew serious. "Now secondly, after I answer your question, what I say goes."

Nu-Nu didn't hesitate to nod her agreement to that condition. She already knew that would be something she'd have to conform to, and she was fine with that.

Kafisa noticed that Nu-Nu was unfazed by her second demand. That pleased her. She believed Nu-Nu would take her lead. "Let's just say you just hit the muthafuckin' lottery and shit fallin' out of the fuckin' sky," Kafisa finally answered.

There was a dead calm in the car for just under a minute, until Nu-Nu's delayed reaction kicked in. Nu-Nu's near window-shattering scream echoed throughout her Lexus. Kafisa put her fingers in her ears to minimize the excruciating sound. Halimah and Laverne followed suit.

"Girl! You bet' not be shittin' me!" Nu-Nu said, regaining her composure.

"No, you better not be shittin' me!" Kafisa rapidly fired back.

Judging by the look on Nu-Nu's face, Kafisa knew her tone was strong enough to convince Nu-Nu that this was not a drill. It was the real thing. She had fallen into a money pot and finally had a chance to deepen her pockets without dealing with some shady-ass motherfuckers.

Kafisa made her first request of Nu-Nu. "Now, call up your homegirl, Niecy, so we can meet her and get this shit flooded in the South." She then reached up and lowered the volume of Nu-Nu's mixed CD. She reclined her seat and watched as Nu-Nu pulled out her phone and dialed her road dog, Niecy. Niecy picked up on the first ring.

"Yo, Niecy. There's people I need you to meet. Holla at me at Tasty's. We on our way now."

"Okay. I'll be there in an hour or so." Niecy hung up the phone.

"Everything is set. Let me show you where the real ballers and shot callers play at," Nu-Nu said as she put her phone back in the middle console.

"I wouldn't have it any other way. Let's do it." Kafisa looked back at Halimah and Laverne with a big smile on her face, letting them know things would be looking all the way up sooner than they had thought. Then Kafisa turned up the volume of Nu-Nu's mixed CD.

# Chapter Nineteen

Tasty's Gentlemen's Club was packed when they arrived. It was doing the damn thing! Strippers flipped upside down on poles, and others paraded around the room half naked, while men and women filled the place, stuffing what little clothing the strippers wore with predominantly one-dollar bills.

Kafisa was not surprised to see just as many women in the establishment as men. Hanging out in strip clubs had become the new thing for females. Kafisa remembered that when she attended college, this club had been called another name, but she couldn't recall what it was. She knew it wasn't a strip club back then, though. Just from the outside alone, she knew it was not the same place it had been.

Nu-Nu had told her it was the new hangout spot for all the local hustlers on all levels in the surrounding area and for money-chasing chicks from all over too. On that particular night, motorcycles, high-priced cars, high-maintenance chicks, and good-looking guys were in force outside and in. It seemed as if the nice weather had brought the whole city out. It felt good to Kafisa to be back around her old college stomping grounds. She thought she recognized some faces from school, but she wasn't sure.

*Damn, I miss the ole days*, she thought while one of the club promoters ushered them inside, enabling them to skip the line wrapped around the building. The crowd of agitated and horny club goers waiting impatiently to see some ass and titties gave them all dirty looks. Nu-Nu ignored the stares and strolled past the crowd and into the club like she owned it. Kafisa knew she was trying to impress her. Although it was her intent to keep a low profile while trying to open up shop, she liked how Nu-Nu rolled. Back home, she would have done the same thing. All eyes were on them as Nu-Nu led the pack.

It was apparent to Kafisa that on a Thursday Tasty's was where you wanted to be if you were getting money and liked to turn up and show out. *The ambiance alone makes you want to spend money, empty yo' pockets in the establishment*, thought Kafisa. A large gold genie's lamp hung from the ceiling, giving off a red glow, which created a sensual atmosphere. The walls were covered with red velvet fabric and pictures of exotic dancers mounted in gold frames.

The bar stretched across the back wall of the spacious room, facing the tables, chairs, and stage. It was fully stocked with every type of liquor imaginable. A curly-haired, brown-eyed beauty stood behind the bar, barely clothed and ready to serve drinks. The stage was a runway and stretched across the front of the room. Everyone had the same view as their neighbor. Access to the stage was easy, so each person could tip his or her favorite stripper accordingly. Two bouncers were seated at each end of the stage, ready to wrestle anyone who overstepped their boundaries and ignored the rules.

As they made their way to Nu-Nu's reserved section, Kafisa couldn't help but notice that in every section, whether next to the stage or in VIP, bottles were being popped. Sexy females in provocative outfits were coming from every direction, with sparklers and bottles in hand. After what seemed like forever, due to the size of the club and the bottle poppers, they finally made it to their elevated VIP section, built against the right wall of the club.

"'Bout muthafuckin' time! It took forever to get in this bitch," Niecy told Nu-Nu. She did a quick scan of Kafisa, Halimah, and Laverne.

"Bitch, we here, ain't we?" Nu-Nu shot back.

Niecy rolled her eyes. She could tell right away that Nu-Nu was in an "I'm here to impress these peoples" mood. Niecy looked at the strange faces before her again, then looked back at Nu-Nu. *This better not be some bullshit*, she thought.

"These my peoples I was tellin' you about." Nu-Nu began to introduce her invited guests. "This is Halimah." She pointed. "That's Laverne." She paused and turned toward Kafisa. "And this is Kafisa," she announced boldly. She wanted to make sure Niecy knew this was who she really wanted her to meet.

"Hey, everybody." Niecy gave a wave with her hand. "Excuse my rudeness, but this bitch been slow forever and a day since I've known her." Niecy chuckled.

Her words removed whatever tension might have been lingering. The New York in Kafisa, Halimah, and Laverne was ready to come out. They had all thought that they were going to have a problem with Niecy. They were all glad when she clarified the reason for the look on her face and her demeanor when they first arrived in the VIP section.

"It's cool," Kafisa said, accepting her apology on behalf of her crew. "Besides, I know exactly what you're talkin' 'bout," Kafisa added with a wink.

"I like her already." Niecy laughed. "What y'all drinkin'?" she then asked. "I got two bottles of white to get us started, but if y'all drink dark liquor, I can order something else," she offered.

Kafisa looked around the club. This time she took a better look. It didn't take her long to figure out who was who and what was what. She knew if she wanted to make her presence felt and have every hustler wondering who she, Halimah, and Laverne were, she had to set the tone.

"We drink Cîroc," Kafisa replied. "No disrespect to you, but that's not enough for us."

Niecy's face twisted a bit. "Okay, balla." She threw her hands up, as if in surrender. "Well, the way my baller account set up . . . ," she joked. Niecy looked over at Nu-Nu, who was just standing there with a humorous grin on her face.

Kafisa let out a light chuckle. "Don't worry about it, ma. I got us."

Ten minutes later, everybody stopped what they were doing and watched as six of the club's baddest chicks came through like a soul train line, toting a dozen bottles of vodka and champagne, accompanied by sparklers. Kafisa had personally requested that the club's baddest girls bring their bottles out. She had tipped healthily to ensure that this would be the case. Kafisa was pleased when she saw the attention their section was receiving. They all sat there while the sexy women of all shades poured them all their first drink, except for Niecy. It was actually Niecy's fourth. When she arrived, she had already had a drink in hand. As time went by, however, they all nearly matched in terms of the amount of alcohol they had consumed.

"Who, me?" Kafisa heard Nu-Nu say, pointing to her chest. Her words were a little slurred. When she turned and looked in the direction Nu-Nu was facing, Kafisa saw a huge, dark-skinned, bald-headed brother, with a shirt two sizes too small on and enough jewelry to light the club back up if the lights shut off, motioning for her to come over to his section.

"Who's that?" Kafisa asked.

"That's Blue. Them the Florida boys I was telling you about," Nu-Nu answered. "But what he tryin'a holla at me for?" Nu-Nu rolled her eyes. "I don't fuck with 'em."

Kafisa shook her head. "He tryin'a holla at you because he tryin'a figure out how the fuck we can afford all these bottles I just ordered," Kafisa said, clueing her in.

Nu-Nu giggled. The liquor had made her a little relaxed. "Ooh! My bad. I guess it's the country in me coming out." She quickly sobered up and stood. Within minutes, Nu-Nu was in between the dark-skinned brother named Blue and another brother, who was two shades lighter than Blue and a few inches taller than him.

Kafisa pretended not to watch as the two men's gold teeth glistened as they talked to Nu-Nu and periodically looked over at Kafisa. She played her position like the boss she was, and sipped on her drink while her girls and Niecy partied. Before she knew it, Niecy had been summoned by another brother, who, she informed Kafisa, was from Charleston, South Carolina, and had the town on lock.

Before the night ended, both Niecy and Nu-Nu had made their rounds to every VIP section in the club. *So far so good*, thought Kafisa as she accepted the check from the waitress. Including taxes and the gratuity, the bill came to $5,600.00. Kafisa pulled a monstrous knot of hundred-dollar bills out of her D&G clutch. She counted out sixty bills and handed them to the waitress.

"Don't worry about the change, sweetie." Kafisa winked at her. She then retrieved one of her business cards from her clutch. "If you ever get tired of doing this, hit me up." Kafisa stared the waitress in her face.

The waitress broke the stare. She had a huge smile plastered on her face. "Thank you. And thanks." She slipped the card in between her breasts and stuck the six grand into the check wallet.

Kafisa stood. Halimah and Laverne followed suit. Kafisa noticed that they had three remaining full bottles and two halves on the table. She leaned in to the closest group of dudes standing by their section. "Hey, y'all can have all this if y'all want." She offered the bottles of liquor with a wave of her hand. The dudes declined. She knew they would. Just like she knew the move would draw the attention of others who were within earshot or who had been eyeing her body language.

*Mission accomplished*, Kafisa said to herself as she led the pack away from the table. She floated through the club, stone-faced, as she made her way to the club's exit.

"I had a feelin' I'd be seeing you soon," she heard someone say just as she reached the exit door.

This time, despite the club's music, she recognized the voice. When she looked to her right, she saw Jameel posted up on the wall right before the exit. Kafisa stopped in her tracks. "Why we keep bumping into each other? Are you following me or something?" Kafisa asked. She wanted to smile, but she knew all eyes were still on them, and she wanted to be sure that she maintained her status.

"I'm the one who lives down here. I should be asking you that last question." Jameel met her blank stare. "As for the first one, I don't know." He leaned in toward Kafisa and hugged her from the shoulders up. "I'm tryin'a see you outside of the club," he cooed in her ear.

Those on the outside looking in wouldn't have known how Kafisa took it. She showed no reaction to Jameel's statement. It took everything in her power not to react, though. She didn't even bother to hug him back. "It was good seeing you. Hit me up sometime," Kafisa said. She then walked out the door. Everybody nodded and waved at Jameel as they trailed behind Kafisa.

Jameel watched as Kafisa and her entourage vanished out of the club. When he turned, he was met by a familiar face.

"Yo, Meel. Who ole girl?" Styles asked curiously.

Styles was one of the few hustlers Jameel interacted with on a business and personal level, so Jameel didn't mind that he'd asked this question. The two had clicked instantly one night when they were eyeing the same girl at another club closer to South of the Border. Styles was the one who had actually turned him on to the small towns off of Interstate 95 in North Carolina, like Dunn, Benson, and Smithfield, but he'd also given him a warning. Styles had shared that his brother had been killed and his right-hand man had gotten life from messing around with some stickup chicks from one of these towns.

Jameel had gone and checked the towns out anyway. All three spots had wound up being lucrative for him, which was why he had a certain love and respect for Styles. Had anybody else posed this question, he would've flipped on them instantly for asking about his personal business.

"She a heavy hitter from up top," Jameel said, offering Styles the only information he needed to know. He had almost referred to her as his ex, but that would be a hater move, and he had nothing but love for Kafisa.

"Where at?" Styles asked, pressing the issue. He was gathering information he knew every baller and small-time hustler in the building wished they could get.

Jameel didn't hesitate to answer. "BK." He realized answering Styles's questions could only help Kafisa in whatever it was she was trying to do.

"That's wassup. Good lookin', my G." Styles gave Jameel dap and a bro hug.

"No doubt, my dude." He returned Styles's handshake and hug.

"Be safe out here, yo," Styles then offered.

"Definitely!" Jameel replied. "You too, bro."

The two went their separate ways. Jameel made his way back over to where he had been sitting up until the time he noticed Kafisa, while Styles returned to his table. The vibration on the side of his hip caused Jameel to pause. When he pulled out his phone, he smiled. He typed in his code and unlocked his screen. He then bent his head after reading the entire message and replying to it.


Halimah and Laverne were giving Nu-Nu her props for the way she had handled her business back at the club. Kafisa sat over in the front passenger seat, in deep thought. She knew that tonight she had played her hand to a T. There was no doubt in her mind that Nu-Nu's and Niecy's phones would be ringing like it was Sunday mass. She had been focused the entire night on creating the impression that she was *that bitch* and her crew was nothing to fuck with. *My game face would have been impeccable, had it not been for running into Jameel,* Kafisa thought.

At the sound of his voice Kafisa had known she had to keep her composure, or else she might have exposed her hand some. There was no way she was going to let anything or anybody stand in the way of what she had to do while she was in the South. There was just something about Jameel that, as of late, had been drawing her in. Kafisa wondered if it was just loneliness she felt, if it had nothing to do Jameel himself. She took a deep breath. *Only one way to find out,* Kafisa told herself.

She pulled out her iPhone, pulled up Jameel's number, and sent him a text. You still tryin'a see me outside of the club? I want u!

Kafisa pressed SEND, then waited for Jameel's response. She held back the grin that tried to force its way onto her face as she read Jameel's immediate response. I would love to see u outside the club. I want u too.

# Chapter Twenty

Jameel went in and out of his ranch-style home in anticipation of Kafisa's arrival. All he thought about was what he was going to show her in the bedroom. He peered down at his watch. Two hours had passed since she had texted him after leaving the club. He had almost given up hope that they would see each other tonight, but then his phone alarm had gone off, letting him know he had a new text message from Kafisa. In her text she let him know she'd be at his house in less than five minutes.

Three minute later her SUV pulled into his dirt drive-way, and he watched as she hopped out. Jameel met Kafisa at his front door.

"I thought you were gonna chicken out." Jameel grinned.

"Not Kafis Jackson's daughter," Kafisa replied with a straight face. "Besides, I'm the one that texted you, remember?" She was still surprised at herself for texting him what she did, but once she'd pressed SEND, she knew there was no turning back.

"True." Jameel chuckled. "And I'm glad you did," he added. "Welcome to my humble abode." He then slid to the side to allow Kafisa access to his crib.

Kafisa accepted his invitation. Her body lightly brushed up against Jameel's as she stepped into his home. She felt a strong magnetic force as she passed Jameel. This was something she had never felt with any other guy. She used to get the same feeling whenever she was around him back in her college days, and she was surprised that the feeling had resurfaced when she ran into him back at the club in New York. Then again, when they met for lunch, she'd felt like a girl with a high school crush.

Once they were inside the house, Jameel helped her get comfortable. He took her jacket, which she had peeled off. "Follow me," he then said as he walked past her and toward his staircase leading upstairs.

As if hypnotized, Kafisa didn't say a word. Instead, she followed Jameel as he led her up the stairs to his bedroom. She staggered a little and nearly stumbled as she walked up the steps.

Jameel turned and asked, "You good?"

"Yes." Kafisa peered up at him. "I'm fine."

Jameel could tell by how glossy her eyes were that she was, at the very least, tipsy.

"No, you're not," he insisted. He grabbed hold of Kafisa's hand and led her the rest of the way up the steps. He escorted her through the hallway until he reached his master bedroom.

Kafisa couldn't believe how passive she was being right now. She wasn't sure if it was because of the liquor, the fact that she was turned on by Jameel's take-charge demeanor, or both. *Either way, it feels nice not to have to lead for a change*, thought Kafisa.

"Have a seat." Jameel pointed to his bed, and she obliged. He then disappeared into the bathroom. He returned with five candles and a lighter. He had rehearsed the type of mood he wanted to set with Kafisa. He set the five candles on top of his dresser. He lit them one by one, then turned off the lights in his room.

Kafisa looked around the room, a bit startled, as if the lights had gone off by themselves. Her ears suddenly heard the sound of one of her favorite former female R & B groups, Floetry. Out of nowhere, one of her favorite songs came flowing out of Jameel's surround-sound speakers. She looked at Jameel, who was now shirtless and was standing by the stereo with the remote in his hand.

Jameel slithered toward Kafisa, snapping his fingers with each step he took. He placed one of his fingers over her lips and then grabbed her hands to pull her off the bed. "You owe me a dance." He smirked. "I saw you in two clubs, and we didn't get to dance neither time," Jameel pointed out.

A huge smile appeared on Kafisa's face. At first, she pretended to resist. She knew Jameel wasn't going to take no for an answer. She realized he was going to dance with her no matter what, even if he had to force her to dance with him. For the first time in a long time, Kafisa let her guard down. Jameel stared into her eyes, wrapped his arms around her hips, and locked his fingers together so that she could not pull away from him. Kafisa responded by throwing her arms around his neck. He turned her on even more by wanting to slow dance in the middle of his bedroom with her. She wondered if he had remembered that she liked to dance or if this was purely coincidental. Together, they swayed back and forth in silence. At that moment, they let their eyes do all the talking.

Kafisa instinctively laid her head on Jameel's bare, rock-hard chest. She closed her eyes but then immediately opened them. The room seemed to be spinning when her eyes were closed. The last thing she wanted was to pass out and not remember a thing. Her eyes trailed down Jameel's chest and rested on his midsection. Kafisa rubbed her hands over all the indentations in his ab muscles. She inhaled his masculine scent and ran her hands down his back. The music had changed to the next track. Kafisa found herself getting lost in his embrace.

It had been a while since she had been in the arms of a man. She had been grinding so hard the past few years that she hadn't had the time or the energy to entertain the opposite sex. Since Jameel, she had gone out a couple of times, but after C-Dub put her in the game, it had been strictly business. Kafisa realized she had longed for the feeling she was feeling at that moment. Without even thinking, she kissed Jameel's chest. She peered up at him immediately afterward, as if she had done something wrong.

"I'm sorry," she said, apologizing in a low whisper.

"Don't be," he replied in a soft but raspy kind of way. He lowered his head and planted a kiss on Kafisa's forehead. He then cupped her chin and planted one on her lips. Kafisa parted her lips and let Jameel's tongue explore her mouth. He could taste the alcohol on her tongue as he kissed her long and hard.

Kafisa followed his lead. Their kiss became more intense. Jameel cupped Kafisa's voluptuous ass with his hands and scooped her up into his arms, the whole while never breaking their lip-lock. He carried her over to the bed and laid her down on it. Kafisa stared at him seductively as he stood in front of her. He gently lowered Kafisa's jeans to her ankles and slid them from around her feet.

She backed up on the bed slightly. *You ready for this?* she asked herself. The mood had gone from zero to one hundred real quick. "Um . . ." She didn't know what she wanted to say.

"Only if you're ready," Jameel said, looking her in the eyes.

*He must be reading my mind*, she thought.

*Damn. I hope you're ready*, Jameel said to himself.

Kafisa nodded. She was all too ready to feel his full lips kissing every part of her body and his firm, large hands gripping her thighs. Her heartbeat increased at the thought. "Of course I want this. That's why I hit you up," she said, running her hand along the side of his beard. Her fingers outlined the shape of his lips, and she examined the passionate look on his face after he heard what she'd said. "It's just been a minute."

Jameel smiled and lay next to her. He ran his hands along the curves of her legs and then rested them on her arms. "No need to be nervous. I got you," he assured her.

Kafisa nodded again. Their eyes met. She got lost in his. Every nerve and sinew in her body began to awaken. Jameel's smoldering looks were overwhelming her. She was now ready to feel every inch of him. "Don't hold back," Kafisa cooed.

"I won't." Jameel kissed her hard. Their kiss led to hands touching every part of the other's body. They freed each other of what few clothes they had on, until they were naked. Kafisa felt good, surprisingly, as she prepared herself to receive what her body had been craving since the night just a short time ago that she had run into Jameel. There was no denying the intensity that had built up since then. Tonight she intended to let it all go in a big way.

Jameel traveled down until he was just above the moist center between Kafisa's legs. He dove in with his tongue. He gently kissed her inner thighs until he was face-to-face with her prized possession. He ran his tongue across her more sensitive area, causing her legs to shake with pleasure. A sensual gasp escaped from her mouth. That turned Jameel on. He increased his pace. Jameel gripped her thighs as he continued to bury his face in her love cave. Kafisa felt as if he was sucking her soul out of her as he tasted her juices with every lick he took.

"Ooh, yes!" Kafisa moaned. She tried to push his head out from between her legs, but he wouldn't budge. Her legs shook ferociously when she felt her first orgasm—a sensation she had not experienced in a long time. "Aah!" she cried.

Jameel pulled away from her. He reached over toward his nightstand and retrieved a Magnum. He licked his lips and gazed into Kafisa's eyes as he tore open the condom wrapper. He then wiped his beard with his right hand and grabbed his stiff dick with his left. After slipping the condom on, he spread Kafisa's legs wider to fit his frame, then guided his pulsating hardness inside of her wetness.

Kafisa's body shuddered from the feel of Jameel's rock-hard dick inside her. His ten inches was giving her everything she desired and yearned for. She arched her back to give his length full access to her sex. She had not felt what she was feeling now in years. Kafisa wanted to savor the moment.

"Go slow," she whispered in Jameel's ear.

"I will," he replied. "I promise I will." Jameel slowed his rhythm. He paused briefly just to absorb the moment. *She feels incredible*, he thought. She was a place that he never wanted to leave. He had waited for this moment for a long time too. He wanted to make it pleasurable for her and worth it. Jameel wanted Kafisa to know that she wasn't a quick bang that he had been waiting to score. She wasn't just an ex-girlfriend; she was his heart, and no one would ever compare to her in terms of the love and the sex.

It just so happened that his favorite track on the CD was beginning. It excited him even more, and he refused to waste another minute. Jameel plunged his manhood deeper into her wet center. The look of ecstasy on her face was turning him on even more. Kafisa's pussy was a bit tender and tight due to a lack of sex. She bit down on her bottom lip and took the pain and the pleasure that followed.

"You good?" he asked her as he continued grinding his wood into her.

"Yes," she sang. Her nails dug into his back as he traveled deeper inside of her.

Jameel was on a natural high with Kafisa's sweet flower. It turned him on so much that with each dig of her nails into his back, his thrusts inside her became harder.

Kafisa's legs quivered with the onset of a second orgasm. She let out a loud moan and let her juices ooze onto Jameel's cock. No longer able to hold on, Jameel pulled out and released himself inside the condom. He jerked the condom until he had nothing left inside of him to release. Jameel collapsed on top of Kafisa. She cuddled him in her arms and planted a kiss on his forehead.

"Thank you," she whispered.

Jameel let out a light chuckle. "Thank you too," he shot back. He found the strength to get up and go into the bathroom to grab them two wet towels. He returned and gently began wiping Kafisa's own juices from between her legs. With the other towel he wiped himself clean, and then he returned the two towels to the bathroom.

"Did you want to shower?" he asked Kafisa after doubling back to his bedroom.

When he didn't hear a response, he crept closer to the bed to see why. The sight of her sleeping on his bed brought a smile to his face. It was beautiful, so beautiful that he had to skip the shower and join her.

# Chapter Twenty-one

The next morning, Kafisa woke up to the early morning sounds of birds chirping and the smell of turkey sausage and eggs in the air. The sun had just risen. The warm rays spread lightly across her beautiful naked body, which was tangled up in the sheets. A cool, refreshing breeze occasionally crept its way through the open balcony door, pampering her. She slowly opened her eyes and stared at the unfamiliar ceiling. She then sat up in a panic as reality hit her. It took her a second to remember where she was. Between the alcohol and the meager rest, not to mention the multiples she had experienced a few hours ago, thanks to Jameel, she had lost track of time and space.

Kafisa had even forgotten that she had come over to Jameel's house late last night. *That's what your ass gets for drunk texting*, she cursed herself, remembering the text she had sent him. She hadn't realized she was as tipsy as she was until she found herself in front of his crib. The next thing she knew, she was naked and Jameel was inside of her. She'd known where the text would lead, but she hadn't expected to be satisfied as well as she was in Jameel's bed last night. That had been her intent, but she hadn't thought she would follow through on it. It had never been her intent to let the sun beat her up. Kafisa shook her head at herself as she let out a light chuckle. She couldn't help but laugh at the fact that her text flirting had gotten real.

She quickly scanned the lavish bedroom for her clothes. They were across the floor, at the far end of the room. She wrapped her body in the sheet and stood up and walked over to pick her clothes up off the floor. When she removed her cell phone from her clutch, she was not surprised to see the abundance of missed calls and text messages from Halimah, Laverne, and Nu-Nu. She figured the 803 area code number she didn't recognize was Niecy's number, since it was in the same sequence as everybody else's missed calls. Kafisa shot a quick text back to Halimah, letting her know she was good, then put the phone back in her clutch. She then began to dress quickly. Just as she was buttoning the last button on her shirt, Jameel came in with a plate laden with sausage, eggs, wheat toast, a glass of OJ, and a bowl of assorted fruit.

"Mornin', Sleepin' Beauty." He smiled. "Hungry? I know you worked up an appetite."

Kafisa noticed he was in a wife beater, basketball shorts, and a pair of Air Max. Judging by the way his muscles were bulging, Kafisa could tell he had worked out this morning.

"Nah. I'm good. I gotta go," Kafisa replied, although she wanted to lie in bed next to him while he fed her breakfast, and let her worries disappear.

Jameel nodded. A grin appeared across his face. "It's cool. I get it," he said.

"Thanks." Kafisa looked around until she located her truck keys on Jameel's nightstand.

"So, when can I see you again?" Jameel asked.

Kafisa snatched up her keys and spun back around. "I don't think that's a good idea." Kafisa looked him straight in the eyes, fighting her need for him.

Jameel lowered his eyes, and that famous smirk appeared. He knew Kafisa was serious and it would be useless to try to change her mind. He had already come to the realization that she was not the same girl he had known her to be back then. The fact that she was now in the South and was the talk of the entire Columbia, South Carolina, region spoke volumes to Jameel. He knew an opportunity when he saw one, and he was determined not to let it slip away.

"Not even for business purposes?" he shot back in a cool manner.

Kafisa wasn't expecting that. His question made her believe Jameel had actually changed his perspective on who she really was. That was all she had wanted from the start—with a side order of sweetness.

"For business, you can hit me directly," Kafisa offered before brushing past him. "I got you." She turned and flashed Jameel a warm smile, then made her way out of his bedroom and down the steps to the entryway.

Once she had exited the house and got into her SUV, she took out her phone. She sent a group text to Halimah, Laverne, Nu-Nu, and Niecy. I'll be there in a few. Afterward, she started the ignition to her truck, then peeled out of Jameel's dirt driveway. Moments later, she was back on the interstate, headed back to her hotel.

# Chapter Twenty-two

*2014*

Kafisa stepped into the three-bedroom house used for bagging up the work she and her crew put into the streets. She had literally gone down South and implemented her New York blueprint there and made it work. Each room in the railroad apartment was infested with different drugs. She had crack and coke in the living room and dope in the bedrooms. The bedrooms were sealed off from the rest of the apartment, and they had air humidifiers, plastic jumpsuits, rubber gloves, face masks, shock caps, and even disposable boot covers. The machines were basic packaging machines.

With Halimah, Laverne, Nu-Nu, and Niecy as manpower, Kafisa ran her operation like the Carter Building in *New Jack City*. She had zero tolerance for any workers getting hooked on drugs. Kafisa didn't know any of the chicks Nu-Nu and Niecy had recruited, which meant she had no real connection to them and wouldn't hesitate to get rid of them one way or another if they threatened what she and her team had managed to build in a short period of time.

Kafisa suited up and entered one of the bedrooms. She nodded her approval in the direction of the nude females who were rubber banding the bundles. The machines were producing ten thousand bags a day, and it still wasn't enough. The operation had grown considerably during the first three months. Between dope, coke, and crack, they made a minimum of ninety thousand dollars a night. Kafisa and her squad were pulling in somewhere between one and a half and two million dollars in profit. Once Kafisa paid off her connect, she was still seeing high six figures.

But the money was nothing in comparison to what Kafisa had managed to rebuild. A week ago she was like a kid in a candy store when Francine sent word for her to meet her in Miami for lunch. During that lunch Francine told Kafisa that she had redeemed her family's name and had become highly respected among the higher-ups as one of the top earners. Francine shared with Kafisa how her numbers were passed around the round table in monthly meetings.

Kafisa had never felt more like a boss than on that day. As far as she was concerned, she was *that bitch* in the South. She was sitting on top of the underworld. She was moving more product than she had ever dreamed of. Francine kept her flooded with kilos of cocaine and bricks of dope by the truckload, as promised, and so Kafisa was able to meet one of the key prerequisites of getting major paper: never running out of product. With a mean connect, she had climbed heights beyond her wildest imagination. If she were to tell it, Kafisa was officially the Nino Brown and Scarface all wrapped up into one in the South, and she carried herself as such.

Out of nowhere she called an emergency drill to see who was really on point. "Clean up and pack up," she ordered, letting them know this was a wrap-up. Such drills were something she had learned from her father, and she had liked to spring them on her team when she was back home. Halimah and Laverne were used to it and acted speedily, but everybody else was slow as shit in Kafisa's eyes. The whole process was done in under ten minutes. Kafisa was used to seeing it done in five. Still, she saw the potential they had and knew their response would get better and stronger as time went on.

"Y'all still gotta tighten up!" she blared.

Everybody in the room nodded in agreement. They had been practicing on their own to get faster, just in case of a raid, because no one wanted to go to jail.

Kafisa left the bedroom and removed her jumpsuit. She made her way into the back room, where she knew she would find Nu-Nu.

Nu-Nu's back was turned when Kafisa entered her office. She stood in the doorway and watched as Nu-Nu wrapped a rubber band around the stack of bills she had in her hand, then toss the stack in the nearly filled duffel bag on her desk. She then picked up the remaining bills and began to count them. Kafisa didn't bother to interrupt. She actually was a little turned on by the scene. Not by Nu-Nu, but by the fact that she was watching her money being counted.

"Nine hundred ninety-seven, nine hundred nine-ty-eight, nine hundred ninety-nine, thirty-five." Nu-Nu slipped a rubber band around the last thousand-dollar stack of money and then placed the stack in the duffel bag.

"You finished?" Kafisa asked, stepping into the room.

Nu-Nu spun around. "Girl, you scared the hell outta me," Nu-Nu confessed. Kafisa's presence had caught her by surprise.

Kafisa noticed the .380 Nu-Nu had tucked in her waist. "Shouldn't have your back turned to the door, anyway," Kafisa reprimanded her jokingly.

"You right," Nu-Nu agreed.

"So how much is it?" Kafisa pointed to the duffel bag.

"This is a hundred thirty-five thousand right here," Nu-Nu replied. "And Niecy said she got another forty-five across town, where she trappin' at tonight. So, I just took it out of my money and put it in there so I wouldn't hold you up," Nu-Nu added.

"I appreciate that, because I'm literally tired as shit." Kafisa was grateful for Nu-Nu's consideration.

"Don't mention it," Nu-Nu shot back. "I know how hard you be going. Shit, I'm tired too, but, like you say, the end justify the means," Nu-Nu said, quoting Kafisa.

"Absolutely!" Kafisa smiled.

Money was flowing like a waterfall, even better than Kafisa had envisioned. The whole while they were locking the city down, they had managed to avoid any trouble with the Columbia PD. Nu-Nu had told Kafisa how even the haters were loving the product and were eating, so they had nothing to worry about as far as someone snitching on them was concerned. Kafisa was glad Nu-Nu had chosen to join her team.

Kafisa knew she couldn't have mounted this operation so effectively and efficiently without Nu-Nu's and Niecy's experience and knowledge of the drug trade in the South. She was also glad that Nu-Nu had been able to put her personal feelings about her aside and focus on the bigger picture, getting bread. In just a short period of time, she had managed to show Nu-Nu more money than she had ever seen in the five years she had been hustling. Kafisa had kept her word and had made sure that Nu-Nu did not regret taking what she called a demotion for the greater good. She made sure Nu-Nu and Niecy had the best and most consistent product around.

As an extra incentive, she had paid off the remainder of Nu-Nu's student loans, had upgraded her 2013 Lexus to a 2015, and had put Niecy in the same model, only a different color. At first she had thought Nu-Nu and Niecy were going to butt heads with Halimah and Laverne, but that was far from the case. Instead, they had formed a sisterhood, one so strong that it was as if they had all grown up together. Kafisa was pleased about that, because their relationship showed in the numbers they were pulling in.

Since their arrival in South Carolina, Kafisa had tried to keep the lowest profile possible, while making sure Halimah and Laverne did the same. With the exception of the business they did with the small circle of people they had met through Nu-Nu and Niecy, Halimah and Laverne saw virtually no one. Kafisa was keeping them close to her until she found the proper places to base them out of. Kafisa had copped herself a double-wide trailer and one for Halimah and Laverne that was not too far from her. But it was not easy, especially since Halimah's and Laverne's buyers' orders kept growing. Only Nu-Nu and Niecy had trap houses and steady areas they supplied. Before Kafisa knew it, she had four jumping houses, and they had the market cornered. Kafisa saw to it that they had the best prices for birds of raw coke and grams of raw dope within a fifty-mile radius, from east to west and north to south. They knew this because that was the distance some hustlers traveled from to cop their product.

With just Jameel's purchase order of fifty keys of coke and ten keys of dope every week, Kafisa knew her product was hitting at least five other states, thanks to Jameel. Their trap houses were bringing in astronomical numbers, and they were bringing in cash like it was 1988 all over again. They were bubbling hard. Business was good, and Nu-Nu and Niecy were major forces behind it. She wondered where she would be if it were not for Francine becoming her plug, Jameel plugging her with Nu-Nu, and Nu-Nu and Niecy doing their hustle.

Back in New York, everything she had worked so hard for in the streets had been taken away from her in the blink of an eye because of one bad apple. Kafisa had had to learn the hard way what her father had meant when

he said, "You're only as strong as your weakest link."
Because of Jazz's weakness, her entire empire had come
crashing down right before her very eyes. Kafisa had also
learned to appreciate the wisdom of another saying her
father liked to repeat. "You're only as strong as your
connect." It was because of her connections that Kafisa
believed she had gotten to where she was in a short
period of time. *Just in time*, she thought, as a special
moment in her life seemed to be rapidly approaching.

"That's wassup," Kafisa said, congratulating Nu-Nu.
She was really impressed with the fluid way in which
Nu-Nu operated. "I'm planning a party for my thirtieth,
which is in six months," Kafisa then said. You could hear
the excitement in her tone. "There's a few things I'm
trying to do and cop when it gets closer, so for the next
few months, I want us to go dumb hard. That day I want
everything to be perfect, and I want us shining harder
than the sun. I already hollered at Limah and Verne, so
you let Niecy know." Kafisa smiled.

"I got you!" Nu-Nu nodded.

"That's my girl." A huge grin appeared on Kafisa's
face. "My shit gonna be the talk of the South," she mused.
"Nobody ever gonna forget my birthday." Kafisa was filled
with excitement.

"Why would they?" Nu-Nu said.

"That's right. Why would they?" Kafisa agreed. "Okay,
ma, let me get out of here and take my ass home." Kafisa
snatched up the duffel bag sitting on Nu-Nu's desktop.
The two exchanged hugs right before Kafisa exited the
trap house and hopped in her Range Rover.

Just as she pulled off, her Bluetooth in her Range went
off. When she saw the name of the unexpected caller
appear on her dash's monitor, she frowned. It had been
so long since she had heard from him. The last time she
had actually spoken to him was when she had reached out

to inform him that she was relocating to the South. Kafisa let C-Dub's call go to voice mail. Although it seemed as if she was ducking C-Dub's call, Kafisa was just not in the mood to talk to anybody or hear about anything that was going on back home in Brooklyn or anywhere else up top. Her main focus, just like when she was in BK, was what she had going on now, and right now she was in the South. Kafisa's voice mail alert went off. She saw that C-Dub had left a message.

Before she could check it, a text message from C-Dub came across her screen. **Call me ASAP.**

Kafisa rolled her eyes. "It can only be about some bullshit," she cursed. She unlocked her screen and shot a quick text back, letting him know she was driving and would call him back when she reached her destination. She ended her text by asking C-Dub what was wrong.

His reply was, **Just hit me.**

Kafisa shook her head. **Okay,** she replied back, then pushed down on the gas pedal, accelerating fast.

# Chapter Twenty-three

"Yeah." Kafisa's tone was dry.

C-Dub laughed. "I see the South hasn't done anything for your attitude. I thought you country girls supposed to be Southern belles and hospitable and shit," C-Dub joked.

Kafisa found no humor in his words. She was not feeling the small talk. She was ready to hear whatever bad news C-Dub intended to lay on her. She was irritated by the fact that C-Dub felt he had to warm her up for what he wanted to tell her.

"I'm not from the South. I'm from BK!" Kafisa shot back. "BK for life, remember?" She repeated the words they had both uttered the last time they spoke.

C-Dub laughed for a second time. "Easy, killa. What's with the hostility?" he questioned. "I call bearing good news, and this is how I get treated?"

Kafisa's eyes lit up at the mention of good news. She was not expecting to hear those words come out of C-Dub's mouth. Her heart rate began to speed up. *Is it over? Can I return to BK? Am I about to get back everything that was taken from me in my own hometown?* So many thoughts raced through Kafisa's mind.

"Good news? What good news?" Kafisa could hardly keep her composure.

"Let's just say, that problem you had has been solved," C-Dub offered.

"What do you mean?" Kafisa wanted to make sure she understood what C-Dub was saying. She didn't think they were on the same page.

"Your girl Jazz," he replied.

It took a few seconds for it to register. She was right. They were not on the same page. She had thought C-Dub was telling her that she, Halimah, and Laverne were in the clear. However, he was actually telling her that Jazz had been killed. It wasn't that she didn't want Jazz to be dealt with. It just wasn't the good news she was looking for. The longer she remained in the South, the less she thought about Brooklyn, but now C-Dub had her in deep thought about her old stomping grounds. Kafisa realized that she had missed her city, despite how successful she had become in the South.

"So it should be over, right?" Kafisa was hopeful.

"It's not that simple," C-Dub replied.

Kafisa let out a breath of hot air into her phone.

"You gotta be patient, Fee. Shit still fresh," C-Dub told her.

"I know," Kafisa agreed.

"In the meantime, in-between time, how you holdin' up down there in the dirty dirty?" C-Dub asked in a joking manner.

Kafisa's body tensed for a moment. She had never lied to C-Dub. She weighed the manner in which he had asked the question. *It seems generic enough to answer generically,* Kafisa thought to herself. "I'm good. We good down here," Kafisa answered and left it at that.

"Cool. Cool. Good to hear," C-Dub said. There was an awkward silence for a brief moment. "Well, you take care down there. It shouldn't be too much longer," C-Dub assured her. "No witness, no case," he added.

"Hope so," Kafisa cooed. "I'm ready to get back up top."

"It doesn't seem like it," C-Dub remarked slyly.

"What is that supposed to mean?" Kafisa wondered where that had come from.

"Relax. I'm just messing with you, baby girl," C-Dub said.

There was only one person in the world she let call her baby girl, and C-Dub was not him. Hearing him say it rubbed her the wrong way. "My bad." she said, apologizing. "Just homesick." She downplayed her feelings. She was ready to get off the phone with C-Dub before she said something she couldn't take back. "I've been runnin' all day. I'ma take it down," Kafisa told him.

"I understand. Get your rest," C-Dub replied. "Give me a call if you ever need to talk," he then said.

It had been a long time since he had extended such an invitation to Kafisa. She appreciated the offer. "Will do," she replied before the two ended their call.

Kafisa made her way to her bathroom. She undressed and turned on the shower. She couldn't help but play some of the tapes in her head of her and C-Dub's conversation. For some reason, he'd been in a playful mood. Too playful for Kafisa's own taste. *Business must be good for him*, she thought as she climbed into the shower. *But business is good for me too*, she reminded herself as she put her head under the showerhead.

# Chapter Twenty-four

*Six months later . . .*

Kafisa, Halimah, Laverne, Nu-Nu, and Niecy stepped into the serene establishment five the hard way. They were greeted with a smile.

"Hello there. Welcome to the Southern Style Spa! What can we do for you today?" asked one of the women at the desk. Her partner handed everybody brochures listing the spa's services.

Kafisa stared at the spa services menu. "This place came highly recommended," she said. "We're getting ready for a special occasion."

"Why, thank you. My name is Daliah, and this is Sue," said the woman who had greeted them. She smiled again. "What's the occasion, if you don't mind me asking?"

"My birthday." Now it was Kafisa's turn to smile.

*Aside from just needing some pampering after all the bullshit I been through this past year*, she thought to herself.

"Congratulations!" both women sang in unison. "So, what would you guys like today?" the first woman, Daliah, inquired.

"We'll take four deep-tissue, full-body Swedish-style massages," Kafisa declared.

"Okay, the number three. Great choice," the other woman, Sue, agreed. "Daliah here is going to take you to the changing room, where you can get undressed, while we start the mineral soak bath for all of you." She rang up Kafisa's order. "Comes to two thousand three hundred sixty-two dollars and fifty cents. Will that be cash or credit?"

Kafisa went into her Michael Kors clutch and pulled out a monstrous wad of money. "Cash," she announced. Daliah's and Sue's eyes widened as Kafisa peeled off twenty-five one-hundred-dollar bills from the knot of cash. Kafisa handed Sue the money. "Keep the change."

"Thank you," Sue said after opening her cashier drawer.

Daliah then led everybody to the changing room. Kafisa stripped out of her clothes, keeping on the bathing suit she had on underneath, and got into the robe the spa supplied. She stuck her MP3 player and her headphones in a pocket. The others followed suit. When they were done, there were four masseurs waiting for Halimah, Nu-Nu, Laverne, and Niecy.

"You come with me," Daliah told Kafisa.

Kafisa and Halimah exchanged humorous looks in response to the brawny woman's request.

"Lead the way," Kafisa told her.

Daliah nodded, then led Kafisa to a private room. Kafisa followed her to a water-jet bath infused with natural minerals. She removed her robe, took out the MP3 player, popped in her headphones, and then lowered herself into the bath, feeling the soothing hot water. She got comfortable and instantly closed her eyes. She soaked in the bath for the next forty-five minutes, easing the minor aches in her muscles. She could tell that her body was replenished when it was time for her massage.

After donning her robe, Kafisa walked up the stairs of the spa and into the white marble room where she would be receiving her massage. She nodded and smiled at the handsome Spanish masseur. She removed her robe but kept on her bathing suit, and he instructed her to lie down on her stomach on top of the massage table, which was covered in a brown plush towel, and to place her head against the leather headrest.

"Did you want to take off your bathing suit?" he asked, knowing some customers preferred to lie naked underneath a towel while receiving their massage.

Kafisa climbed onto the massage table. She shook her head with a smile. "No, no thank you," she answered. She sat on the edge of the massage table.

The masseur smiled, noticing her demureness. "I just asked because it's almost like a policy. You'd be surprised how many people would rather receive a massage with nothing on. Let's get started."

Kafisa lay down on the table and let the Spanish masseur knead her back muscles. The curative nature of the massage was immediately apparent to her. She had once been skeptical about massage therapy, but no more. She could attest to its power. The masseur's hands lightly stroked her neck and shoulders, then descended to her spinal column. He poured aromatherapy oil on her midway down her back and rubbed it into her backside. His hands then moved down to her thighs and legs, and he rubbed in the oil in a circular fashion. The massage was so ardent that Kafisa almost thought the masseur was making love to her with his hands.

When her Swedish rubdown ended, she thanked the masseur and tipped him graciously. She went back to the changing room to change into her clothes. She realized her bathing suit was still wet, and decided she'd just throw on her miniskirt and showcase the top of the one-piece.

With her MK clutch in one hand and her shirt in the other, Kafisa stepped out of the room and made her way back to where her girls were. Everybody had a relaxed expression plastered across their face. Kafisa was pleased that her crew seemed to have enjoyed the pampering at her expense just as much as she had. After all, they had been working and going just as hard as she had.

They left the spa and piled into Kafisa's Range Rover. After she dropped everybody off, Kafisa headed home to prepare for what she believed would be an unforgettable night. *Yeah, tonight's definitely gonna be a night to remember*, she told herself. She had no way of knowing just how memorable a night it would be, though.

# Chapter Twenty-five

*Later that evening . . .*

All eyes were on them as Kafisa and her entourage stepped out of the cranberry-and-silver Maybach. Kafisa noticed all the stares through her Dior shades as she and her crew breezed past both the regular and the VIP line. She wasn't sure at first whether the crowd was more impressed with her and her four-woman team or with the luxury car, but judging by the looks on their faces, she could tell it was a combination of both. Just like she could tell it was the first time the majority of the club goers had ever seen a Maybach outside of a rap video or magazine. When she'd treated herself to the car, she knew it would be a head turner.

*Now is a better time than any other*, she thought. Tonight was her night, and nothing was too expensive when it came to making her happy. Lately, as the December 31 date was nearing, Kafisa had been feeling some type of way. So much had happened since she had left New York.

Overall, she had weathered the storm and had become stronger than ever, and tonight it would show. She had worked hard, and now she wanted to play hard. She had been stacking her money, the way she had learned from her father, and it had all been worth it. Her work ethic was impeccable. She was like the Energizer Bunny when it came to her grind. Money was her motivation.

She hadn't slept for a good twenty-four hours combined throughout the entire week to ensure nothing got
in the way of her weekend plans. Either she'd been on
the highway, driving to some other state, or she'd been
on a plane, flying somewhere. Her peoples in North
Carolina and Virginia were copping bricks like they were
going out of style, and her team in the South Carolina
area was moving so many pies, they should open up a
bakery. Thanks to Francine's drug pipeline, supplying
enough drugs to meet the demand had her constantly on
the move. The raw coke and heroin that she was getting
from Francine were definitely in demand throughout the
South, but if her buyers did not place their orders and
pick them up by the weekend, then they would be ass
out. Kafisa let everybody she supplied know that she was
about to close up shop for this weekend. Tonight was a
celebration without any concerns or worries about street
shit.

Between the Maybach she had purchased and the real
Queen B pendant she had had made especially for her
platinum chain and matching bracelet, not to mention
what she had paid out for this night, she had spent just
over three quarters of a million dollars. To many, that was
a lot of money, but to Kafisa, it was nothing. Money
was the least of her worries. She had it and plenty of it.
After all, she was that chick who was winning.

Not only was she winning, but so too was her crew. It
was no secret that she and her squad were some of the
most talked about females in the dirty, but by the way
they were all dressed, you never would have known that
these five enticing women who had entered the club
were some of the most dangerous of their kind. *Sexy*
and *deadly* would be the best words to describe Kafisa
and her girls. Between the five of them, they had over
a million dollars in ice around their necks, in their ears,
and around their wrists.

As they were escorted to their VIP section, other women envied them, while men lusted after them. The five of them were indeed a sight to see. As soon as they reached their VIP section, the energy of the club increased. There were bottles awaiting them.

"Damn. We haven't been out in a while," Niecy reminded them.

"Right!" Nu-Nu and Laverne chorused.

Kafisa and Halimah looked at each other. Kafisa was the oldest of them all, followed by Halimah, so they didn't feel the same way that their three crew members felt when it came to going out. But tonight Kafisa intended to show them all how to party on another level.

"What's up, ladies? Can I take your picture?" a well-dressed light-skinned brother with a camera asked them over the music, interrupting them.

"Come back in a few," Kafisa replied on behalf of her squad.

The cameraman nodded, smiled, and attempted to make his exit.

"Matter of fact, hold up. You can get us now, before these bitches start disappearing and get white-girl wasted," Kafisa told him, changing her mind.

"Got you." The cameraman smiled.

Within seconds, the cameraman began to do his thing. Onlookers stared as he snapped what seemed like a hundred different shots of Kafisa and her crew. Each pose was different as they raised up drinks and bottles. He even managed to take a few of Kafisa tossing a stack of singles in the air. Once he was done shooting, he showed them his photography equipment, and they all leaned in to get a look at his high-tech digital camera, which replayed the photos with a push of a button.

Kafisa gave a nod of approval.

"You like 'em?" the cameraman asked.

"Definitely," she answered for them all.

"Which ones you like?" he then asked.

"Yeah, we like 'em all," Halimah said, chiming in.

Kafisa smiled. "Yeah, we like 'em all. Give me all of 'em," Kafisa said, backing Halimah up.

The cameraman could not believe his ears. He was used to people he had photographed liking all the photos, but no one had ever wanted to buy so many at one time, especially not women. He knew they were not your average chicks. He did a quick calculation in his head and told Kafisa the price for all the photos.

Without hesitation, Kafisa pulled out her stack of money and peeled off two crisp hundred-dollar bills and handed them to the photographer. "Take this now and come back and take another two hundred dollars' worth later, once we get some more bottles and everything."

"I appreciate that," he said, pocketing the money. "Thanks. I'll be back with your flicks."

Kafis nodded. She sat down and leaned back. The rest of her crew did the same, except for Niecy.

"Oh, this my shit right here!" Niecy shouted as the sounds of Chief Keef's latest jam filled the air. She instantly broke out in her famous two-step.

"Aye!" Halimah threw her hand up in the air and snapped her fingers to the music. Nu-Nu and Laverne joined her as they cheered Niecy on.

Kafisa let out a light chuckle. She enjoyed watching her girls have a good time. Just then, two male servers appeared out of nowhere, carrying cranberry, orange, and pineapple chasers, along with two metal buckets of ice. Kafisa had already called and made arrangements ahead of time as to what she wanted. As if on cue, what seemed like a soul-train line full of servers made a beeline over to Kafisa's VIP section. Partygoers cleared a path as six sexy females of assorted flavors came through with a bottle in each hand, accompanied by sparklers. The first three females possessed different flavors of Cîroc, while the last three toted bottles of rosé.

"What are you having?" asked the sexy server closest to Kafisa, leaning in.

"Peach Cîroc with a splash of orange juice."

The girl immediately cracked a bottle of peach Cîroc.

"And a glass of sparkling rosé," Kafisa added.

"Got you." The girl gave her a wink and a smile. After she poured Kafisa's drinks, she attempted to take everybody else's order. It was too late. Halimah had already cracked a bottle of rosé for herself, while Niecy, Nu-Nu, and Laverne had all helped themselves to the other bottles of Cîroc.

Kafisa smiled. "We good," she told the server.

The girl returned Kafisa's smile before exiting the VIP section. Kafisa scanned the club. Once again, she noticed all eyes on them as she and her crew turned up. Her eyes rested on the section across from theirs. She made eye contact with one of the dudes in that section. It was apparent from the six bottles Kafisa observed that he and his two boys had come to turn up as well. The dude raised his glass in Kafisa's direction and slipped her a sly smirk. Kafisa pretended not to see him and focused back on her own section. At first glance, she hadn't recognized him, which meant he was a nobody, as far as she was concerned, because she already knew everybody who was somebody.

"Who ready for two-K-fifteen? South Carolina, where y'all at? Make some noise!" the DJ shouted into the mic.

"Whoo!" The crowd broke into a thunderous roar that could be heard throughout the body-infested club.

Kafisa glanced down at her iced-out Franck Muller Rolex. In ten minutes it would be a New Year, and she would be a new woman. The rosé had her feeling nice, but before the year 2014 ended and the New Year came in, she wanted to be white-girl wasted like everyone else. She poured herself another glass of the sparkling wine and tossed it back. After repeating this two more times, her bottle of rosé was empty. She placed it upside down in the ice bucket.

"Limah, hand me that bottle." She pointed to the closest open bottle of rosé.

Halimah smiled and enjoyed the fact that her boss was finally relaxing. Since she'd hooked up with Kafisa, every birthday had turned better than the last. "Look at you. Tryin'a handle it like a real bitch!" she teased.

"I *am* a real bitch!" Kafisa wasted no time shooting back. Her words were a little slurred, but her tone was firm. Joking or not, her father had told her never to let anyone downplay or assassinate her character, no matter who it was. Although she knew Halimah had meant no harm, she still had to check her.

Halimah knew she had crossed the line, just as she knew the reason for this was her liquor.

"Yes, you are, boss! And any muthafucka that says different, they gonna get dealt with." Halimah's words came out with conviction.

Kafisa felt the love. She smiled. "Bitch, don't get all mushy on me. Pass me a damn bottle."

Halimah chuckled and snatched up the bottle of rosé from the metal bucket.

As Kafisa took the bottle, she noticed another dude in the section across from them eyeing her. She raised her eyebrows, as if to ask what he was staring at, then just waited for a response. The dude answered her with a chuckle, then turned his head and returned to sipping his drink. Kafisa was tempted to step to him, but she decided against it. Tonight was her night, and she was not going to let anything or anybody ruin it.

"Okay, everybody! Thirty seconds till the countdown," the DJ informed the crowd.

Kafisa stared at her ice beveled timepiece. As the seconds hand approached the ten-second mark, the DJ began to count down.

"Ten . . . nine . . . eight . . . seven . . ."

The crowd joined in. "Six . . . five . . . four . . . three . . . two . . . one! Happy New Year!" The crowd cheered as confetti fell from the ceiling of the Columbia, South Carolina, nightclub. Champagne flutes, bottles, and cups with assorted light and dark liquors filled the air.

"I'd like to wish a special Happy Thirtieth Birthday to the queen bee of not only the South but also the BK! Kafisa the Don! I see you, baby girl. If you don't know, you better know now, 'cause she one badass bitch!" Mister Cee, the DJ, shouted through the microphone as he switched songs. "This one's for you, ma!" he added.

Just then the sounds of Biggie Smalls's classic "Juicy" boomed through the massive speakers that lined the club's walls and shook the building. It was her thirtieth birthday, and Kafisa felt she deserved to go all out and splurge on her special day.

In her VIP section Kafisa held her glass up even higher than she already had it raised, and nodded. Her birthday was one of the best times of the year for her, as she had been born on New Year's Day. The two hundred grand she had dropped to rent out the club and pop bottles of Cîroc and rosé all night was nothing to her, especially on her special day. She knew the DJ, Mister Cee, personally from back home and had flown him in to rock her party, which was why she was not surprised to hear her favorite song by one of her hometown's hip-hop legends.

Her female entourage followed suit. They held their glasses in the air to toast with their boss. Kafisa turned and smiled approvingly in her team's direction. The whole while the cameraman shot away. His flashing lights added to the ballin' ambiance surrounding Kafisa and her female entourage. They were indeed the center of attention in the upscale club.

Kafisa held her hand up to her eyes to block the flash from the camera as she raised her glass to her lips. Between all the rosé she had consumed and the flashing lights, she was getting light-headed. She dismissed the cameraman with a wave of her hand. He nodded and directed his attention to the crowd.

Kafisa took a sip of her rosé. Just before she tilted her head back, something caught her eye. In a New York minute, she went from party mode to combat mode. Her smile was quickly replaced with a scowl at the sight of the two bodies standing up in the VIP section next to theirs. The glare from the chrome weapon one of the men was brandishing was what caught Kafisa's attention. One look at them and she knew they weren't local. Kafisa instinctively reached for her weapon tucked in her LV belt, despite the fact that the two unidentified gunmen already had their weapons raised and pointed in her direction. By the time her crew realized the imminent danger surrounding them, Kafisa had already sprung into action, and the sound of gunfire filled the air.

L and Moe had waited patiently for long enough. For the past four months they had been preparing for this moment. It had cost a lot of money to stage the scenery they had put in motion, but the job had paid well, and so they could afford what they had spent. Between the money they had dropped on bottles and on inviting all the sack-chasing chicks into their section, they had paid a pretty penny to blend in. On several occasions they had seen a potential opportunity but hadn't taken advantage of it. They had been tempted to run down on their target when she first pulled up in front of the club by doing a drive-by but had sided against it. Instead, they had waited for the perfect opportunity. Now was as perfect a time as any, given all the flashing lights being directed at their intended target. They immediately sprang into action.

Moe was the first to draw his SIG, followed by L, who pulled out his .40 caliber. Moe's eyes locked with Kafisa's the moment he raised his gun. He immediately noticed the Beretta Kafisa pulled out of her belt. He wasn't expecting that. He let off two wild shots and scurried to the left. The first shot that whizzed through the air shattered one of the bottles of Cîroc in one of the metal buckets. The second one took a wild trajectory and found a final destination in the side of Niecy's head. She never knew what hit her. The impact of the shot caused her to lunge into Nu-Nu and Laverne. Nu-Nu was clueless as to where the shots had come from, but she was the first to draw her .38 revolver after she noticed Kafisa pull out hers.

Kafisa wasted no time returning three shots herself. The first 9-mm bullet pierced the soft flesh of L's upper left side, separating two of his ribs. The burning sensation ignited his insides, letting him know he had been shot. He grabbed his gun with two hands, his finger on the trigger, and then aimed in Kafisa's direction, desperately trying to let off his last shots. Her second shot caught him in the neck, and blood squirted all over a hysterical chick beside him in his section. The chick scrambled to get away.

L saw murder and knew he was the victim. Kafisa's third shot slammed into his chest like a sledgehammer, knocking him back onto the VIP couch. He managed to get off three shots before reaching the couch, but he never got to see where his bullets landed. But Kafisa did. The first one came dangerously close to a woman's ducking head, another broke a glass in a man's hand, and the third grazed Kafisa's own flesh.

Suddenly, a bullet ripped into Laverne's back and pierced her heart, killing her instantly.

"Fuck!" Kafisa yelled as she scurried over toward L's semi-lifeless body. She pumped three more shots into L's face, then looked around. By now the club was in an uproar, and pure chaos reigned. Kafisa had lost sight of the second shooter.

"I see him!" Halimah shouted. She wasted no time hopping over the VIP section with her .380 in hand. She took up pursuit as she waved her gun around to part the crowd.

Kafisa couldn't believe what had just happened. Two of her girls were dead, and apparently, somebody wanted her dead. *But why*? she wondered. She made her way over to where Niecy lay, lifeless. "Nu-Nu?" she called out as she moved Niecy's dead body off of Nu-Nu.

"I'm good," Nu-Nu confirmed.

Kafisa helped her up. "Let's get the fuck outta here!"

The parking lot was infested with bodies when Kafisa and Nu-Nu burst through the exit. Kafisa retrieved a fresh clip and reloaded her weapon.

"Where the fuck is Halimah?" she asked immediately.

She looked around with her gun in hand, ready for whatever might happen, while Nu-Nu backed her up with her own gun. Just then a teal-green Ford Explorer pulled up in front of them. Kafisa cocked her Beretta.

"Get in!" Halimah yelled as the driver-side window of the Ford Explorer came down. Both Kafisa and Nu-Nu wasted no time hopping in.

"Good job," Kafisa acknowledged after climbing into the front seat.

"Where's Verne and Niecy?" Halimah's face was covered with concern.

Kafisa just shook her head. "They didn't make it."

"Muthafucka!" Halimah bellowed. "I got that bitch-ass nigga in the back. He gonna tell us something." She couldn't believe two of her girls were dead. She floored the stolen SUV's gas pedal and made a mad dash out of the club's parking lot. She pumped the brakes twice when she saw a police car headed in their direction.

Kafisa peered over at Halimah. Her words had both impressed and surprised Kafisa. She waited until the patrol car passed them by before spinning around and looking in the back of the SUV. In the darkness she couldn't see the body lying in the back, but seeing Nu-Nu rise up and hog spit in the back of the SUV confirmed he was back there.

Kafisa turned back around. "Even better." She nodded in Halimah's direction, showing her distaste for home-girl's killer.

# Chapter Twenty-six

"Agggh!" The piercing sound could be heard through-out the soundproof room in the basement. Even if the room wasn't noise resistant, Moe's cries still would have gone unheard, thanks to the Meek Mill track "House Party," which filled the air. The sudden excruciating pain he felt instantly brought him back to a conscious state and caused him to scream out in agony. The sting from the blow Halimah delivered to his right cheek with her gun sent an electrifying sensation throughout Moe's entire body.

"Who sent you?" Halimah wasted no time tearing into a tied-up Moe.

Moe chuckled. "Get the fuck out of here," he spat.

Halimah launched another assault with her gun.

"Motherfuckin' bitch!" Moe bellowed. This time the butt of the gun caught him upside the head. The blow gave him an instant gash. His head was throbbing, and he had a headache that had Excedrin written all over it. You could literally see his veins pulsating on his forehead. He could smell and feel blood oozing out of the right side of his face, but not even his headache or the open wound he had received from the blow could compare to the pain he was feeling on the side of his face. He inhaled and exhaled repeatedly to fight the pain from the battering he was enduring. They had caught him slipping, and he knew it. He cursed himself for getting caught slipping. Where he came from, if you got crept on, that mean you were sleeping. He was the one who was used to catching people sleeping. Now he was on the receiving end. He wondered if L had gotten away.

"This muthafucka ain't talkin'!" Halimah turned and looked at Kafisa. "Let me blow his fuckin' face off," she pleaded out of anger.

Moe let out a chuckle.

"Something funny, nigga?" Halimah spun around and delivered a right hook to Moe's midsection.

The punch caught him off guard. Tears leaped out of his eyes, and snot shot out of his nostrils. Before he could regroup from the punch, Halimah followed up with another blow. This time its destination was his sack. Moe's cries confirmed the excruciating pain he felt. His breathing increased, and his heart kept beating like a drum up against his flesh. He growled through clenched teeth and closed his eyes. He lowered his head and tried to shake off the pain all in one motion, but to no avail. This time there was no relief in sight.

The impact of Halimah's blow nearly drained what little strength he had left, but still he managed to hold on. "You're muthafuckin' dead," he spat as he did his best to get a grip on the pain she'd inflicted.

That was Kafisa's cue. She had listened to him long enough. She had immediately picked up on the fact that he had a New York accent, but the way he had pronounced the word *muthafuckin'* was all the confirmation she needed to know that he was from Brooklyn and that whoever had sent him was possibly from BK as well. *The question is, who?* thought Kafisa. With that in mind, Kafisa emerged from behind Halimah.

Moe's eyes grew wide, and the muscles in his jaw stiffened. Out of nowhere, a grin appeared across his face. "You 'bout no real bitch or boss. You ain't shit." He smiled just before he spit out the blood that had filled his mouth.

"You's a real gangsta, huh?" she retorted, with sarcasm in her tone.

"Believe that, bitch!" Moe barked.

It was now Kafisa's turn to smile. "Well, let me show you what I do to gangstas who come for this 'ain't shit' bitch."

"Fuuuck!"

The shot had come out of nowhere. Moe had never even noticed the SIG Kafisa had in her hand. The bullet had ripped through Moe's designer jeans and had torn into his inner left thigh. The impact of the blow had transformed Moe's tough persona and he'd given a childlike scream.

Spit flew from his mouth as he continued to screech. He was now breathing heavily. "You think you're gonna get away with this?" Moe spit out some more blood.

"Like you thought you were gonna get away with that bullshit you and the dead fuck boy tried to pull off back at the club?" Kafisa shot back.

Hearing that his right-hand man, L, was dead infuriated Moe. "You's a dead bitch!" he spat.

The second shot she let off slammed into Moe's knee, splitting it into two pieces. She let off a third shot into his other knee. The pain nearly caused Moe to pass out. Kafisa moved in closer toward Moe. She grabbed a fistful of his Mohawk hair.

"You know you're gonna die, right?" she taunted. She then placed her weapon inches from his face. "You might as well tell me who sent you, so he can meet you in hell," she added.

Moe knew Kafisa meant business. He couldn't believe that a bitch, of all people, had gotten the drop on him. All the thoughts and plans he had once had began to fade. It didn't take a rocket scientist to figure out he was a dead man. His only thought now was whether he should answer the question to which she was demanding a response. He quickly weighed his options. His last thoughts on the matter seemed the most appealing to him. For a tenth of a second, Moe felt like he was about to snitch, but his conscience convinced him he was making the best choice, considering the situation and the circumstances.

"What's it gonna be, nigga?" Kafisa moved her weapon over to Moe's temple. She knew if she killed him without him giving her the information she needed, her chances of finding the person who had sent him would become slim to none. She knew she could reach out to her uncle Fran to find out, but she would feel like less of a boss, since she hadn't had to reach out to him in a long time. That wasn't something she was willing to do. Kafisa pressed the SIG up against Moe's temple.

Moe's eyes grew cold. He sucked his teeth, as if he had something stuck in between them. "C-D—" His first word was cut short by the shot that entered his skull.

But Kafisa had heard enough to know who was probably behind the hit. Her heart nearly burst out her chest as Moe's blood and brain matter flew everywhere and sprayed her face, but she had killed before, so she was unfazed by the life she had just taken. Her heart reacted because she had heard the first letters of the name of the person who, according to Moe, had sent him and his boy at her. Her adrenaline was now at an all-time high.

Apparently, Halimah had figured it out also. Nu-Nu had a clueless look on her face.

"C-Dub sent these niggas!" Halimah was the first to say something. It was more of a statement than a question.

"Who the fuck is C-Dub?" Nu-Nu wanted to know.

"The reason why we came down to this muthafucka in the first place!" Halimah bellowed.

"One of y'all peoples?" Nu-Nu had a crooked look on her face.

"Supposed to be more than just our peoples. We family!" Halimah bellowed. She was still heated over her partner, Laverne's demise.

"That's fuckin' crazy." Nu-Nu shook her head. She peered over at her boss, who said nothing.

Kafisa was still in shock from Moe's utterance. She didn't want to believe it, but her gut was telling her Moe had not lied. She stood there, in a daze. *Betrayed* would be the best word to describe her mood at that moment. Her mind made a quick trip back in time. *It was right in front of me the entire time,* Kafisa thought to herself. She had listened as Halimah had ranted and raved. *She's fucking right,* Kafisa said to herself. Her reason for leaving New York was linked to C-Dub. *But why?* Kafisa wondered. All types of crazy thoughts invaded Kafisa's mind. She had a lot of questions that she wanted answers to.

One thing was for certain. Kafisa knew her next move would be to find out what the fuck was going on. The only way she knew she could do that was to return to Brooklyn.

# Chapter Twenty-seven

"Stupid muthafuckas!" C-Dub cursed out loud for the umpteenth time at no one in particular as he banged his fist against his desk. He still couldn't wrap his head around how two of his top shooters had fouled up the fifty-thousand-dollar hit he had put on Kafisa's life. *A whole fuckin' year of planning down the drain*, C-Dub thought to himself.

When he had caught wind of Kafisa hustling and getting paper in a major way in South Carolina, behind his back, he had made his decision. Before he jumped the gun, he'd given her an opportunity to tell him what she had going on—with the expectation that she would cut him in on the action as a token of her respect and appreciation. But she never did. He had a clue why. C-Dub had never felt that Kafisa respected him the way everybody else in the streets did.

C-Dub felt it was because she was the daughter of his mentor and she thought he'd never measure up to the legendary Kafis Jackson, Kafisa's true teacher. This was the main reason why he had stripped her of everything she'd worked so hard to build in the streets. C-Dub had noticed that Kafisa was getting too big for her britches, and he had decided that she had to be humbled in the worst way. When one of his little manz had told him he was fucking Jazz, one of Kafisa's top earners, C-Dub had known it was the perfect opportunity to bring Kafisa back down off her high horse.

The hit on Kafisa couldn't have been planned any better, thought C-Dub. When Kafisa had informed him that she was going down South to lay low, he hadn't thought anything of it. He'd been too busy gloating over pulling the plug on Kafisa's whole BK operation. It hadn't dawned on him that she had already mapped out her plan to relocate to South Carolina and open up shop. The way he had heard she was moving in the dirty, he believed Kafisa hadn't made him aware of her down South activities for the same reason her father had managed to rise in the game, which was also the reason he had lost his life—his connect.

C-Dub felt slighted that Kafisa had felt the need to keep him out of the loop. Because of that, he had put Kafisa on his hit list, and she had become public enemy number one to him. He had taken her actions as disrespect. It wasn't something he tolerated. He had killed people for less, which was why he had felt no remorse when he called in L and Moe for the job.

Now he had gotten word about the club shooting in South Carolina, which had left three dead and four wounded. One of the males fit the description of L, and two of the females were a part of Kafisa's team, but neither Moe, Kafisa, Halimah, nor Nu-Nu was among the dead or wounded. That was what concerned C-Dub the most. The last thing he needed was for the attempt on Kafisa's life to be linked to him. C-Dub knew that if Kafisa was still running around, very much alive, he had to make a beeline for Moe before the sun came up.

# Chapter Twenty-eight

Kafisa had been driving for the past three hours, ever since she and Halimah had switched positions at the Maryland House, a rest area on Interstate 95. Since then, I-95 North had been congested. Kafisa steadily made her way through the early morning traffic she had been fighting since they crossed the Delaware Memorial Bridge.

It seemed as if the traffic would never ease up, but Kafisa wasn't complaining. For the average person, the stop-and-go traffic probably would have been annoying and frustrating, but Kafisa took it all in stride. She was a New Yorker, so she was used to it. She was just happy to be out of South Carolina and to be getting closer to home. The years in the South had done her more good than she could have ever imagined. It had made her a stronger person in more ways than one. The closer she got to New York, the stronger she felt she became, only this was a different type of strength. This strength was fueled by rage.

Given all that had popped off recently back in South Carolina—the attempt on her life and the death of two of her girls—all Kafisa thought about now was revenge. She knew her return to New York was a huge gamble, but that was the world she lived in, so she was prepared to bet it all on herself. She knew that once she returned to Brooklyn, there could be no half stepping.

Kafisa shook her head in disgust as she darted over into the passing lane. The more time she had to think about it, the stupider she felt. C-Dub had been playing her the entire time, and she wanted to know why. She knew all her answers resided back in Brooklyn.

Kafisa peered over at Halimah in the passenger seat and then took a quick glance in her rearview to check on Nu-Nu. The two were knocked out. She had just reached the top of the New Jersey Turnpike. She thought more about what needed to be done. Kafisa knew it wouldn't be easy, but it had to be done sooner than later.

"You straight?" Halimah asked through a stretch and a yawn.

Kafisa hadn't even noticed she'd woken up. "Yeah, I'm good," she answered. "Go back to sleep."

"Nah. I'm up. Damn, traffic is crazy out here."

"Yeah. It's been like this for almost two hours," Kafisa agreed. "Y'all asses were knocked out most of the way." She smiled for the first time since they had left South Carolina.

Halimah smiled back. "Yeah, I think I went out as soon as we hopped back on the road."

"Both you bitches did." Kafisa let out a light chuckle. "Sounding like two howling dogs."

Halimah broke into laughter. "Stop playin'," she shot back. She massaged her left shoulder. Her tone switched from playful to serious. "Had to get that in," she added in her own defense. "Gotta be well rested for when we get back. We got shit to do."

Kafisa glanced over at her in admiration. As time had gone by, she couldn't deny the fact that Halimah reminded her of her own self. There was no doubt in her mind that Halimah had her back through thick and thin.

"Absolutely." Kafisa nodded approvingly.

"So, what's on your mind?" Halimah asked her.

"Everything," Kafisa admitted in a low tone. "And it's not gonna rest until that nigga answer some questions before I put him in the dirt. That nigga gotta go." Kafisa's words were stern.

Halimah shook her head in agreement.

Nu-Nu woke in the middle of Kafisa replaying for Halimah her memory of what had happened.

"I always thought he was an old bitch-ass nigga," Halimah noted after Kafisa had finished. "I ain't never tell you, but he tried to holla at me one time on the low up in Sue's," Halimah admitted, recalling the evening she had been up in the famous gentlemen's club and had run into C-Dub and his entourage.

"And you just saying something now?" Kafisa looked over at Halimah through squinted eyes. *Another sign showing me that C-Dub has been a snake on the low the whole time*, thought Kafisa.

"It wasn't about nothin'. I shut that shit down and fell back. If it was more, I would've brought that shit straight to you. I just didn't want to make something out of nothing," Halimah explained. "It was around the time all that shit was going on with Jazz. You had enough on your plate at the time, and it seemed like he was helping you get right, so I didn't want to create no unnecessary tension between nobody." Halimah sighed. "Now I wish I would've just put it in your ear. Maybe all of this could've been exposed sooner."

*The plot keeps getting thicker and thicker.* Kafisa shook her head. *This muthafucka been comin' for me for a long time. I just wasn't paying attention*, she thought.

"It's cool. You handled it the best way you felt." Kafisa understood Halimah's decision. "And I know you would have told me if it was more to it," she added. She knew

Halimah wasn't a snake or a slouch, and she was sure she had handled the situation exactly how she said she had. "We family, and that's what family do."

Halimah smiled.

"Don't worry. Him and everybody rollin' with him gonna pay," Nu-Nu said, joining in from the backseat.

She was just as heated as Kafisa and Halimah were. She too had lost someone dear to her, and the name C-Dub was attached to the reason why. She had never been to the Big Apple before and hated the reason for her first visit. As far as she was concerned, if C-Dub was behind her best friend getting killed and he was in New York, then that was where she needed to be. It wouldn't have mattered to her if she had to travel to China. There were no lengths to which she wasn't willing to go to avenge what she believed was Niecy's unnecessary death. C-Dub had become just as much her enemy as he was Kafisa's and Halimah's, even though she had never met the man.

"When we get back to BK, muthafuckas gonna have serious fuckin' problems!" Halimah exclaimed. Just like Kafisa, she was anticipating the return home.

They were all more than ready to touch New York's soil. Kafisa had already decided that once they got back to Brooklyn, she wasn't going to waste any time getting to the bottom of what had pulled her out of what had become her comfort zone. She had already told herself she wasn't leaving her birthplace until she had handled her business and tied up any and all loose ends, starting with C-Dub. Kafisa had also decided that after all this was over, and before she headed back down South, she would reclaim her position in the streets of BK. This time she was going after an even higher position and a new spot: C-Dub's.

Kafisa reached for her sun visor and pulled out a twenty-dollar bill as they steadily approached the Holland Tunnel. *You done crossed the wrong fuckin' chick*, Kafisa thought to herself as she came one step closer to showing C-Dub that she was Kafis Jackson's daughter and what that really meant in the streets of Brooklyn.

# Chapter Twenty-nine

When Kafisa, Halimah, and Nu-Nu walked in the club, all eyes were on them. Just what Kafisa had wanted. She knew she was taking a huge risk, and it was dangerous exposing herself like this. Just like she knew someone was bound to reach out to C-Dub, letting him know they were there, if he wasn't in the lounge himself and hadn't already been informed of their presence by someone. At this point she didn't even care. It was going to be what it was going to be. She had chalked it up to the game.

Two weeks had gone by, and still they weren't any closer to tracking down C-Dub. They had been searching high and low and doing everything they possibly could to flush C-Dub out. By now the word was out that Kafisa was back in Brooklyn and that she had a beef with him.

After hearing the sucker shit C-Dub had tried to pull, sending shooters at Kafisa, the hood had mixed feelings about him. Thanks to her father's encouragement, prior to fleeing to the South, Kafisa had done exactly what Kafis had asked of her. She had earned the love and gained the respect from those she needed to in Brooklyn. Because of that, the streets had remained neutral. Nobody wanted to touch the situation out of respect for Kafisa, Kafisa's father, and C-Dub.

To show her appreciation, Kafisa had made it real sweet for all the major money getters and shooters, so it was easy for them to maintain their position in this matter. She had spread the word throughout the underworld that she had the keys to the best coke and dope around, and that she was letting them go for half of what C-Dub sold his for. She had also hit all the shooters she could think of with both money and product and had offered them an opportunity to make more money by spreading the news to all the shooters she might not know or had missed. She didn't care how much it took: she was willing to give it all up to humiliate C-Dub publicly and regain control of what her father had built and run for years, until his demise.

In total she had dished out over $350,000, not including product, to keep the beef between her and C-Dub hot. It was easy to dissuade his buyers from doing business with him by pacifying their greed. It was a tactic she had seen her father utilize successfully during some of his street wars. Kafisa was determined to flush C-Dub out. She had the word out that she was looking for him and was paying for information. That was how they had landed in Lou's Lounge off Nostrand Avenue.

Kafisa did a quick scan of the intimate lounge spot, which used to be one of her, Halimah's, and Laverne's hangout spots. *This muthafucka used to never come here,* Kafisa thought to herself.

Unfortunately, there was no C-Dub in sight, which she already knew. The fact that shots weren't fired the moment they walked in the door was enough confirmation for Kafisa that he wasn't present. As the stares continued, Kafisa wondered who would be the snake that slithered off to let C-Dub know they were in the building. Kafisa was met with head nods, waves, and fist pumps as she made a beeline to her old section and positioned herself and her crew. She was better able to survey the room now that she could see it in its entirety. That was the main reason why this section used to be her favorite.

Just as she'd thought, a snake began to slither in the grass. Kafisa took a mental picture and made a mental note to remember the girl who tried to pretend she hadn't just been staring in her direction. Kafisa played along and pretended not to notice the girl watching her. Then Kafisa shifted her attention to an approaching body. She looked up and smiled at the short, pudgy man, someone for whom she had much respect.

"Hey, Lou," Kafisa called, greeting the owner of the establishment.

"Hello, Fee." Fifty-eight-year-old Lou Jones embraced her.

Judging by the look on his face, Kafisa knew he was concerned. Lou Jones was a retired old-school gangsta. It was rumored that he had killed more people than the worst serial killer, and the money he had gotten paid to do so, he had poured into his lounge. Kafisa knew the truth, though. This was all he had and the only thing, they said, Lou Jones loved. In the twenty-odd years he'd had the lounge, no matter what the situation was, no one had ever beefed or killed anyone on or inside his property. A tussle might have started there, but it had never ended there. That was out of both fear and respect for Lou Jones. Kafisa's father had been the one to tell her that every rumor she had ever heard about Lou Jones was true. He had also told her that Lou Jones was the most dangerous man he had ever met in his life and that it wouldn't be wise for anybody to cross him. Kafisa had never forgotten those words.

"Don't worry, Lou. My respect for you is too high for me to ever disrespect you or your place of business," Kafisa said, giving him her word. "I know this is your baby." She shot him half of a smile, accompanied by a wink.

That made Lou Jones smile. "I sure wish your Fis was here." Lou Jones shook his head in mock disbelief. "None of this foolishness would be going on. He always kept the peace."

"I know," Kafisa said solemnly.

Halimah, who had been silently shadowing Kafisa, nodded in agreement.

Nu-Nu, who had been trailing Halimah, listened, wide eyed. It was the first time she was really hearing about Kafisa's background.

"Hey, but as long as I'm here, he's here," Kafisa added, clarifying the matter.

Lou Jones lit up. "Spoken like a true Jackson." He paused briefly. "Whatchu drinkin'? It's on me," he then said.

"I think we're gonna do shots. Patrón," Kafisa replied. "Bring the bottle and pineapple juice. I got it," she informed Lou.

Lou Jones waved her off. Moments later, the same girl who had been eyeing Kafisa from behind the bar appeared with glasses, a half gallon of Patrón, and a carafe of pineapple juice. She began pouring shots from the bottle for Kafisa, Halimah, and Nu-Nu.

"You from Brooklyn?" Kafisa asked the girl, glancing at her name tag, which read CARMEN.

The question caught the girl off guard. "Uh. No. Why you ask?"

"Just asking." Kafisa's tone was level.

Both Halimah and Nu-Nu watched the exchange as they tossed their first shots back.

"Long Island," the girl said with a smile.

"Carmen from LI." Kafisa let the words come out of her mouth slowly, as if she was wondering where she had heard the name before. But that was not the case. She wanted the bartender to know she was onto her. The way Carmen's wrist shook as she refilled Halimah's and Nu-Nu's glasses let Kafisa know she had gotten the hint.

"We're good," Kafisa said, dismissing her. "You can go back to doing whatever it was you were doing behind the bar." Kafisa flashed her a smirk.

Carmen smiled back, broke her stare, and scurried back over to the bar.

"What the fuck was that all about?" Halimah asked, beating Nu-Nu to the punch.

"That's the bitch that let C-Dub know we here," Kafisa replied, then tossed her shot of Patrón back, chased it with some pineapple juice, and poured herself another drink.

# Chapter Thirty

Yo, just relax, were the words C-Dub used to begin his text message. You shouldn't have said nothing to that bitch. Shit! After finishing his text, he pressed SEND.

When he had gotten the text from his young bartender chick that Kafisa and her crew were up in the local lounge, he'd been appreciative of the heads-up. Fortunately for him, the young tenderoni, whom he had just sent home in a taxi, had delayed his arrival at the lounge, or else he might have walked right into Kafisa and her squad. Now he cursed the fact that he had to actually go down there on his own and put his own work in.

"Little smart bitch," C-Dub said out loud. Out of all the places she could have picked to post up, she had to pick the best one. The type of reputation that Lou's Lounge had was no secret to C-Dub or anybody else. It was the reason that he himself had started hanging out in there after he muscled Kafisa out of Brooklyn.

Aside from that, he couldn't get anybody in the entire BK to pick up the bounty he had on Kafisa's head. She had managed to keep all the shooters from the BK borough at bay. C-Dub knew that he couldn't bring in anyone from out of town to handle a Brooklyn beef. Not unless he really wanted the entire BK to turn on him. He knew it was one thing to send shooters from his borough to another area, but it was another thing altogether to bring outsiders in for the very same reason. It was forbidden, an unwritten rule in BK, and Kafisa knew that.

Two hours later C-Dub's phone rang, waking him from the nap he had fallen into at his desk. He looked at the caller's name on the phone's screen and picked up the call just before the last ring.

"Wassup, love?" a voice said.

"Wassup," C-Dub hollered into the phone. The caller spoke. He peered at his watch. "Damn," he cursed. It didn't seem like he had been asleep that long. "Keep me posted if anything changes." C-Dub ended the call.

He wiped his face with the palms of his hands and then sprang up from his chair. C-Dub walked over to his wall safe and opened it. He retrieved the twin sixteen-shot blocks from the safe. He stuck one under the front part of his belt; the other he tucked under his belt at the small of his back. He then pulled the bottom of his shirt over the bulges and smoothed it out.

*Let's see how this little bitch really built,* C-Dub thought as he snatched up his car keys and exited his brownstone.

# Chapter Thirty-one

It was approaching 3:00 a.m. when Kafisa, Halimah, and Nu-Nu polished off the last of the half gallon of Patrón. Kafisa hadn't even realized so much time had passed. They had been at Lou's Lounge for nearly seven hours and still no sign of C-Dub. Kafisa thought he'd at least show his face, given the way she had been calling him out. She knew his reputation was at stake. It was something he lived for, and she had challenged it. Up until this moment, she had taken only two shots of the liquor. She had wanted to make sure that nothing prevented her from seeing who was coming and going at Lou's. She had also wanted to be ready for whatever, in case C-Dub did happen to show up and be on some bullshit.

Although nothing had ever popped off in Lou's establishment, with all that C-Dub had done to take everything from her in Brooklyn, she wasn't taking any chances. *Anything is possible when dealing with a coldhearted snake*, she thought. Kafisa glanced down at her watch. By now they were pretty much the only ones left in the lounge besides the bartender Carmen, Lou, security staff members, and a couple who were indulging in conversation in the corner opposite from where Kafisa sat.

"That nigga ain't showin' up tonight," Kafisa concluded. She snatched up her glass with the remainder of her drink, tossed it back, and then stood to retreat. "Let's get the fuck outta here." She was more disappointed than anything. She had really thought that by using the tactics described in the book *The 48 Laws of Power*, she was going to force C-Dub out of hiding. She had followed them to a T, but still no C-Dub.

*Pussy*, Kafisa said to herself as she began to make her way toward the entrance to the lounge. Halimah and Nu-Nu both hopped up and followed suit. Kafisa looked to the right of her. She and Carmen made eye contact. Kafisa could see the nervousness in Carmen's eyes. She grilled her the whole time she was making her way toward the exit. There was no doubt in her mind that Carmen had reached out to C-Dub and had informed him of their presence. Her source had never been wrong before when providing information, so she knew somebody had given C-Dub the heads-up, and Kafisa believed that somebody was Carmen.

Had it not been for Lou's no-nonsense policy, Kafisa knew she would have gone behind the bar and pistol-whipped Carmen until she was unconscious with the baby 9 mm she had tucked in her lower back. Kafisa let out a light chuckle before breaking her stare with Carmen.

"Bitch!" she heard Halimah shout in Carmen's direction just as she reached the front door.

Kafisa turned around just in time to see Halimah stop in front of the bar. Nu-Nu had posted up on the side of Halimah. Kafisa saw Lou approaching in her peripheral, and so she doubled back over toward the bar.

"Limah!" Kafisa called out.

Halimah stared long and hard at Carmen before turning to face Kafisa. Kafisa shook her head and made a waving motion with her hand in front of her neck. She was telling Halimah to dead whatever it was she had in mind.

"She good," Kafisa told Lou, vouching for Halimah.

"All right now," Lou announced. "I don't want no shit up in here."

"I gave you my word." Kafisa nodded.

The exchange between Kafisa and Lou was enough to make Halimah disengage. The Patrón had her feeling a little more aggressive than normal, but she knew enough about Lou Jones to know that he was a man of few words. Halimah had heard too many people in the street say that if he had to talk, usually something serious would follow, so she knew that nothing good could come out of him opening his mouth now. Halimah did not want that at all. Their beef was with C-Dub, not Lou. She couldn't help but take out her anger and frustration on the person Kafisa had told her had reached out to C-Dub. She was itching to pull out her .380, which was strapped to her ankle, and shove it down Carmen's throat. She decided against it, out of respect for both Kafisa and Lou Jones.

"Pardon me, Lou," Halimah said.

"Apology accepted," Lou replied. "Y'all get home safe, ya hear?" Lou waved his hand.

"Thanks, Lou." Kafisa smiled. "Let's go," she then said to Halimah and Nu-Nu. Kafisa waited until they had walked in front of her before she made a beeline over toward the entrance. She couldn't wait to tear into Halimah.

"Are you fuckin' crazy?" Kafisa stormed once they were outside and heading down the street to where she had parked her Range Rover. "What the hell were you thinking?"

"I know. I know. My bad," Halimah replied. "But that bitch was lookin' at you crazy once you walked past," Halimah informed her. "I couldn't let that shit slide."

"Yeah. I caught it too," Nu-Nu said, joining in. "I was about to say something myself."

"Fuck her!" Kafisa spat. "We not checkin' for her. We lookin' for C-Dub's punk ass!" Kafisa reminded them both.

Like a wish come true, the familiar voice came out of nowhere, catching them all by surprise.

"Here I go right here, bitch!" The shot that then rang out sent them all diving for cover.

C-Dub had been sitting outside in his Chrysler 300 for the past two hours, waiting patiently for Kafisa and her crew to come out of Lou's Lounge. When his phone vibrated in his lap, he knew it was the text he had been waiting for. He smiled and nodded. "It's on now, mutha-fuckas," C-Dub said under his breath. He leaned over to the passenger seat to retrieve his MAC-10 semiautomatic. He cocked the MAC to put one bullet in the chamber. Just as he removed the safety, out walked Halimah and a female he didn't recognize. He rose up when he saw Kafisa hurry out the door. "Yeah, got your ass now, bitch!" C-Dub proclaimed.

He knew he couldn't just hop out in front of Lou's spot and gun them down. That would be asking for trouble he didn't need. So instead, he waited, hoping they'd go in a direction that took them away from Lou's Lounge. As luck would have it, Kafisa, Halimah, and Nu-Nu started walking in the direction in which C-Dub was parked inconspicuously. "Yeah, come to Papa." He nodded. C-Dub hit the UNLOCK button on his Chrysler. He cracked open his driver's door, then leaned his seat back some. Just as they approached, C-Dub hopped out of his whip and sprang into action.

The four wild shots that followed C-Dub's sudden out-burst gave Kafisa and Halimah enough time to take cover. Nu-Nu, on the other hand, was not so lucky. The side window of the car she had chosen as a shield was pene-trated by one of the shots from the rapid firing of C-Dub's MAC-10, and the bullet tore into her left shoulder.

"Shit!" C-Dub cursed when he realized three bullets had gone astray and now his cover was blown.

By now, Kafisa, Halimah, and a wounded Nu-Nu had their weapons drawn. They immediately began to return fire. This was not how C-Dub had envisioned things. He had gotten the drop on them and had fouled up the opportunity. He let off eight more shots in succession as a diversion, then hopped back in his whip. As he sped off, the back of C-Dub's car was met with a barrage of bullets. He lost control of the vehicle and slammed into a parked car.

Kafisa watched as C-Dub's car crashed. Before she made her way up the street to his car, she did a quick survey of the area. She saw that Nu-Nu was down and Halimah was now by her side.

"I got her. Go get that muthafucka!" Halimah bellowed.

Kafisa nodded. She didn't waste another second. She rushed up the block to finish the job.

C-Dub had lost consciousness, but he regained it a minute later. Reality set in. He knew Kafisa and her crew were not too far behind. He reached for the car door handle. The door wouldn't open. "Come on!" he yelled, but the door remained stuck. C-Dub pressed his weight up against the door and began to push forcefully. The car door opened a few inches, but not quickly enough.

"Don't you fuckin' move, pussy-ass muthafucka!" Kafisa spat.

When C-Dub peered up, he was met with Kafisa's weapon just inches away from his face. A smile appeared across C-Dub's face. "So this how it ends, huh?" he asked.

"Nigga, shut the fuck up!" Kafisa's emotions were running wild. She couldn't believe that she had finally tracked C-Dub down, and now the moment of truth was here. She leaned in and snatched C-Dub's weapon out of his hand as she kept her 9 mm aimed at his head. She tossed C-Dub's MAC-10 behind her and cocked her own weapon.

"Before you pull that trigger . . ." C-Dub cleared his throat. "There's something that I think you should know," he stated with a heinous smirk.

"Nigga, ain't nothing you can say to get the fuck out of this," Kafisa assured him. Her grip tighten up on her 9 mm.

"I swear, you're gonna wanna hear this," C-Dub insisted. "It's about your father."

The mention of her dad sent Kafisa over the deep end. "Don't you ever fuckin' mention his name!" Kafisa spat. "If he were still alive, he'd kill you himself!" she shouted.

"Well, he ain't shit." C-Dub let out an insane laugh. "Because I got his ass killed, you stupid fuckin' bitch!"

Before she had time to react, C-Dub shifted all his weight onto the door and it flew open. The moving door caught Kafisa by surprise and knocked her back. Her gun flew out of her hand as she plunged to the hard concrete. C-Dub hopped out of the crashed vehicle. He quickly looked around for his gun but could not locate it. He did, however, see Kafisa's gun lying across the street. Just as he was about to head over toward it, he saw Halimah rushing up the street, headed his way.

C-Dub grimaced. "Bitch!" He kicked Kafisa in the mid-section. "I'll see you another time, bitch. I promise you that," he thundered. He fled up the block to the sound of sirens in the distance.

"Fee!"

Kafisa heard Halimah call out to her. When she opened her eyes, she saw Halimah hovering over her. She grabbed the back of her head with her right hand and her stomach with the other.

"That muthafucka got away," Halimah informed her.

Kafisa didn't say a word. She was still trying to process what C-Dub had said to her. Tears began to stream out of her eyes as she continued to sit in the middle of the street.

"Fee, what's wrong?" Halimah kneeled down to help her up.

"I'm all right!" Kafisa pulled away. She stood up on her own and cleared the big lump that had formed in her throat. She wiped her face with her hands several times, but despite her efforts, uncontrollable tears continued to pour out of her eyes.

"Fee, what the hell is wrong?" A concerned and confused Halimah wanted to know what was causing this outpouring of emotion. She threw her arms around Kafisa's shoulders. Kafisa looked to the sky and shook her head. She tried to find the words. She closed her eyes, then opened them. She had been given another reason to hate C-Dub and want him dead. What had started out as just business had now become personal for Kafisa. She cleared her throat for a second time. She turned and looked at Halimah.

"That motherfucka killed my father!" Kafisa bellowed.

All Halimah could do was stand there in shock as Kafisa dropped the news on her about her father.

# Chapter Thirty-two

*Weeks later . . .*

C-Dub rose up out of bed. He jerked his head from side to side. He could literally hear his neck cracking. He planted his feet on the plush carpet and then slipped them into the house slippers on the side of the bed. He stood and stretched. The same noise that had come from his neck could be heard coming from his back. Ever since he had run out of the painkillers for the injuries he'd sustained in the car crash, the result of fleeing from the barrage of bullets Kafisa and her crew were firing at him, he had been waking up sore and stiff.

Luckily, he had managed to escape with just a flesh wound on his right shoulder. C-Dub slipped his arms into his shirt and slowly buttoned its buttons. He glanced back at his bed when he heard the sound of his covers rustling.

"Where you going?" Carmen's head popped out from underneath the covers.

C-Dub ignored her question. He continued to dress.

Carmen sucked her teeth. "You didn't hear me?" she questioned.

C-Dub looked down at her. "Yeah, I heard you."

Carmen rolled her eyes.

C-Dub continued to dress slowly.

Carmen reached out and grabbed hold of C-Dub's hand, preventing him from buckling his belt. "You should come back to bed," she suggested. She was already pulling down C-Dub's jeans zipper.

"I'm hungry," C-Dub announced abruptly.

"So am I," Carmen cooed seductively. She slipped her hand in C-Dub's jeans through the parted zipper.

"Chill." C-Dub made a failed attempt to push her hand away.

Carmen slid closer to the edge of the bed. Before he knew it, she had C-Dub's partial hardness poking through the slit of his boxers. C-Dub started to protest again, but the warmth of Carmen's hand wrapped around his dick caused him to lose his train of thought. Carmen replaced her hand with her mouth. She sucked C-Dub's dick to a full erection.

"Shit," C-Dub moaned. He placed one hand on Carmen's head and the other on his hip. Between her lip service and the pain from his injuries, it was a task just keeping his balance as Carmen went to work on his shaft.

Carmen licked around the helmet, then up and down the spine of his rock-hard dick. She then pulled his boxers down below his waist to expose the full length of his manhood and licked his sack. She knew that drove him crazy. It took all his strength for C-Dub's legs not to give way under him. His knees weakened as she sucked on his nut sack. She then glided her tongue back to the head of his member and put him back in her mouth. She expertly began deep-throating C-Dub's pulsating dick.

"Yeah," he uttered, encouraging her. He placed his hands on her shoulders for balance.

The sounds of the slurping as Carmen sucked him like there was no tomorrow had C-Dub turned on. He began to sex her mouth roughly. His thrusts matched the rhythm of her lips. He could feel himself building up each time the head of his dick touched the back of her throat and her tongue touched the bottom of his length. Carmen sucked his dick vigorously as she jerked the rest of him with her hand. C-Dub closed his eyes and threw his head back. Images of him pounding her from the back flashed in his mind as that familiar sensation began to emerge.

"Right there," he whispered, just loud enough for Carmen to hear.

Carmen worked her lips, tongue, throat, and hands even more upon hearing C-Dub's request. C-Dub's nails dug into Carmen's shoulders as the inevitable took control of his body.

"Aagh," he blurted out. His juices exploded and sprayed the inside of Carmen's mouth.

She continued sucking until C-Dub's sex pistol was empty. She swallowed every ounce of him until there was none left. Even when he had gone limp, she still continued to taste his dick. She knew how sensitive it became when he busted a nut. She looked up and saw the look of satisfaction on his face. Carmen smiled. She slid back onto the bed and parted her legs so he could see the juices dripping from between her inner thighs. Her pussy hairs glistened from her own climax.

C-Dub looked at her hot box oozing with her juices. He bent down and pulled up his boxers and jeans. "I still wanna go get some breakfast." he I said dryly. His mood had quickly changed back to a cold one.

Carmen frowned. She couldn't believe how unappreciative C-Dub seemed of the oral she had just performed on him. "Why should I have to cook when we can afford to eat out? Besides, I just gave you dessert," she said with attitude. She pulled the covers over her and switched subjects. "And speaking of affording, you were gonna go to breakfast without me?" she whined.

"Does it matter?" C-Dub spat. "You up now. Get dressed."

Carmen rolled her eyes. She was just about tired of C-Dub bossing her around and treating her like shit.

After all, were it not for her, he probably wouldn't be alive. That was what Carmen believed. She flung the covers off her naked body and slithered into the beige sundress she had worn the night before.

"And you drivin' too," C-Dub announced.

"I knew that was coming, anyway." Carmen cut her eyes over at C-Dub. Then she made her way into the bathroom and freshened up some.

Moments later, she and C-Dub were making a beeline for his 2015 black Camaro. Carmen hit the alarm button on C-Dub's key chain to unlock the doors to the muscle car. She opened the front passenger-side door for C-Dub. Once he was secure, she made her way around to the driver's side.

"Shit!" C-Dub cursed.

"What's wrong?" Carmen turned and looked over at C-Dub.

"I left my piece in the house." C-Dub grimaced. "I'll be right back," he told Carmen. He then opened the car door and climbed out.

"Hurry up, ole man. I'm starvin'," Carmen teased.

"I got your ole man," C-Dub replied, not bothering to look back.

If Carmen had heard him, he'd never know. The impact of the explosion caught C-Dub by surprise. The pieces of debris from his Camaro tore into his flesh like hot slugs after the bomb that was connected to his ignition blew the car to smithereens. C-Dub's body was tossed up against the front of his house. He could hear his rib cage crushing as his body slammed up against the house. C-Dub's limp body fell to the ground, but not before a metal object that was obviously from his car smashed into the side of his face and entered his skull. That was the last memory C-Dub would have before his eyes closed.

***

Kafisa watched from afar as C-Dub and the girl whose name she remembered was Carmen exited the Long Island home. Thanks to her, Kafisa had been able to track C-Dub down. She had remembered that Carmen had told her she was from Long Island. She had been following Carmen ever since the girl had popped back up at Lou's Lounge in the days after Kafisa, Halimah, and Nu-Nu had run down on C-Dub. She'd known it was a long shot when she began tailing her. Several times she had considered running down on her and forcing her to give up any information she had on C-Dub's whereabouts, but she'd decided against it. She hadn't wanted to take the chance of someone seeing anything.

The entire day she found him, she had exercised patience. As luck would have it, her patience had paid off. She had thought her eyes were deceiving her at first when she saw an image appear from behind the blinds of the front window of the house. It had happened so quickly, Kafisa wasn't sure, but there had been no mistaking his identity when C-Dub poked his head out and looked left, then right, before kneeling down to pick up the newspaper on the front porch. Kafisa had hunched down low in the silver Challenger. Had C-Dub looked forward and taken a closer look, he might have seen her lurking in the cut, but that had not been the case. Kafisa had waited until C-Dub closed the front door before she pulled off. She hadn't even bothered to tell Halimah or Nu-Nu she had tracked him down. After the close call with Halimah getting shot, she had decided to handle the situation on her own.

Once Kafisa had locked in on where C-Dub had been holing up, she'd frequented the area for the next few days, until she'd learned the normal flow of operations in the neighborhood. She knew Long Island was not somewhere where you wanted to get caught out of pocket doing anything. Of course, they had their bad areas, but this was not one of them. She knew she had to map out strategically how she was going to go about killing C-Dub.

It wasn't until she had met up with and spoken to Francine that an idea had come to mind. She wanted to send a message to everybody who was down with or rolled with C-Dub, and she wanted it to be heard loud and clear. It was Francine's idea as to how she could do that. The next day, she had received a package at her hotel. Hours later she'd been on Long Island, waiting for the sun to go down and the community C-Dub resided in to take it down for the night. Going unnoticed, Kafisa had cautiously scurried over to the car she knew belonged to C-Dub and had done exactly what the instructions she received with the package told her to do.

Now she sat and watched as C-Dub and Carmen exited the house. Kafisa hadn't anticipated that Carmen would come out with C-Dub. Not that she cared. She couldn't help but shake her head as Carmen helped C-Dub into the passenger seat, then made her way to the driver's side. "This bitch!" Kafisa cursed.

*Casualties are a part of war*, Kafisa thought, chalking Carmen's presence up to that. She was sure that Carmen knew the risks of fucking with somebody like C-Dub. As far as she was concerned, Carmen's life was a small price to pay for C-Dub's. Kafisa gripped her gun tightly in her hand, in case something went wrong. She watched as Carmen climbed into C-Dub's driver's seat. The next thing she knew, C-dub was getting out of the Camaro.

"Fuck!" Kafisa spat. She removed the safety from her gun, then grabbed her door handle. There was no way she was going to let C-Dub get away. Kafisa opened her car door, but before she could get out, the Camaro burst into flames.

Luckily for her, the explosion didn't reach where she was parked a short distance up the street. Other cars were not that fortunate. The street was flooded with dust and smoke. Kafisa squinted her eyes in an attempt to see through the fog. At first she couldn't see a thing. She tucked her gun into her waist and exited her vehicle at a rapid speed. She knew she didn't have much time. Kafisa could hear the Camaro's alarm going off as she jogged over toward C-Dub's house. She brought her hands up to her eyes and mouth as she fought through the smoky fog. As she got closer, Kafisa saw who and what she was looking for. She drew her weapon. Although the smoke had begun to settle, it was still difficult to get a clear view of anything, but there was no mistaking C-Dub's limp body lying sprawled out on the semi-burned lawn.

Kafisa knew she didn't have much time. She knew it was just a matter of time before the area was crawling with cops, firemen, ambulances, and nosy neighbors. She was surprised no one had come out yet. Kafisa speed walked over to where C-Dub lay. *Damn! This nigga look fuckin' dead as shit*, she thought to herself, seeing C-Dub's face and now clothes-free body covered in blood, burns, and ash. Still, she wasn't taking any chances. She had gone to great lengths and had been through too much just to track down and kill C-Dub.

"This for me and my father and all the people you crossed, bitch!" Kafisa spat on him.

She pumped six rounds into C-Dub's body. She noticed that aside from rocking from the impact as the shots tore into his body, he never moved. Satisfied, she rushed back to her parked car. She quickly started it, then looked left and then right before peeling off. A quick left and then a sharp right, and moments later Kafisa was back on the highway.

"Justice served," she said aloud to herself as she navigated the stolen Dodge Challenger to reclaim what she believed was rightfully hers—Brooklyn.

When he opened his eyes, all he could see was a bright white light shining down on him. He felt like he was floating on air. His first thought was that he had died and had somehow made it to heaven, but he shot that theory down quickly, because he knew there was no way he could have made it to heaven, unless God was grading on a mean curve. C-Dub closed his eyes again and then opened and closed them several more times. His vision was blurry. He thought he was dreaming, but he wasn't. An incessant reverberating beeping sound could be heard in the distance. C-Dub looked around and then down at himself. He could feel something sticking in his arms and pinching him between his legs. He had no idea where he was or how he had gotten there. He was still somewhat discombobulated. Then suddenly he remembered.

The explosion appeared in his head as if it were happening at that very moment. *What the fuck happened?* he wondered. Everything was pretty much a blur to him. He struggled with his thoughts. He had no idea how long he had been wherever he was or how he had gotten there. The last thing he remembered was going back into the house for his gun before he heard the loud boom. *Carmen,* he thought. C-Dub wondered if she had made it out alive. *How the hell did I even make it out alive?* he wondered.

Just then he heard a voice. Instinctively, C-Dub reached nowhere in particular for a weapon, but to no avail. Instead, he was met with sharp pains throughout his entire body. He let out an agonizing cry.

"Try to relax, sir." The doctor came over and placed his hands on C-Dub's shoulders. "It is not wise to move around so quickly after the surgery," he informed C-Dub.

His words caused C-Dub's eyes to widen. He tried to fix his mouth to ask, "What surgery?" No words came out.

The doctor must have read his mind. "We were able to remove five of the bullets successfully, but the one in your calf, we chose to leave. It was just too risky. So we decided to let it just fall out on its own," the doctor told him. He had no way of knowing that C-Dub's ears went deaf after hearing the word *bullets*.

An image began to appear slowly in C-Dub's head as he played back the tapes of his memory. "Son of a bitch!" he cursed aloud. He'd realized that his last recollection was not of heading back into the house. The beeping sound of the heart monitor C-Dub was hooked up to began to speed up. C-Dub became furious as a picture of Kafisa standing over him invaded his mind. The last explosion C-Dub remembered was from the first bullet that had exited Kafisa's gun and slammed into his chest. The doctor had mentioned five additional shots, though.

C-Dub counted his blessings. He knew he was still alive only by the grace and mercy of the Creator. *Thank you, God.* He looked up. *But when I get out of here, you ain't gonna never see me up there*, C-Dub thought, continuing his discussion with his higher power. *Because when I get back to Brooklyn, I'm gonna kill that bitch and everybody down with her.*

C-Dub closed his eyes and drifted off to sleep.

ORDER FORM
URBAN BOOKS, LLC
97 N. 18th Street
Wyandanch, NY 11798

Name (please print):_____

Address:            _____

City/State:         _____

Zip:                _____

| QTY | TITLES | PRICE |
|-----|--------|-------|
|     |        |       |
|     |        |       |
|     |        |       |
|     |        |       |
|     |        |       |
|     |        |       |
|     |        |       |
|     |        |       |
|     |        |       |
|     |        |       |
|     |        |       |
|     |        |       |

Shipping and handling-add $3.50 for 1st book, then $1.75 for each additional book.

Please send a check payable to:

**Urban Books, LLC**

Please allow 4–6 weeks for delivery

## ORDER FORM
## URBAN BOOKS, LLC
### 97 N. 18th Street
### Wyandanch, NY 11798

Name: (please print): _____

Address: _____

City/State: _____

Zip: _____

| QTY | TITLES | PRICE |
|-----|--------|-------|
| | 16 On The Block | $14.95 |
| | A Girl From Flint | $14.95 |
| | A Pimp's Life | $14.95 |
| | Baltimore Chronicles | $14.95 |
| | Baltimore Chronicles 2 | $14.95 |
| | Betrayal | $14.95 |
| | Black Diamond | $14.95 |
| | Black Diamond 2 | $14.95 |
| | Black Friday | $14.95 |
| | Both Sides Of The Fence | $14.95 |
| | Both Sides Of The Fence 2 | $14.95 |
| | California Connection | $14.95 |

Shipping and handling-add $3.50 for 1st book, then $1.75 for each additional book.

Please send a check payable to:

**Urban Books, LLC**

Please allow 4–6 weeks for delivery

# ORDER FORM
## URBAN BOOKS, LLC
97 N. 18th Street
Wyandanch, NY 11798

Name (please print):_____

Address:　　　　　_____

City/State:　　　　_____

Zip:　　　　　　　_____

| QTY | TITLES | PRICE |
|-----|--------|-------|
|  | California Connection 2 | $14.95 |
|  | Cheesecake And Teardrops | $14.95 |
|  | Congratulations | $14.95 |
|  | Crazy In Love | $14.95 |
|  | Cyber Case | $14.95 |
|  | Denim Diaries | $14.95 |
|  | Diary Of A Mad First Lady | $14.95 |
|  | Diary Of A Stalker | $14.95 |
|  | Diary Of A Street Diva | $14.95 |
|  | Diary Of A Young Girl | $14.95 |
|  | Dirty Money | $14.95 |
|  | Dirty To The Grave | $14.95 |

Shipping and handling-add $3.50 for 1st book, then $1.75 for each additional book.

Please send a check payable to:

**Urban Books, LLC**

Please allow 4–6 weeks for delivery

# ORDER FORM
## URBAN BOOKS, LLC
97 N. 18th Street
Wyandanch, NY 11798

Name (please print):_____

Address:            _____

City/State:         _____

Zip:                _____

| QTY | TITLES | PRICE |
|---|---|---|
| | Gunz And Roses | $14.95 |
| | Happily Ever Now | $14.95 |
| | Hell Has No Fury | $14.95 |
| | Hush | $14.95 |
| | If It Isn't love | $14.95 |
| | Kiss Kiss Bang Bang | $14.95 |
| | Last Breath | $14.95 |
| | Little Black Girl Lost | $14.95 |
| | Little Black Girl Lost 2 | $14.95 |
| | Little Black Girl Lost 3 | $14.95 |
| | Little Black Girl Lost 4 | $14.95 |
| | Little Black Girl Lost 5 | $14.95 |

Shipping and handling-add $3.50 for 1st book, then $1.75 for each additional book.

Please send a check payable to:

**Urban Books, LLC**

Please allow 4–6 weeks for delivery

ORDER FORM
URBAN BOOKS, LLC
97 N. 18th Street
Wyandanch, NY 11798

Name (please print):_____

Address:           _____

City/State:        _____

Zip:               _____

| QTY | TITLES | PRICE |
|-----|--------|-------|
| | Loving Dasia | $14.95 |
| | Material Girl | $14.95 |
| | Moth To A Flame | $14.95 |
| | Mr. High Maintenance | $14.95 |
| | My Little Secret | $14.95 |
| | Naughty | $14.95 |
| | Naughty 2 | $14.95 |
| | Naughty 3 | $14.95 |
| | Queen Bee | $14.95 |
| | Say It Ain't So | $14.95 |
| | Snapped | $14.95 |
| | Snow White | $14.95 |

Shipping and handling-add $3.50 for 1$^{st}$ book, then $1.75 for each additional book.
Please send a check payable to:
**Urban Books, LLC**
Please allow 4–6 weeks for delivery